"I'm your son."

She blinked. The young man stood still, as if frozen, while his words replayed themselves in her mind. He'd just said he was her son. He couldn't be.

Sara clutched the door with both hands and leaned against it, her gaze never wavering from the young man standing just outside.

Who was this boy claiming to be the child she'd given away so long ago? This child she'd worried for, grieved over and daydreamed about ever since. This young man named Ryan.

"Should I go?" he asked.

"No!"

"You're shocked. How could you not be?" His voice was filled with strength, compassion and a tremble of fear.

Years of training drove her to respond. She held out her hand.

"Nice to meet you, Ryan."

Dear Reader,

Most of us will never face Sara's challenges, but we almost all have to make the same choices she does. The choice to play it safe, to exist—or to take the big risks, to reach for everything, to live fully. We have to be willing to not only face our fears, but to walk right into them if required, so we can get through them to whatever awaits us on the other side.

I'm often asked where I get the ideas for my stories. Sometimes I have specific answers. I have no idea where this story came from. It doesn't quite fit the usual boundaries or genres. But it wouldn't go away. I spoke to my editor about this story. She didn't seem shocked or even hesitant as she told me she thought it would work and asked me to write it. I didn't question her acceptance any more than I questioned myself about the original creation.

And then, halfway through the book, I questioned everything—mostly myself. What had I done? How was I going to get a romance out of this? How was I going to get *anywhere*?

I was scared. I'd taken a risk and felt I was about to fail. I considered calling my editor and telling her we'd made a terrible mistake. And then Sara spoke to me. Was I going to work my way through the fears and let her find her happily ever after? I cared about her. And for her, I sat down every day and I wrote.

I didn't take Sara to her happily ever after. She took me. I hope you'll join us on this journey.

Tara Taylor Quinn

TARA TAYLOR QUINN
Sara's Son

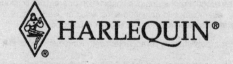

TORONTO • NEW YORK • LONDON
AMSTERDAM • PARIS • SYDNEY • HAMBURG
STOCKHOLM • ATHENS • TOKYO • MILAN • MADRID
PRAGUE • WARSAW • BUDAPEST • AUCKLAND

ISBN-13: 978-0-373-78173-7
ISBN-10:   0-373-78173-3

SARA'S SON

Copyright © 2007 by Tara Taylor Quinn.

All rights reserved. Except for use in any review, the reproduction or
utilization of this work in whole or in part in any form by any electronic,
mechanical or other means, now known or hereafter invented, including
xerography, photocopying and recording, or in any information storage
or retrieval system, is forbidden without the written permission of the
publisher, Harlequin Enterprises Limited, 225 Duncan Mill Road,
Don Mills, Ontario, Canada M3B 3K9.

This is a work of fiction. Names, characters, places and incidents are
either the product of the author's imagination or are used fictitiously,
and any resemblance to actual persons, living or dead, business
establishments, events or locales is entirely coincidental.

This edition published by arrangement with Harlequin Books S.A.

® and TM are trademarks of the publisher. Trademarks indicated with
® are registered in the United States Patent and Trademark Office, the
Canadian Trade Marks Office and in other countries.

www.eHarlequin.com

Printed in U.S.A.

ABOUT THE AUTHOR

Tara's first book, *Yesterday's Secrets,* published in October 1993, was a finalist for the Romance Writers of America's prestigious RITA® Award. Her subsequent work has earned her finalist status for the National Readers' Choice Award and the Holt Medallion, plus another two RITA® Award nominations. A prolific writer, she has more than forty novels as well as three novellas published. To reach Tara, write to her at P.O. Box 133584, Mesa, Arizona 85216 or through her Web site, www.tarataylorquinn.com.

Books by Tara Taylor Quinn

HARLEQUIN SUPERROMANCE

1189–NOTHING SACRED*
1225–WHAT DADDY DOESN'T KNOW
1272–SOMEBODY'S BABY*
1297–25 YEARS
    (anthology with Margot Early & Janice Macdonald)
1309–THE PROMISE OF CHRISTMAS
1350–A CHILD'S WISH
1381–MERRY CHRISTMAS, BABIES

HARLEQUIN EVERLASTING LOVE

THE NIGHT WE MET

HARLEQUIN SINGLE TITLE

SHELTERED IN HIS ARMS*

MIRA BOOKS

WHERE THE ROAD ENDS
STREET SMART
HIDDEN
IN PLAIN SIGHT

*Shelter Valley Stories

For my father, Walter Wright Gumser.
Because he always did his best.
I love you, Daddy!

CHAPTER ONE

May 24

1:00—Lunch

2:00—Interview (It's the retired cop. Credentials in folder.)

2:20—Meeting with Rodney Pace. (Presentation schedule included in red folder on desk.)

6:30—Dinner with partners from Mr. Calhoun's firm. Hanrahan's.

Note: Proof Sheriff Lindsay's book. Sign checks and contracts before leaving. (In blue folder.)

Further note: Don't forget to eat.

SARA CALHOUN SMILED as she read the final line Donna had jotted on the daily agenda, which sat atop a newly readied pile of folders on her desk at the National Organization for Internet Safety and Education early Thursday morning. The red-eye she'd taken from a PTA conference in Anaheim had just landed at Port Columbus International Airport half an hour before. She couldn't remember the last time she'd eaten.

If she'd gone straight home to shower without stopping at the office first to review the day's materials, she could have had breakfast with Brent.

Glancing at the plain gold watch on her wrist—a college graduation present from her parents—Sara sat, pulled the pile of folders onto her lap and started to read.

THE DOORBELL RANG just as she was finishing her makeup. Stroking a couple of coats of mascara onto her lashes, Sara quickly dropped the tube in the sectioned container on her dressing table and raced to the stairs. Maybe it was just a salesperson, but she couldn't stand to not answer.

She never let the phone ring, either.

It was five to nine. She'd spent so long at the office already that she was now late for work. But the sun was shining, May flowers were in bloom and an entire lovely summer stretched ahead.

Sara slowed at the bottom of the stairs, taking a deep breath to compose herself as she smoothed a hand down her slim brown skirt and brushed the pockets of her jacket. Dignity and class were her mantras. Always.

Brent expected this from her.

"Can I help—" The ready smile froze on her lips. A cop was standing on her doorstep.

Something had happened to her dad. Or Brent.

The young man's mouth moved, but at this moment Sara couldn't concentrate sufficiently to make out his words. "What?" she asked, willing herself to hear what he was saying. "What happened?"

"Are you Mrs. Sara Calhoun?"

"Yes." She wished she weren't. Law enforcement officials never came to deliver good news. She ought to know. She'd grown up with one.

"You are." The young man's gaze deepened, studying her.

"Yes," she managed to say, bracing herself.

And nothing happened. Officer Mercedes, according to the thin nameplate above his left pocket, just stood there, apparently at a loss for words.

"Can I help you?" she finally prompted, mystified. She was the one getting the bad news—wasn't she?

"I…uh…I've been planning this moment for a long time and I thought I was completely prepared. But now I have no idea what to say."

Planning this moment? One didn't usually plan to deliver bad news.

He looked so lost, so young, Sara's heart caught. "You're sure it's me you want to see? I'm Sara Calhoun, formerly Sara Lindsay. I'm married to Brent Calhoun. He's an attorney...."

Relief made her talkative.

"Antitrust. Yes, I know," the tall, well-built officer said with a rueful grin. And a nervous twitch at the left corner of his mouth.

He ran his hand through his short sandy-colored hair, his raised arm drawing her attention to the belt at his waist—and all the defensive paraphernalia strapped there. That gun looked heavy.

"And, yes, you're the one I'm looking for."

The kid was young, his green eyes switching back and forth between innocent and knowing as he stood there, shifting his weight. He couldn't be much more than twenty-one, which made her thirty-seven seem ancient.

"What'd I do? Forget to signal a turn? I have a habit of doing that, though I'm working on it," she said, brushing a strand of hair back over her shoulder. This had to be his first house call.

He frowned and then, glancing down, his face cleared. "Oh, the uniform," he said. "I'm not here on official business. I work the night shift in Westerville—just got off duty and finished my paperwork."

Westerville, a north Columbus suburb a bit west of the New Albany home she and Brent had purchased six years before. There was a park within walking distance of every home in their area. Barely thirty when they bought it, she'd still believed that her workaholic husband was going to agree to have the children they'd always said they were going to have.

"Speaking of work, I'm late," Sara said now, suddenly anxious to be on her way.

"I can come back another time."

"No." She shook her head. What could a young cop possibly have to do with her that would justify a second trip out? Or any trip? "I'm listening."

"And I'm finding that there's just no way to say this except outright."

She waited.

"I'm your son."

She blinked.

The young man stood still, as if frozen in stone, while his words replayed themselves in her mind.

He'd just said he was her son.

Her son.

He couldn't be.

Twenty-one years of fighting for dignity and

grace served her well enough to keep her standing. Sara clutched the door with both hands, leaned against it, her gaze never wavering from the young man standing just outside it.

He shifted, his hands folded together as if in military or pallbearer stance. Had he ever been in the military, this boy who was standing there claiming to be the child she'd given away so long ago? The child she'd worried for, grieved over and daydreamed about ever since.

Had he, too, suffered the pain of losing one he loved?

"Should I go?"

"No!"

"You're shocked. How could you not be?"

His voice was deep, not at all that of the little boy she'd imagined so often that he seemed completely real to her.

This voice was filled with strength. Compassion. And a tremble of fear.

Or was she only losing her mind? After all these years, all the determination and trying, the counseling, all the self-flagellation, was the past finally going to undo her, anyway?

"I'm… I'm sorry," she finally managed, straightening. "I just…"

"I know," he interrupted, his hands still folded

together. "I tried to come up with some easier way to do this, but I guess there isn't one."

No. Not easy. Nothing about Sara's life had been easy since the morning after this boy—if he was her son—had been conceived. Nothing had been quite real. She'd lost things then that she'd been too young to even know she'd prized.

"I... What did you say your name was?"

"I didn't. It's Ryan—Ryan Mercedes."

Ah. Yes. *Officer Mercedes.* Seemed like years ago that she'd read that name tag.

He was staring at her openly now. Counting the lines on her face? Finding her wanting? Wondering what kind of woman she was who would give away her newborn son?

Years of training drove her to respond. She held out her hand. "Nice to meet you, Ryan."

Was she insane? *Nice to meet you?* With a handshake?

He glanced at her hand, looked up to her face. She thought he was going to refuse her offering. And then he reached out, took her hand and held on.

Sara started to cry.

AFTER A QUICK GLANCE behind him, Ryan reached with his free hand to wipe the tears from his mother's face—and his own. He'd imagined this moment, of course. Many times.

He'd just never thought she'd be such a beautiful woman. Or that she'd look so young. He'd known she was thirty-seven, but he'd pictured someone more like his mom. Harriet Mercedes. Fifty-one. Graying. Twenty pounds heavier than she'd been when he was little.

Brent Calhoun was a first-class fool.

Shoulders tensing as a car passed behind him, Ryan said, "May I come in?"

He didn't want her neighbors talking, asking her awkward questions. Didn't want to make life harder for her than he already knew it was going to be.

"Um, of course."

She turned and backed up, breaking eye contact with him. He was shocked at the loss he immediately felt. Of course, he'd expected to have some feelings for this woman—she'd given him life—but he'd imagined his reaction would be protective, rather than deeply emotional.

He had a mother and father whom he adored. They'd raised him, provided for him, loved him. They'd given him all the support and encouragement any kid could ever hope for.

He didn't need Sara Calhoun. At least not emotionally.

She led him through a formal living room with carpet so plush that the sides of his black regulation shoes sank into oblivion—the maroon-trimmed cream silk furniture was obviously not used much—past a shining, stainless-and-granite kitchen to a large, more comfortable room at the back of the sprawling custom home.

Though they weren't millionaires, the Calhouns' yearly income more than doubled that of Ryan's parents. He'd never been inside such a nice house.

Or expected her to have such long, dark hair. Was the color natural?

"Have a seat." His birth mother was standing in front of a sliding-glass door that revealed an acre or more of freshly manicured green grass out back.

Ryan chose one end of the couch, not wanting to risk choosing Brent Calhoun's chair out of the three in the room. Assuming the man had a special chair. There was only one chair in the family room at his folks' house—his dad's recliner. His mom used the couch, as did the two Labs. That left him the floor or the love seat when he visited. He used both, depending on his mood.

His perusal of the room complete, he turned back to the woman who'd seated herself at the other end of the couch—and was leaning heavily on the arm. He almost wondered if she was afraid of him.

Kids were, sometimes. When he was in uniform. He didn't like it then and he didn't like it now.

He didn't want Sara Calhoun to fear him. He wanted her to like him, to approve of him.

And that's when he knew he'd been kidding himself.

Pathetic as it was, what he needed was for her to love him.

"I ALWAYS THOUGHT I'd recognize you if I ever saw you." Sara was completely out of her element. Every moment in her life was carefully planned, scripted. Often rehearsed. How did you do "tragedy from the past catching up with you" with dignity and class and the peculiar level of withholding yourself that dignity and class required?

"I think I have your chin. At least, that's what my parents say."

"They know me?"

He shook his head. "I showed them the pictures that I found of you."

This was becoming completely surreal.

"What pictures?"

"Some I found in a newspaper article on the

Internet. You'd just won the Ohio State alumni woman-of-the-year award."

A miracle was happening. Or a catastrophe. And they were talking about the Internet.

"What makes you think I'm your mother?" She should have asked sooner. Would have, if she hadn't been afraid she'd find out she wasn't.

"You gave permission for your name to be made known, if I ever sought you out."

She nodded. "I gave up hoping that would happen years ago." She'd never given up the grieving, though. Not one day between then and now had passed without an awareness of the weight inside her.

He slid his hands along his thighs, to his knees. "So you don't mind?"

"Mind?" Her face stiff, Sara smiled. Until her lips started to tremble. "I've mourned not knowing you every day of your life!"

"I'm sorry."

"Sorry! For what? You were a helpless baby!"

"You were mourning and I've known about you for seven years."

He'd have been fourteen then. He'd known about her since he was barely a teenager. From the time she was thirty. Before she bought this house—when she'd still been counting on having another child.

"And you owed me nothing," she told the son she'd had when she'd still been a child herself. "Don't you ever feel sorry for your part in any of this. Not ever." She carried around enough shame, anger and grief for all of them.

He nodded and she sat back, studying him further, finding every aspect of his face fascinating. And the way he held his hands, as if he was always aware of them, always in control of them.

"What do you think?" His question startled her, embarrassed her.

"That you're everything I've imagined you to be. And more."

"You don't even know me yet."

"Based on what I've already seen, I know that you can be kind. Compassionate. Gentle. You're working in an admirable profession and obviously have lived your life in such a way that allowed you to pass the rigorous background checks necessary to be a law enforcement officer."

"Just like your father was."

She drew back, frowning. "Just how much do you know about me?" It was disconcerting, having this perfect stranger, this flesh of her flesh, aware of facts of her life—while she, who'd been yearning for even one word of him for more than twenty years, knew nothing.

He glanced down, his cheeks turning red, and when he sought her gaze again, his expression was pleading. "Can we start over? Or at least go back a little bit? I honestly had this whole thing planned and... I don't know..." He shrugged. "Being here, meeting you. It's not at all like I thought it would be."

He was a planner. Just like she was. Except that she hadn't been—until that awful night so many years ago.

"How did you think it would be?"

He made a face. "Businesslike."

Her heart dropped. "Is that what you'd like it to be?"

"No!" Ryan sat forward, his hands on his knees, as if ready to push off. She expected him to stand, but he turned to look at her instead.

"I... Can I start at the beginning?"

Pleased by his strong need to stay, Sara smiled. "Of course. Especially if you're going to tell me about you. It's strange having you know things about me, when I don't know anything about you beyond the fact that you made me sick to my stomach for three months straight, kicked like a soccer player and were so eager to be born I barely got to the hospital in time."

And she also knew that he'd been a perfect

baby boy. That he'd weighed seven pounds even. Been born at 3:58 a.m. And had a full head of sandy-colored hair.

"Really?" He grinned. Sat back. "I never knew that."

"How could you?" Not even her parents knew that. They'd been out of town for the weekend, leaving Sara home alone with a neighbor on call next door. She hadn't been due for another three weeks.

She'd taken a cab to the hospital. And called them after her son had already been whisked away.

Having Ryan had been something she'd had to do on her own.

Right now, he looked as if he was waiting for her to elaborate. She wasn't prepared to go back there. Not yet. She'd spent twenty-one years running in the opposite direction.

"You were going to start at the beginning."

Ryan told her about the youthful rebellion that had ended with his parents encouraging him to pursue finding her, if that was what he needed in order to have a sense of identity.

"I was shocked," he said, one knee up on the couch as he turned to face her. His arm stretched along the sofa back until he was almost touching her shoulder.

Sara relished the closeness, the warmth of his fingers nearby. She wished she had the right to hug him, to fill the emptiness she'd felt in her arms since the day he'd been born.

"I knew I was adopted. I've always known. But I never asked about my birth parents, figuring it would hurt my real parents' feelings."

He stopped. Sara raised her brow.

"I was going to apologize."

"They're your real parents, Ryan. Never doubt that. I played a biological role in your life, nothing more." The words just came out.

"How can you say that?"

"It's what I've been telling myself more than half my life."

It was the only way she'd survived without him.

"Do you really believe that?"

They were traveling backward again—to places that hurt a great deal.

"I believe I want to hear the rest of your story."

He studied her a moment longer and then, to her relief, he continued.

"My mom called the adoption agency for me and a couple of weeks later I came home from school to find a letter waiting. It told us your name, and that you lived in Maricopa."

A town just outside Montgomery County, near

Dayton. A little over an hour from Columbus. She'd grown up there.

Ryan had been born there.

He pulled a document out of his back pocket and handed it to her. "And there was this." A copy of his birth certificate. The official one with her name on it, next to the words Baby Boy Lindsay. That piece of paper would only have been released to one person—her son.

"I came to Columbus to go to Ohio State, got married and never left," she said inanely, so disoriented she couldn't think straight.

He nodded. "I know."

There it was again. That knowledge he had.

"You never wanted to contact me?" God, she sounded pathetic. And the question was completely unfair.

He grimaced, shrugged. "Sure I did—some of the time. But I knew you were married. I didn't know if he knew about me, or if you'd welcome the idea of a potentially painful reminder from your past showing up on your doorstep."

"I would have welcomed you. Instantly. Any time."

She couldn't speak for Brent. Wouldn't speak for him. They didn't share the same feelings about children.

Hers. Or anyone else's.

Though, for years, she'd thought they had.

"I also didn't want to hurt my folks," Ryan admitted next. "They were completely open about finding you, but I could tell my mom was a little worried, too."

Understandably. Sara had a strong urge to meet the woman who'd been such a good mother to the boy she'd birthed. To tell her thank you. And to tell her not to worry.

To find out if the woman could accept her—or if she hated her. To find out if some of the jealousy she'd avoided acknowledging all these years could be put to rest.

But what if it intensified?

"Do they know you're contacting me now?"

She'd jumped ahead. There was so much in between.

"Yes."

That was all. Nothing more.

"I was kind of geeky growing up," Ryan said then, obviously sensing that they had to go back to go forward. "I played Little League and high school football…."

"Were you good at it?"

"Good enough." He shook his head, as if his sports successes were inconsequential. "I enjoyed playing, and my father encouraged it, but what I loved most was reading. And surfing the Net."

"AOL would have been in full swing by the time you were in high school."

"I was a junkie on Genie," he said, naming an Internet connection source that had been out of business for several years.

"I'm assuming you know what I do for a living?"

"You're executive director for NOISE, a national nonprofit organization that teaches Internet safety to kids, which your father, Sheriff John Lindsay, founded after his first book on the subject was published. You're not supported by taxpayers' money, but you get more than half of your funding through state-paid programs that contract your services."

"Is there anything about me you don't know?"

He glanced away and, for the first time since he'd come into her house, Sara felt uneasy with him there.

She realized she hadn't called the office.

CHAPTER TWO

"EVERYTHING OKAY?" Ryan asked when Sara came back into the room and sat. He was sitting on the couch, right where she'd left him when she went to phone Donna. "Do you have to leave? I can come back another time."

She shook her head, wondering how she was going to answer the questions her executive assistant was sure to ask when she finally did make it in to work. "I had an early flight from California this morning, so my schedule is clear until one."

Everyone who knew her at all would find it odd that she wasn't in the office, anyway—she'd been gone for three days.

But at the moment, she didn't really care. For the first time in many years, the office, her father, what people thought of her, didn't matter.

"Would you like something to drink?"

"I'm good, thanks." He shook his head.

"You were starting at the beginning."

"Yeah." Head bowed, he didn't speak right away. Then, looking up at her, he said, "This is kind of strange, isn't it?"

Sara chuckled. "To say the least. I'm nothing to you—I don't even know you. And yet I look at you, know that you're my son and I feel like a mother. I'm thirty-seven years old and I don't recognize myself."

"I kinda feel like I know you, too."

"Sounds like you know quite a bit about me."

The thought was a comfort, given the seven years it had taken him to come and meet her.

"I've always loved puzzles, solving riddles and mysteries. When I was a kid I preferred old detective reruns to cartoons and all the action-hero shows the kids at school talked about."

She could picture him, a much smaller version of the man sitting beside her, with skinny arms and legs, innocent eyes and the same freshly cut hair, lying on his stomach in front of a television set, his chin in his hands. The vision was so bittersweet it echoed the ache that accompanied her everywhere, every day.

"I don't really know how it all started," he continued. "It's not like I ever made a conscious decision, but somehow, after I learned your name—and decided that I wasn't going to try to see you—I started looking you up on the Internet."

Sara's chest tightened. Her entire life was a secret, built on air—and on her determination to protect herself, make amends, never be hurt or hurt anyone ever again. She would not allow herself to falter.

But no one knew that. In this area she had no confidants.

"There was no Internet when I was growing up. And I'm a behind-the-scenes kind of person. I imagine that search bored you fairly quickly."

Ryan shook his head. But it was the compassion shining from his eyes that scared her to death.

He knew. That one look from her son brought back all the shame. The dirtiness. The fear and anger. The guilt.

She didn't want him to see her like that. Didn't want to be that person. She'd worked so hard to leave sixteen-year-old Sara Lindsay behind.

"When I typed in your name, nothing came up. But birth records are public and it didn't take long to find out that your father was the sheriff of Brighton County."

Court cases were probably public record, too. And if someone was savvy enough to know how to access them…

"It was actually through his name that I found the old newspaper articles."

"How old?" The Internet hadn't been around that long.

"Twenty-two years. The *Maricopa Tribune,* like a lot of newspapers, hired someone to archive their past issues and you can access the collection on their Web site."

She'd had no idea. Had never seen the articles to begin with, though she'd heard about them. Her parents had pulled her out of school that year and her mother had homeschooled her. They'd done all they could to help her recover from the tragic consequences of her great rebellion—including arranging counseling.

Still, despite all their efforts—and her own—the damage remained.

Ryan hesitated, and now it was Sara's turn to look away. How did a son broach such a subject with his mother? Especially one he'd just met?

He shouldn't need to.

And yet it was clearly important to Ryan.

"It was my fault." She hadn't meant to say the words. And knew logically that they couldn't possibly be true. Everyone who'd been around then, who'd had anything to do with her, had adamantly insisted that she hadn't been to blame.

And yet she'd deliberately disobeyed her parents. She'd lied. She'd put herself in danger....

"You were raped. Three guys were convicted and sent to prison! How can you possibly think that was your fault?" Ryan's words echoed those she'd heard so many times before.

"I should never have been at that party," she said softly. "It was stupid teenage rebellion. Growing up the only child of a sheriff—especially when you're a girl—isn't always easy. My father was pretty strict, seeing danger in everything."

"I can imagine."

Glancing at his uniform, she was sure he could. And with twenty-one years' hindsight—heck, with one more day's hindsight—she'd been able to understand, as well.

But if they had to talk about this, she needed it done as quickly as possible, with as little discussion as possible.

"I'd wanted to go to a concert in Cincinnati at Riverfront Stadium with a group of girlfriends, and my father said no. I was the only one who couldn't go and they all had a great time. Talked about it the entire week afterward. I felt left out. And so uncool. Like a little kid hanging out with girls who were growing up without me. And it just so happened that that following weekend one of my friends told me about a frat party that a group of college guys were having down by the lake a few miles outside of town. Her older brother was going. I'd been to the lake a hundred times, we all had. I saw this as an opportunity to show them all—most particularly my dad—that I was growing up, too. And so, pretending to be older than I was, I went to that party. Turns out there was only one other girl there and I don't know how long she stayed."

She cringed, even now, as she thought about the stupid young girl she'd been—so hell-bent on running her own life, she'd damaged it irrevocably.

Hers and many others.

"The paper said you'd been found there the next morning."

"By my father." Of all people. "All I can remember is having two bottles of some wine thing. And the next thing I know, my dad's shaking me awake. I was already wrapped in his coat. And wearing little else."

Ryan's gaze fell momentarily. "The newspaper article didn't mention that part."

"There were empty beer bottles all over the ground." Sara continued her recitation as if he hadn't spoken at all. "And whiskey bottles, too."

She'd do this once, and never again. For the child who'd been conceived that night.

"My father was determined to find the guy who'd taken advantage of me."

"It was a lot more than that." Ryan's voice was stronger, coplike.

Arms around her waist, Sara shivered, in spite of the heat. "Maybe," she allowed, and then nodded. "Probably, considering the fact that until that point I hadn't even been kissed. Guys didn't fool around with Sheriff Lindsay's daughter."

She'd been the quintessential virgin. She'd never even had her breasts touched through her clothes, and suddenly she'd been naked for all the world to see.

"There was a guy at the scene who I guess wasn't as drunk as the rest. He apparently named the three guys and the hospital was able to confirm that all three of them had been…with…me."

Problem was, she couldn't remember if they'd simply had sex with her. Or raped her.

"I didn't even have to testify," she continued, lost in her thoughts with that young girl again, trying to make sense out of a world gone mad. "I couldn't remember anything, but it didn't matter to my father or the court. I was underage. It was rape. Statutory or otherwise."

"The evidence was pretty clear that it'd been otherwise."

She'd been badly bruised in places a girl should never be bruised.

"For all I knew, I got wild when I drank."

"You'd never gotten drunk before?"

She shook her head. "And I've never been drunk since."

"You don't drink?"

"Socially." One glass of wine, if a host was serving her. And only if the circumstances were completely controlled.

"According to what I read, none of the men convicted remembered much about what happened, either. Or at least, that was their defense."

That's what she'd been told. She hadn't been present to hear any of the testimony.

"Based on the number of bottles found at the site and how sick we all were the next day, I'd guess we were all somewhat to blame."

But she hadn't lost her freedom for it. She hadn't been sent to prison at eighteen, to be God-knew-what by the hardened and deranged prisoners who were spending their lives behind bars.

And if it had been only statutory rape, if she'd been a willing participant in the sexual antics that night, she was at least somewhat to blame for their incarceration. They'd been sent up on charges of having sex with a minor and she'd told them all she was twenty-one. Dressed as if she'd been twenty-one, with a bra that had pushed up her breasts and a low-cut blouse that showed more than it left to the imaginations of a bunch of horny college guys.

"Do you know if any of you were checked for drug use?" Ryan sounded all cop.

"Did the papers say we had been?"

"It wasn't mentioned."

"If we were, I wasn't told about it. I sure didn't see or hear anything about any drugs at the party. These guys were there to drink, but that's all. Why do you ask?"

He shrugged. "PCP, for instance, is a dissociative street drug that's been around since the fifties and it's still used by about two and a half percent of high school seniors today. One of its side effects is loss of memory."

He was well-trained. And seeing things that weren't there because he knew too much?

"I'm sure if my father suspected drug use, we were tested," she told her newfound son. "But passing out from an overdose of alcohol can also result in loss of memory, and I know for certain that there was an ample supply of that on hand."

"So you think you passed out drunk, and then they had sex with you?"

Her body temperature rising from her feet to her ears, Sara concentrated on taking long, calming breaths. Distancing herself, as she'd been taught in her counseling sessions all those years ago.

"I try not to think about it at all," she told her son honestly. "I woke up, spent the day vomiting and crying, and six weeks later I found out I was pregnant."

"I was afraid of that."

"Afraid?"

He shrugged, looked down. "The papers, the trial transcript, said nothing about a pregnancy. I kind of hoped my conception was a separate incident."

"I was sixteen."

"I know. But you'd been to the hospital. They'd have taken precautions to prevent pregnancy."

"There's only so much they can do. It happens that way sometimes."

"My folks said tests were never done to determine which of the three was my father."

Since she had no memory of any of them, the three had kind of morphed into one in Sara's mind.

"I'd say I was sorry, except that then I wouldn't be here," Ryan added.

"I'm definitely not sorry you're here," Sara told him, looking him straight in the eye. And she wasn't. At all. She'd given life to a remarkable human being—given a son to a childless couple who'd clearly loved him well.

"You might be."

That sounded ominous. "Why?"

"I haven't told you what I'm doing here."

He'd come out of a desire to finally meet her. Hadn't he?

"So tell me." Sara couldn't imagine anything worse than what they'd just been through.

"First, I don't think the story of that night ends with you having me and three young men going to prison."

Of course it did. It was over, done.

"I think the whole rape thing was a cover-up."

The idea was so ludicrous she couldn't even consider it. Ryan was young. A rookie cop, over-eager. Needing to put a different light on the night of his conception.

Because the facts as they were were unsatisfying—and ugly.

Because he felt the need to exonerate his birth mother? Or to pretend that he wasn't the offspring of a rapist?

"A cover-up? For what?"

"Murder."

"Whose murder?"

"I don't know yet, but I intend to find out. Some bones were found on the other side of the lake later that year after a huge flood washed away much of the bank. The local coroner dated them to within a few weeks of the night of that party."

In her mind, it was the night she was raped. The night of his conception. The night that changed her life forever. But if he wanted to refer to it as the night of the party, that was fine with her.

She remembered the flood. Had been glad to hear that the site of her foray into hell had been washed clean.

"Were the bones identified?"

"No. From what I can see, the townspeople were questioned and requests for information posted, but no one came forward. Apparently, there were not only no witnesses to the death but no one reported a missing person, either. You can't match dental records without a possible identity to begin with. And Ohio has only been using DNA testing on a regular basis since the late '80s. There were no matching missing-persons reports in the state during the three months prior, or two years after, the approximate time of death."

She wasn't going to ask him how he knew

that. Maricopa wasn't in his jurisdiction. But he was a police officer. He had ways to get access to information that most people wouldn't even know existed.

Still…

"So how does this all tie in? You think someone was murdered that night at the lake? Surely someone would have reported a missing college kid."

"The dead man was in his late thirties to early forties."

Ryan's earnestness, his conviction, was endearing. "And the tie-in?"

"That's what I have to find. But think about it. The sheriff's daughter, a conservative young woman, by all accounts, is suddenly having sex with three men—and all four of you have no memory of the incident. There's ample physical evidence, and a baby, to prove what happened. This is a case that will consume every ounce of the sheriff's attention, focus and energy. An open-and-shut case that won't require digging into anything else that might have happened that night. You have to admit, it's convenient."

Not a word she'd ever associated with that night.

"Too convenient, if you ask me," Ryan continued. "Most cops don't like coincidences, and I don't like conveniences. Crimes aren't usually that easy to wrap up."

"And this…convenience…is what you're basing your murder cover-up story on?"

He nodded, fingertips tapping together. "That, the unidentified bones, and…" he glanced away and then back, giving her a sheepish look "…I've read some of the police reports."

"Did you find something unusual?"

"Not necessarily, but I've got some questions and am hoping to get the whole file. I'm studying to become a detective and I've asked to look over the case for practice."

Just as she thought. A young cop playing sleuth. And where was the harm? If he needed to reshape the events that surrounded his conception, she wasn't going to try to stop him.

"That's actually not why I'm here," Ryan said then, as if he knew she wasn't buying his theory.

There was more? She wasn't sure she had the emotional or physical resources to handle anything else at the moment.

She wanted to know how old he was when he took his first step. And whether or not he liked peas. Or if he had a girlfriend?

He wasn't wearing a wedding ring.

But this wasn't about her. She'd given up her rights to Ryan's life the day she'd let them whisk him away, never to be seen by her again.

A newborn baby rejected by the woman who'd given birth to him.

At least she'd given birth to him. Her parents had spent weeks trying to convince her to terminate her pregnancy.

It was evidence of her overwhelmed state that it took her several minutes to realize Ryan wasn't talking anymore.

"So why are you here?"

"I haven't wanted to intrude on your life," he answered slowly. "But neither have I been able to forget you."

She smiled and he smiled back.

"So I've sort of been watching you."

She sat up. "Spying on me?"

"No!" Ryan stood. Faced her.

He was a lot taller than she'd pictured him these past couple of years. An inch or two over six feet.

"Watching *out* for you, I should have said."

Sara couldn't help smiling again. While she'd been going through the motions of living, her long-lost son had been protecting her, kind of like her own private guardian angel.

Which was overstating things, she was sure.

But the calming sensation moving slowly through her sure was nice.

"Thank you."

"Don't thank me." His face was grim.

"What?" Sara sat forward, frowning. "Something's going on at NOISE that I don't know about? Tell me."

"It's not NOISE."

"What, then?"

Her father was retired. Still living in the house in Maricopa where she'd grown up. Nagging her about NOISE. Writing the books on adolescence and Internet safety that had made the organization such a success.

"Your husband."

"Brent?"

Ryan nodded. Waited. Almost as if he couldn't bring himself to tell her what he'd gone through all of this to say.

"He's gambling again?" She'd warned him. One more time and they were through.

He shook his head. His eyes warming again. And she knew. Ryan was like her own self-appointed private eye. And everyone who watched the old detective shows knew what kind of information they were usually hired to ferret out when it came to marriages.

She said the words so he didn't have to. "He's having an affair."

MARK DALTON ROSE when his name was called, walked across the front of the large hall on the Ohio State University campus and accepted his Juris Doctor. Circling around, he resumed his seat in the great hall at the law school he'd been attending for the past three years, immune to those around him. Some might not know who or what he was. Many probably no longer cared. He'd long since ceased to allow such things to bother him.

He'd have left, if not for the fact that his mom and sister were sitting with the family members of his classmates behind him. He'd told them they needn't come. The two-hour drive from Cleveland, where they'd relocated twenty years before, wasn't hard, but his sister—a waitress at a well-to-do club—had to work that night.

And his mother's eyesight wasn't good enough for her to drive alone in the dark.

Besides, Mark was going to work, too, as soon as he got home and changed out of the conservative shirt and tie he had on under his academic robes. He had a '52 Corvette to deliver the following day and some finishing touches to put on his workmanship.

The rich and famous in the car world didn't

mind doing business with a known sex offender, when he was also one of the best vintage car restorers in the country.

No one worried about him assaulting an engine.

Charles Granger, dean of Ohio State's College of Law, ended his closing remarks and the ceremony concluded with a whoop of congratulations. Mark waited for his chance to leave.

"Good luck, Mark," Sharon Rose said from beside him, squeezing his hand.

She was forty, divorced and starting a new life. She'd been hired by the county attorney's office.

"You, too," he told her.

"Give me a call sometime."

He nodded, knowing he wouldn't.

Filing out, Mark was greeted by many of the other students and professors, all gathered there to celebrate new beginnings. He waved at his mom, who was wiping her eyes.

For Mark, this was an end. Unlike most of his classmates, he didn't have a job lined up with a firm or with the state, or any kind of a law career ahead. He'd done this simply because it had been one of the most important goals in his life back when his life had been his own. There were many doors closed to him now, but getting the degree was not one of them.

As to the rest of that dream—to practice public law, prosecute for the state of Ohio, as Sharon was going to do—it had died a long time ago.

Registered sex offenders were not permitted to take the bar exam. Nor to hold any position in society that required a professional license.

But he could drive a car.

And he was free.

CHAPTER THREE

SARA WENT TO DINNER with Brent and his partners Tuesday night, as planned. She made small talk with the wives, ordered steak and pretended to eat, and sat silently while her husband talked business. Brent was the rainmaker—the one who sought out business for his firm. And his partners were excellent attorneys.

She had one glass of wine.

And she went home to bed with Brent. They talked about the dinner as they moved around each other almost in choreographed motion, Sara washing her face at her sink while he brushed his teeth at his, meeting together over the dirty clothes hamper in their room-sized closet. She reached for her nightgown off one hook as he grabbed his pajama bottoms from the matching designer hook beside hers. They walked into the bedroom, turning off the lights as they went. She raised the blinds so the moon could shine in.

Brent was pleased with the evening. His partners were pleased with the amount of revenue he was bringing in for them, and they expected very little in the way of actual lawyering from him. He had a young attorney who worked for him who did most of his work—and, according to Ryan, did other things for him, as well. Intimate things. And what she didn't do, his law clerk handled—workwise, anyway.

"I'm glad the evening went so well," Sara said, pulling back the covers on her side of the bed to slide beneath them. As Brent clicked off the last light and joined her, she checked the alarm, making sure it was set to go off.

Brent turned, gave her a quick peck on the lips. "Me, too. You were great, babe, thanks."

"You're welcome," she said with dignity and class. And then rolled over facing the wall opposite him, just as she did every single night.

But instead of willing herself to sleep, she lay awake, long into the night, alternating between joy and despair, tears rolling silently down her face onto her pillow.

She'd met her son. After twenty-one years of longing and agony, she'd looked him in the eye, held his hand. Hugged him goodbye.

And after fifteen years of marriage, she had

to face the fact that no amount of pretending or trying or waiting was going to repair her marriage.

This day had changed her life.

SATURDAY MORNING DAWNED at 6:09 a.m. Sitting at her kitchen table with a cup of coffee, Sara was waiting. Brent always woke as soon as the sun began to stream into the bedroom window. He'd take a quick shower, because he had a golf game scheduled. And then he'd be down for coffee.

A twisted sense of humor lurking in the part of Sara that had been detached from life since the morning after her rape, prompted the thought that she should take bets with herself as to whether or not he'd make his game.

Twisted thought he would. Kind—or dead, she wasn't sure—guessed he wouldn't. She gave up the attempt to pretend she could joke about this, in any way, even to herself, when the tears came again.

She couldn't be crying when he came down. Tears made him uncomfortable, defensive. Tears would only make this harder than it already was.

Mostly, she couldn't believe it had come to this. His refusal to have children, after telling her for so many years that he wanted them, too, as soon as they were solvent, had been rough.

Putting up with his lack of satisfaction with their physical life hadn't been easy, either.

But she'd comforted herself with the knowledge that she wasn't alone—and he wasn't, either. They had each other. They had trust and loyalty.

And she'd been willing to settle for those. They were comfortable. Safe.

After the rocky start to her adult life, safety and security had been priorities to her.

Sara heard the shower. Sipped her coffee. Waited. How could she be so calm, when inside she was falling apart? Devastated? Scared to death?

"You're up early," he greeted her with a quick kiss on the cheek, smelling of the musk aftershave she'd been buying him for years. His thick, dark hair was still damp.

"I couldn't sleep."

Pouring his coffee, he turned, cup in hand, to frown at her. "Aren't you feeling good? Cramps?"

She'd had her period the week before.

"I know about Chloe."

His entire demeanor changed, stiffened. His shoulders closed in on his tall, lanky form. Cup in hand, he pulled out a chair at the table, not his usual one. One reserved for guests.

Sara catalogued his every move. Watched his

long legs slide under the table, wincing as he sipped hot liquid, too much, too fast. Noticed his Adam's apple as he swallowed. She watched herself watching.

"Who told you?"

The emotional weight dropped deeper into her stomach, making her queasy. Bringing on panic so intense she could hardly breathe.

So it was true. Her zealous, young son hadn't been jumping to conclusions. Amazing how a life could fall apart without even making a sound.

And he wanted to know who had told her. "Does it matter?"

His gaze held hers for long seconds and then dropped. "I suppose not."

He sipped. She watched. She had coffee, too, but she was pretty sure she'd choke on it.

"How long has it been going on?"

His face stiff, he stared at her. "Does it matter?" He repeated back to her.

"Yes, I think it does."

When he glanced away, she knew she'd won. And lost everything. "A year."

Jitters spread through her, just beneath her skin—and deeper. "As long as she's been there?"

He acknowledged the statement with one tip of his head—as if this wasn't all that big a deal to him. As if infidelity was just another little bump in the road—like stealing away, with false promises, her chances of ever bearing a child she could hold in her arms, nurse, raise.

And then, struck with horror, she realized something else.

"There've been others, haven't there?" How stupid of her not to have considered that fact. How amazingly blind. She wanted to crawl into a hole.

"A few."

Sara hadn't figured there was enough left of her heart to be further crushed.

"They don't mean anything, Sara."

That made her angry. "Of course they do!" She raised her voice—something she almost never did. "They mean you've been unfaithful to me! To the vows we took. They mean you're untrustworthy."

Didn't he understand that loyalty and trust were all they had? And now they had nothing at all?

"They mean that I have needs you aren't willing to meet."

Sucking in a breath, she nodded. She'd heard about that before. Countless times. Couldn't take it again—not right then.

Leave it to Brent to make this her fault. Just as

it had been her fault that she hadn't understood that when he said he wanted children later, he'd meant he didn't want them—ever.

"I've never turned you away when you've asked for sex."

"Who wants to have to ask?" His voice was quiet, his expression tired. "I want a woman who's eager to be in my arms, Sara. One who enjoys my touch."

"I enjoy it."

"Sometimes," he allowed. "And other times, you lie there and make the right moves and wait for it to be over."

Didn't every woman? When she was tired? Feeling taken for granted?

Is that how it had been for her the night of Ryan's conception? Had she lain there, her thoughts and emotions separate from what they were doing to her body?

Sara shook her head, pulling her thoughts back from places she'd left behind long ago. She hadn't considered that night for years. At least not for more than a second or two. Ryan's visit was costing her greatly.

"If you were eager, Sara, you'd want to experiment."

She stared at him, knowing she should speak up. Knowing there were things she needed to say.

But she couldn't bring them to mind, couldn't focus. All she could do was hold back the tears.

"We've been married fifteen years. And in the same standard missionary position, with the same foreplay, for all of them. If you were doing more than your duty, feeling more, you'd need some variety, something to keep things fresh and new."

"Why?" she suddenly spouted, not recognizing her own voice. "When apparently you've been getting fresh and new for years?"

His shoulders dropped more.

"I'm sorry," she said, out of years of habit—and because she meant it. "That was beneath me."

"Just think about what I'm saying for a minute," Brent said, his voice soft, almost pleading, and Sara wondered if he actually wanted her blessing for his actions. Her approval. Maybe even a go-ahead to continue? "When's the last time we made love?"

She tried to remember. Picturing them in bed. At night. On Sunday mornings. The last time they'd been in a hotel together.

"You can't remember."

Her mind scrambling, she stared at him.

"Can you?"

Sara shook her head.

"I can," he surprised her by saying. "It was two months ago. On a Saturday morning. You'd had a bad dream and cuddled up behind me. I actually thought you were finally making a move on me and before I realized that you were still half asleep, I'd already gotten your attention and you finished what you'd inadvertently started."

She remembered. Not the dream—that was long gone. But how she'd felt, needing comfort. Needing to be held. And having to have sex instead.

She'd taken comfort from the fact that making love was something that she and Brent shared that no one else had a part in; that it was something that he gave only to her, and she to him.

She hadn't needed it often. But she'd valued the connection.

"How do I know you haven't given me some kind of infection or disease?"

"I always use a condom," he said, as if that made the fact that he'd been screwing his assistant while sleeping with Sara, too, okay.

It wasn't. Right now it felt as if nothing would ever be okay again.

Finding it harder and harder to breathe, Sara considered her options. And she couldn't find any.

"I'm filing for divorce."

He set his cup down. "You can't be serious."

Maybe not. Maybe she wasn't strong enough.

But… "I am." She waited for fear to make her take it back. To apologize. Or compromise. And it didn't.

It sent fresh shards of panic through her, however, mingling with the despair. She couldn't see beyond the hopelessness. But something inside her wouldn't let her lie down, either.

She'd been a victim for such a long time. She just couldn't do it anymore.

Brent sat forward, taking both her hands between his, holding them on her lap. "Don't be ridiculous, Sara. We're partners. We're good together. We've built a great life."

Drawing a strange kind of strength from the warmth of his hands, Sara listened to him. She recognized the words—they were the way she'd have described their relationship, too. A week ago.

"We've got a beautiful house," she said slowly, as though waking from a deep sleep. "A healthy bank account. And a routine that works."

When they weren't eating out, she did the cooking. He did the dishes. She went to the grocery store and did the laundry; he looked after the cars and paid the bills. They took turns putting things back in place after the housekeeper had been in to clean. And they moved gracefully around each other in the bathroom every morning and night.

"Yes," he said, sounding relieved.

And the things she'd been feeling since she'd found out about his adultery didn't change at all. She might have been blind for a lot of years, but she wasn't anymore.

"That's an arrangement, not a relationship."

"You're just tired. Overwrought. I'm sorry you found out about Chloe, but this doesn't change anything, Sara. Things are just as they were last week and the week before. You weren't unhappy then."

Wasn't she? She hadn't asked.

"You certainly weren't thinking we needed to divorce."

He was right. She'd never even considered the possibility. Despite the fact that she'd wanted children more than anything and he'd led her to believe he did, too, until it was too late for her to do much about it. Regardless of how unsexy he made her feel with his dissatisfaction.

Until two days ago, she'd been existing.

Her entire world had changed in the past forty-eight hours. She didn't know how that could happen; how an inner self that had been complacent and exactly the same for more than twenty years could suddenly wear a completely different face. She just knew she wasn't the same person she'd been when she'd run to answer the door two days before.

Funny how it seemed to be the unexpected instants in life that irrevocably changed things. Not the planned-for and worked-toward events.

"Are you going to stop seeing her?"

His hands dropped. So did his head. But when he looked up, she saw resolution in his eyes. "I will, if that's what it takes to keep this together."

What was "this," exactly?

"For how long?"

Brent didn't answer immediately. But she knew him well enough to know that he was attempting to be honest. "I can't make any promises, Sara," he finally said. "I'd like to tell you forever, but I just don't know that. I guess it depends on how much you're willing to do."

"Me?"

"We could see a therapist. Work through your sexual issues and maybe…"

Sara stood, took her cup to the sink. "I've been through enough counseling sessions to write a book on the topic. Probably two," she said. "I am what I am, Brent. A woman who doesn't think sex is the be-all and end-all of life. I enjoy it when the timing is right. I can't make the feelings come at random."

He looked over at her. "I'm not asking you to."

"What are you asking?" Arms folded, she leaned back against the counter.

"I don't know." He swore. "That you lighten up a bit, I guess. Be willing to experiment a little."

Breathing wasn't easy. The tightness in Sara's chest had grown into a physical pain. She felt inadequate—in so many ways.

"Wild and crazy is not fun for me, Brent. It's frightening."

He stood, too, pushing his chair back to the table. He rinsed his cup. Put it in the dishwasher, and then took her shoulders between his hands.

"We'll work this out, Sara," he said, looking her straight in the eye. "I'll end things with Chloe and we'll go from there. Okay?"

She almost nodded. Wanted to nod. Her instincts told her to nod.

She asked a question instead.

"Do you love me, Brent?"

"Of course I do." His gaze dropped to her lips.

"Are you in love with me?"

Letting go of her, he ran a hand through his inch-long hair—still the California blond it had always been. "I don't even know what that means," he said, obviously frustrated with her. "It's a pretty phrase some woman made up, I'd guess. I'm a good provider, Sara. Our bills are paid on time. We live in a nice house in a fine neighborhood. We can afford to vacation where and when we want and eat out every night of the week if we choose to. I clean up after myself and am always here when I say I will be. I don't know what else you want from me."

She wanted him to think she was enough just as she was. She wanted him to be trustworthy. To be loyal to her. She wanted him to be sufficiently in love with her that he couldn't look at another woman.

She wanted from him the things she gave to him.

He grabbed her hand again and as she studied their interlocked fingers, her skin started to burn. Those fingers had touched her intimately. Been inside her.

And inside other women, too.

"I want a divorce."

WHILE BRENT PLAYED GOLF, Sara packed every suitcase they had, as well as a few moving boxes they'd kept in the garage, loaded as much as she could into the back of their dark blue Ford Expedition and rented a furnished apartment near OSU, just off High Street. She'd go back to New Albany on Sunday to get the rest of the stuff she'd packed. And see about finding a more permanent residence—probably in a little better area. She'd been complacent for most of her adult life, but suddenly she couldn't move fast enough. Couldn't even recognize herself.

It was almost as though, if she slowed down, she'd fall.

In her new place she hung her clothes and unpacked bathroom essentials. Leaving everything else, she went to the nearest mall to walk around, be among people, find enough diversion to keep her from sinking into hell beneath the weight of her thoughts.

She thought about calling her father.

Or going to work.

Instead, she bought a beautiful teapot. It was fine bone china. Ivory with gold trim and exquisite little roses hand-painted across its belly.

The teapot reminded her of happy women. Of birds and beauty and things that were more powerful than money or marriages or even death. It brought tears to her eyes.

As soon as she had her purchase in hand, she left.

BACK IN HER TEMPORARY HOME, Sara tried the teapot in several locations, on the ledge inside the front door, the only door, in the middle of the dented, half-sized stove; on the back of the toilet;

and ended with it on her nightstand, so she'd see it first thing when she woke up in the morning.

And then, at 8:42 p.m., according to the cell phone that was doubling as an alarm clock, she crawled into bed, pulled the cheap bedsheets up over her shoulders and cried until her ribs hurt so much she couldn't move.

A SCREAM FROM UPSTAIRS woke him. Mark listened, trying to determine if he needed to get up and help. Call an ambulance.

"I don't give a rat's ass what your mama said, this is my house and I'll damn well leave my shit on the floor and anything else I want to…"

Mark pulled a down pillow over his head. The newlyweds who'd moved into the apartment above him were at it again.

"Uncle Mark?"

Hell. He'd forgotten he had Jordon with him for the weekend.

"Yeah?" Sitting up, Mark flipped the switch he'd installed in the wall beside his cherry-wood headboard, to see his thirteen-year-old nephew, wearing basketball shorts and nothing else, standing in his bedroom doorway.

"Shouldn't you do something?" Jordon gestured to the ceiling. "Call someone?"

He'd been playing surrogate dad to his sister's kid since Jordon was two and her husband, a firefighter, had lost his life in a warehouse fire. Mark took Jordon camping, drove to Cleveland to go to ball games, taught him how to fish. He just never brought him home to Columbus with him.

"They'll stop soon enough," he said now, wishing he'd done as Dana had suggested and stayed with Jordon in Cleveland while she went on an overnight trip with her new boyfriend on his cabin cruiser along the Ohio River.

He'd been afraid having the boy around while she was getting ready—maybe asking questions—would make her change her mind about going. Ken, a widowed doctor she'd met at the club where she worked, was the first guy his sister had dated since her husband's death.

"You're nothing but a pig and a jerk and I can't believe I married you…"

Jordon glanced up again, his brow furrowed. "He might hit her."

Possibly. But Mark didn't think so. If this evening went true to form, Jordon was soon going to be hearing something else his sister didn't want her adolescent son listening in on.

"Don't you touch me, you…"

Yep, here it came. Mark jumped out of bed.

"How about some ice cream?" he asked, pulling on shorts and a T-shirt over the briefs he slept in.

"It's almost midnight!"

"So?" he said to the boy. "I know a shop that's open until one from May 'til September. You saying you don't have room for a banana split?"

Jordon loved banana splits.

"Sure!" His nephew said, just as the sounds overhead started to change. "I've always got room for that."

"Then get your rear next door and grab a shirt and some shoes."

Moving out to the tiny space that served as a living room, Mark raised his voice, ostensibly to be heard from the spare bedroom next to his, avoiding the sight of the wrought-iron bars on the windows—a necessity in this neighborhood—as he grabbed his keys.

He had Jordon out of the apartment and onto the street before the going really got good upstairs. And he took the long way to the ice cream shop two blocks away. He figured he had at least an hour to kill.

"WHY DO YOU LIVE in that place?" Jordon asked, when his boat-shaped dessert dish was completely empty, as Mark nursed a cup of decaffeinated coffee, regardless of the eighty-degree temperature outside.

"I'm too lazy to move," he answered the boy.

"You, lazy? Give me a break."

"I've done a lot a work on the place," Mark tried again, wondering how such short hair got so rumpled as he ran his hand through it. "What about that entertainment system? Can't beat that, huh?"

"'Cept the room's so small you get kinda dizzy watching such a large screen."

Yeah, he hadn't anticipated that consequence.

"It's 'cuz of that stupid sex offender stuff, isn't it?"

He shrugged. "It does make things a little difficult."

"It's not fair, Uncle Mark. You didn't do anything."

His family had never tried to hide from the horrible turn Mark's life had taken that night at the lake, not far from Wright State University during his freshman year of college. He and Dana had told Jordon about Mark's past as soon as they'd thought the boy was old enough to understand.

They'd thought that was preferable to him hearing about it somewhere else. From someone who maybe wasn't in possession of all the facts.

"Yes, I did, son. There was forensic evidence to prove that I did."

"You were at a party with a bunch of college kids."

The place was empty except for the old guy working in the back room.

"I had way too much to drink." Readjusting his long legs beneath the short, square table, Mark tried not to think about the bed he'd just left.

"And you haven't had anything to drink since."

"Doesn't change the fact that I broke the law."

"Yeah, and served your time."

Though Jordon's voice was changing, he still looked young for his age. Even with the too-long hair and baggy clothes.

"Some crimes you pay for for a lifetime."

"The girl said she was twenty-one."

"She was bruised." He squinted against the harsh fluorescent lighting.

"There were two other guys with her, too." Jordon's hazel eyes—a family trait he shared with Dana and Mark—were wide and glinted with emotion. "They had to have hurt her. You wouldn't have hurt her."

"But I can't remember what happened." He'd tried everything from revisiting the scene to hypnosis, and still not one clear recollection of the latter part of that night came to him.

"You know you wouldn't have hurt her."

He did know that. Which was the only reason he could sleep at night. But he also knew he'd had sex with a sixteen-year-old girl at the same time that there were two other men having sex with her. Had they taken turns, watched each other? Had two of them touched her at once? The thought sickened him.

Stopped him in his tracks.

"I think you should move. You got the money."

He did well for himself.

"There's no law against it, is there?"

"No. I'd have to let the sheriff know, and reregister with my new address."

"Then why not do it?"

Jordon was growing up, choosing to tackle mature issues. Mark decided to be honest with him.

"Because if I did, everyone in the new neighborhood would be notified about me being there. I'd likely have hate mail, things thrown at my house, signs put in my yard and people running scared with their little kids."

"That's bullshit!"

"It's life."

His life, anyway.

"I'm comfortable where I am, son. People know me."

"It's a ghetto."

Not quite. But close.

"You could get gunned down taking out your trash."

"We'll stay in Cleveland next time your mom leaves town, okay?"

"I think you should move."

Mark gave up trying to convince his nephew of things he had a hard time accepting himself.

CHAPTER FOUR

AMAZING, REALLY, how quick and easy it was to disassemble something that had taken fifteen years of hard work to build. Agree to split all assets in half, file papers, wait thirty days and the state of Ohio dissolves a union once destined to last a lifetime.

Sara hadn't even been able to fully wrap her mind around the idea before the marriage was legally ended.

Providing male oversight on the last day of June, while the movers took her half of the household out of the home in which she'd hoped to raise children and grow old, her father gave her hand a squeeze.

She nodded.

And that was the end of any conversation they were going to have on the subject.

"When do you close on the new place?"

"A couple of weeks." The new house had been

vacant and the owners were letting her rent it until the paperwork was complete.

Retired sheriff John Lindsay stood up straight, staring out the front window toward the moving van. "Brent seen it yet?"

"No. Why should he?"

"Has he found a place?"

"Chloe has a place on a lake. He's moving in with her for now."

"She got kids?"

"Two." *Don't let it show,* she ordered herself. *Don't let it show and it won't hurt nearly as long.*

Her father's nod said more than she wanted it to. He saw the irony in the situation. Her husband had refused to have babies with her— a woman who desperately wanted to have a chance for do-overs in that department—and yet he was willing to take on another man's children for someone else.

She couldn't stand his pity. All her life she'd had her father standing over her, watching her hurt. The pattern had to stop.

"Have you called him? Seen if he's changed his mind?"

Sucking in air, Sara counted to ten, squeezing fingers to her thumb as she did so. "No."

Two brawny, sweaty, unshaven young men

were loading her dresser. Part of a set that was now split up.

"Don't you think you should?"

Her father wanted what he thought was best for her, she reminded herself, while her mind screamed silently.

The man was unfaithful to me! An adulterer, dammit. More than once. For years. How could you want him to ever come near me again?

"He chose Chloe."

"You're better for him. He's going to realize that."

But he's not better for me.

"I wouldn't be too sure about that. She's going to be a high-powered attorney someday."

A furniture pad went over the dresser.

"He has his own power. What he needs is a woman on his arm who knows how to make him look his best."

As much as Sara cringed at the description, she knew that her father had just paid her his idea of the highest compliment. How he survived in today's world, with his chauvinistic views, she had no idea.

"I guess he doesn't think so."

One nightstand was next.

"Did you split the mattress set, too?"

"No. I gave him the set in exchange for the bed

frame. I didn't want the mattress we shared, anyway."

"What about the cars?"

"I got the Lexus." Leaving Brent the Expedition. She'd had to give up the boat, too, but it was worth it. She had no use for a recreational vehicle she could neither get into nor out of the water by herself.

"Good for you."

With a nod, her father was gone—outside, giving last-minute instructions to the crew he'd hired.

BY SIX THAT EVENING—the first of July, a new month, a new life—all boxes and belongings were off the truck. Just as the Two Man Movers van drove away, the pizza delivery guy pulled up. Paying him and taking the hot cardboard box, Sara climbed over cartons on the way to her new kitchen.

The walls were green, but they were going to become yellow before the week was out.

"Dinner's ready!"

She grabbed a beer for her father and a glass of diet cola with lots of ice for herself. Then she collected paper plates, tore paper towel off the roll to serve as napkins and fell onto an elegant dining-room chair in her ceramic-tiled kitchen.

Brent had gotten the kitchen set, in spite of the

fact that Sara didn't have a formal dining room. So…eclectic was in. The set was made of hand-carved cherry wood and the seats were extremely comfortable.

"TV, VCR, DVD and stereo are all hooked up." John Lindsay came in, stopping by the sink to wash his hands.

She nodded. Half of the components were new. As was the entertainment center in her small sunken living room.

Unscrewing the beer cap, he sat across from her, apparently unaware of the incongruity of sitting in his jeans and sweaty T-shirt in an informal kitchen on velvet brocade chairs. He loaded his paper towel with pizza slices. Took a hefty bite. Looked over at her empty plate.

"Eat."

"I will." Maybe after he left.

But probably not. She'd had a banana a couple of hours before. And cereal for breakfast. She'd stay alive another day.

"Now." His dark-eyed gaze bore into her.

Sara picked up a slice of pizza and watched her father eat. John Lindsay, retired and in his sixties, was still an intimidating man. Tall, lean, even now, with broad shoulders that never seemed to hunch, he commanded respect.

He loved her. Sara had never doubted that.

He glanced up and caught her staring. "What's on your mind?"

She could shrug, tell him nothing, and no more would be said. Or…

"I met my son."

Hand on his beer bottle, he froze.

"I'd given permission for the agency to reveal my identity, if he ever asked."

"Why didn't your mother and I know about this?"

"You wouldn't have approved."

His glance was searching. And then he nodded, started to eat again.

"He's a cop, Daddy," she said softly.

"Where?"

"Here. With the Columbus police. He's on the Westerville beat."

"I know some guys over there."

"I figured you would."

"You want me to ask around about him?"

"Would it matter if I said no?"

"Probably not."

She grinned. "I didn't think so."

He finished his pizza. Wiped his mouth. And sat back with his bottle of beer in his hand.

"How long ago did you meet him?"

"Over six weeks," she told him and then

quickly added, "I've only seen him once, when he showed up unannounced on my doorstep."

"Did he say why?"

"He's known about me since he was fourteen and he's been keeping a watch over me, he said." With a deep breath, she continued, "Which is how he found out about Brent and Chloe."

John frowned. "He's the one who told you?"

Nodding, Sara played with her pizza crust, twirling a thin piece back and forth between her fingers. "He thought I should know."

Her father didn't look as if he agreed with her son's decision and Sara was struck once again with her awareness of something she'd always known. Her father would tell her only what he thought was for her own good, withholding everything else. And his idea of what was good for her wasn't necessarily hers.

"What's he like?"

Sara smiled and held back the tears that arrived every time she thought about the handsome young man who'd shown up on her doorstep and turned her life upside-down. In so many ways.

"Taller than you. Broad. Blond, with green eyes. Like any good cop, he seemed to take in the whole room at a glance."

And he'd given her things to think about that

were compelling enough to take her mind off the fact that life as she'd known it was over—that the man she'd trusted to be loyal to her, hadn't been.

"His name's Ryan. Ryan Mercedes."

John sipped his beer slowly, gaze intent, though he didn't seem to be focusing on anything in front of him.

"I don't think it's just chance that he's in police work."

"What?" Her father asked, turning that gaze on her. "You think it's hereditary?"

"I think he's a young man with an analytical mind like yours, an unbending view of right and wrong and a sense of responsibility to do what he can to fight evil. He's known since he was fourteen that his grandfather was a sheriff, and I think some emotional need to connect with his biological roots, combined with his traits, has led him to his chosen career."

"You got all this from one meeting?"

"I've had a lot of time to think about him."

And the things he'd told her.

"You going to see him again?"

The sun was setting, though it would be another hour or two before it got dark outside. Evening shadows were creeping into the kitchen.

"He left his number."

"I take it you haven't called."

"I've been a little busy."

SARA ALMOST CALLED Ryan Saturday night. Now that her father knew, hadn't tried to deny that she'd ever been pregnant and given up her child or denied that he had a biological grandson, Ryan's existence seemed all the more real.

She picked up the phone a couple of times, but always put it down again. She had no idea what she'd say. If he'd be at home on a Saturday night—or what he'd be doing if he was.

Did one leave a message for one's child that one had given away? What did she call herself? *This is your mother.* Her mind played out various messages and rejected them.

Mrs. Mercedes was Ryan's mother. Sara was Sara. Nothing more.

HER FATHER WAS BACK again on Sunday, seemingly undeterred by the seventy-five-minute drive from Maricopa to Columbus, to unpack her half of the tools in her garage. He'd brought along a Peg-Board and broom-holder bar to hang for her.

And when that was done, he came inside to help, moving boxes, putting together the new daybed in the room that was going to serve as her study and guest room. After which, he installed two new toilet seats in her bathrooms—Sara's mother had always insisted new toilet seats were mandatory when moving.

Sitting on the edge of the tub, watching as he lay flat on his back on the tile floor, his head underneath the tank while he worked an ornery lug nut, Sara knew the time had come.

Ryan's appearance in her life had prompted many changes. And because she was starting to obsess about some of the things he'd told her—the things left unsaid—she was going to have to do something.

"Tell me about that night."

He didn't miss a beat. "What night?" The words came out almost as a grunt as he gave the wrench a hard tug.

"The night I was raped."

John Lindsay bumped his head on the bottom of the toilet tank. He didn't swear. Barely acknowledged having done so. Just went back to the bolt. With one more tug, after ten minutes of struggling, it was free.

"I need to know, Daddy."

"No, you don't."

Twenty years ago that would have been that. Hell, twenty days ago it might have been.

"I'm thirty-seven years old. Old enough to determine for myself what's important to me."

"You don't know what you don't know."

She'd known this wasn't going to be easy. Her insides were shaking. She'd always gotten knots in her stomach at the thought of standing up to him. But this time anxiety wasn't going to stop her.

"I'm not going away on this one. I can't anymore," she said softly, as much for herself as anything else. "I've just spent the past twenty years of my life doing as you wanted, as Brent wanted, and look where it got me. Right back where I was at sixteen, trying to pick up the pieces of my life, with my father there taking care of everything for me. Except, this time, I also have the memory of an ex-husband so dissatisfied with me that he had no hesitation breaking our marriage vows."

"He's a fool—and a man. He'd have gotten over it."

"I don't think so." And it wouldn't matter if he had. The trust was gone.

The second bolt was loose with one twist and soon the new seat was securely in place.

"You sell yourself short," he said, gathering up his tools. "You run a nationally recognized organization, one built almost entirely by your efforts.

You have the respect of many of this country's most important movers and shakers."

That said, he left the room.

After unrolling the new purple-and-green bathroom rugs she'd bought to go with the shower curtain, towels and light purple paint that would soon be on the walls, Sara followed him. He was in the laundry room now, hooking up the washer.

"If you don't tell me, I'll ask someone else."

She received a long under-the-arm glance for her efforts. But the usual look of steely determination that he used to perfection was not there.

Sara's hands started to shake.

THEY ENDED UP in the kitchen with glasses of iced tea. Sara couldn't remember a time when she and her parents had had any serious discussion any place other than the kitchen table. If you had to talk, that's where you went. Period.

That's where they'd discussed the results of the pregnancy test and, ultimately, the adoption. The college she'd attend. It had been over a Sunday steak dinner that she'd introduced them to Brent. And lasagna on a Friday night, when she and Brent announced their engagement.

It had been at the kitchen table, five years before, that her father had told her about the car accident that had killed her mother. She'd received a call at work, asking her to meet him at home. All the way from Columbus to Maricopa she'd imagined what she might find there. From her parents selling everything and retiring to Florida, to one of them finding out he was ill, she'd run the gamut. And come up horribly short.

"What do you want to know?" Her father's question was brusque.

"Everything."

Sitting up straight, his fingers tapping the sides of his glass, he frowned. "I don't see how, after all these years—"

"You and Mom were still asleep that morning when the call came."

"That's right."

"Who called?"

"Chris Watson."

"I don't know him."

"Neither did I. He was a freshman at Wright State, new to town, and he came to the party with the rest of them."

"How many people were there?"

He stared at her for a long time and Sara realized she shouldn't have done this. Not because she didn't need to know. She did—should've asked years ago. But she shouldn't have done this to him.

Never once, in all these years, had she looked at that night and the months that followed through the eyes of a man who loved his only daughter. When she'd seen her father's part in it all, it had been as her father, the enforcer, the sheriff. The big, strong man who always did the right thing and made damn sure those around him did, as well.

"Twenty-three for at least part of the evening," he finally said. "Twenty-one of them male. I questioned everyone who'd been within half a mile of that lake, from the family who'd driven down to do some stargazing and left when they arrived to find a party in full swing, to the gas station attendant down the road who'd seen cars go by. And everyone who'd known about the party, as well, whether they attended or not. I'm certain there wasn't a person in the vicinity I didn't talk to."

She'd known her father had worked exhaustively on the case. And she would have tried to find out more at the time if she'd been in any state to think for herself. In the months immediately following the rape, she'd been adamant about one thing. She was not going to have the abortion her parents were pressuring her to consider.

For everything else, she did as she was told. Ate the foods her doctor recommended, studied the lessons her mother prepared, visited with the two girlfriends her father encouraged her to see.

"In the end, the physical evidence did the work for us," he said now, bending over his iced tea glass. There were lines around his eyes she'd never noticed before.

As soon as he left, she'd hook up her computer—she'd been planning to, anyway. And then she'd do what she'd never allowed herself to do before and begin to dredge up the past. She'd find the articles Ryan had found—articles that, until he'd told her about the small town news archives, she'd never even considered having at her disposal. She'd read about the night that had stolen away her childhood. It had taken an unfaithful husband, meeting her son for the first time, the shock of a quick divorce, but she was finally ready to rock the boat she'd been floating in precariously ever since that horrible night.

However, there was at least one thing she wouldn't find in old newspaper articles.

And she had the chief investigator right here.

"Aside from the…incident…with me, was there anything else unusual about the party? Any fights? Or evidence of misconduct?"

"Other than littering?" her father asked. "No. By all accounts, and believe me I heard them all, the goal was to get trashed. It was the week before finals and they'd brought cases of whiskey, beer and wine to drown themselves. They put their car keys in a can, buried it and drank until they puked. Repeatedly, judging by what we saw at the party site the next day."

"Were they smoking pot?"

John shook his head. "We found cigarette butts, but no drug paraphernalia of any kind."

"Was anyone tested for drugs?"

"No. There was nothing to indicate drug use."

"What about the fact that at least a few of us couldn't remember anything the next day?" Ryan's doubts confused an already blurry situation.

"You reeked of alcohol and were obviously passed out, drunk. With the number of empty bottles, divided by the number of people at the party, added to the fact that you'd mixed beer, wine and whiskey, we were more concerned with getting you awake and sober."

And dealing with the rape. Sara filled in the blanks her father's expression left hanging there.

"And you have no doubt that nothing else happened there that night?"

"Honey, I know the details of that party so well I could have been there myself."

She wanted to believe him.

CHAPTER FIVE

OTHER THAN GOING to work on Monday and Tuesday, Sara devoted the next two days to searching. The archived articles provided surprisingly little information. They were frustratingly vague and she saw her father's influence in that. Just as he'd kept news of her pregnancy out of the papers—and out of the trial. The young men might have gotten longer than five years, if evidence of the hardship she'd suffered had been presented at sentencing; but then she'd have had to be there, to testify before the jury. Her parents wouldn't allow it.

John was busy on Wednesday, the Fourth of July, riding in the back of a convertible in Maricopa's annual parade and helping the Fraternal Order of Police with their sausage booth at the festival that followed. He'd invited Sara to attend with him—as he'd done each of the five years since her mother's death.

This year she'd declined, claiming a load of unpacking still to be done. And she *did* have a large amount of unpacking to do. She hadn't done any since he'd left on Sunday.

Picking up the phone that morning, hoping that if Ryan was going to be celebrating with friends and family it would happen later in the day, she dialed her son's number.

And this time she held on while the rings sounded on the line.

"Hello?"

"Ryan?"

"Sara?" She was thrilled that he recognized her voice, until it dawned on her that he'd have caller ID.

Whoa, girl, she cautioned herself. Hang on to the emotion here. You can't afford not to.

"Are you busy?" It was the polite thing to ask. And at least now she knew what he was going to call her—Sara. As if they were friends.

Of course, the people who worked for her called her that, as well.

It meant nothing. Except that she wasn't mother. Or Mom. Or Ma. Or even Aunt something.

"I just finished having my cereal and I'm heading to bed."

"You were on duty last night?"

Did he know it wasn't healthy to eat right before bed?

"Tuesday, Wednesday, Thursday and Friday nights."

"Do you sleep the other days, too, to stay on schedule?"

"Nah, I stay up on Saturday, so I can be on schedule with the rest of the world when I'm off."

He'd be working that night, when the rest of the city had been partying all day and many people would be shooting off illegal fireworks—after drinking.

There'd be drunks on the road. Fights. Car accidents.

"Do you wear a vest?" Her father rarely had.

"Yeah. They're mandatory."

"And you call for backup before you get out of your car?"

"Yes, ma'am."

She was ma'am, now. Sara paced her small study, glancing out the window at a backyard in need of mowing.

She'd chosen the house for the white picket fence and flower garden that took up one corner and most of the back of the lawn. The colorful blooms were magnificent. And they needed weeding.

Her son needed to get some rest.

"I've been reading those articles you told me about."

"And?"

"I… Is there anything we can do, *I* can do, to help find out if anything else happened that night?"

She'd been stripped of dignity, of an ability to love openly, of confidence in a sexuality that still hadn't blossomed. She'd spent more than twenty years tormented with guilt over the possibility that three young men had gone to prison instead of college because she'd lied about her age. If she'd been a willing participant in what had happened…

The idea that there might have been another cause for what had happened that night than just alcohol, reckless choices by a stupid, recalcitrant, rebellious girl and male violence was one she couldn't let go of.

"You could talk to your father. He was the investigating officer."

"I already have."

The pause on the line was telling. She simply wasn't sure what it implied. Didn't trust her judgment where this young man was concerned.

"You told him about me?" Ryan's voice was less confident as he asked this question.

"Yes."

"What did he say?"

"That he's positive nothing else happened."

"You asked him about the bones? Did he say if he'd ever made a connection between them and what happened to you?"

"No." She slowed herself down. Picked some lint off the new maroon-and-rose coverlet on the daybed. "I didn't tell him anything you said about the night of the party." She hadn't been ready to push him that far.

"I just told him I'd met you. That you told me about Brent and Chloe."

"What's going on with that?"

She'd half expected him to know. But court records were filed slowly.

"I'm divorced," she said, the words still a shock to her system.

"Already?" His voice rose. "It's only been six weeks!"

"I know." Sara swallowed back tears. "I had no idea it could happen so quickly." And then, when the silence lasted too long, when she began to worry that he was blaming himself, because it was what she would have done, she added, "We had nothing to fight about. We split our assets in an afternoon, wrote it all down, filed the papers, and thirty days later it was final."

He still said nothing.

"I've bought a house just off 161." She told him the name of the subdivision just outside Westerville.

"That's my beat."

She'd wondered. And she was glad he couldn't see how wobbly her smile was. At least he'd be close by, even if she never saw him again.

"So you're living alone?"

"Yes."

"You have a dog?"

"No."

"An alarm system?"

"No."

"You need to get one."

She would look into getting a puppy. After she found the silverware. And unpacked the keepsakes that were stashed in the attic.

"An attractive woman living alone is an invitation to the crazies walking around out there."

"I haven't seen any in my neighborhood this week."

"You're blowing me off."

"I have had a cop as my father my whole life," she said, rubbing her forehead. "One, I might add, who's already scheduled the installation of the alarm system and signed a two-year contract for service."

"Good."

Ryan sounded like his grandfather. But coming from him, the tone didn't raise her hackles so much. It brought a curious warmth instead.

"Did he also tell you that eighty percent of all burglaries take place in residences without dogs?"

"That statistic's gone up." She'd always wanted a dog. Her mother had been allergic, and Brent wasn't a dog person. He didn't want drool on things, and he said their feet got dirty every single time they went outside, which meant they tracked filth through the house.

"I'm wasting my time, aren't I?" She heard a chuckle in his voice—one she'd never heard in her father's.

"No," she told him, relenting. "It makes me happy to know you care enough to say something."

"If you saw what I've seen…"

"I know." And where did a faltering conversation go from there, with a person you didn't know at all, had only met once and loved with all your soul?

"So, what can I do?" she asked, as if she was at work putting together a new project.

"You busy this afternoon?"

"Just unpacking."

"How about I stop by around six and we can

talk. I'll tell you what I know and see what we come up with."

"Can I make dinner for you?"

"I never turn down a free meal. Or a home-cooked one, either, for that matter."

Sara liked his honesty.

Truth was, she liked everything she knew about him.

MARK WAS GETTING READY to leave for the shop just after ten on the morning of the Fourth of July when he heard a knock on the door of his apartment. He couldn't remember the last time he'd had a visitor.

Solicitors didn't venture into neighborhoods like his.

Peering through the peephole, checking his back out of habit, Mark considered pretending he wasn't home when he saw Sharon Rose standing outside.

She looked great. Blond hair silky and clean, curling around slim tanned shoulders left mostly bare by the tank top she had on. The white shorts she was wearing showed off her legs to perfection.

"Sharon, hi." He had to pull open the door. She wasn't safe out there alone.

Blushing, she stared him straight in the eye. "I

know this is forward of me and I'd apologize, except that I'm not sorry."

"Would you like to come in?"

"Yes."

For three years he and Sharon had been studying together, along with three other students in an informal group they'd formed. Three years of meeting at coffeehouses, on campus and once or twice at someone's home. But never his.

He'd ask how she'd found him, but he already knew the answer. He was registered, and she knew it.

Waiting for her to state her business, he kept his feet firmly planted on the four-by-four section of newly laid tile that served as his foyer.

"Nice place you've got here."

The words were trite, clichéd even, but the surprised and pleased intonation she added gave them meaning just the same.

"Thanks." He'd paid his bills that morning. And had enough cash left for the pecan hardwood he'd had his eye on for more than a year. It should take him a week, tops, to get it laid throughout the apartment. "How've you been?"

"Fine. Busy. I would've waited for you to call, but I knew you weren't going to."

Mark slid his hands into the pockets of his

jeans, which were a little tight because of the swim trunks he had on underneath them. After he finished work he was driving up to Cleveland. "There's not much point."

"I don't agree."

Standing at the door, Mark frowned.

"You just put it all out there, don't you?"

"I've never been good at playing games."

He'd never had a chance to find out if he was.

"School's out." He gave her the same respect she'd given him. Honesty. "We're not class-mates anymore."

"That doesn't have to matter." She didn't move any closer. Didn't do anything that could even covertly be construed as a come-on.

"Yes, it does."

"Why, because you made a mistake as a kid?"

"A mistake that carries lifetime penalties."

"Come on, Mark. We all do things we regret. I'm guessing if you polled all the guys in your freshman class, at least half of them would admit they'd partied too hard and had unplanned sex as a result."

"Undoubtedly. But the issue here isn't the partying or the sex. You think it wouldn't bother you to be hooked up with a sex offender, but until you've lived the life you have no idea."

"Then let me live the life."

He was tempted. Damn tempted. Law school had given him a rare opportunity to actually get to know people, to see people with whom he had much in common on a daily basis. He was probably going to miss that more than the chance to practice law.

"You've already got a hard climb ahead of you, a woman in the legal field; added to the fact that you're starting out midway through your working life. How do you think it would affect your future clients' faith in your judgment, if they knew you hung out with a registered sex offender?"

"They wouldn't have to know."

"I'm required to register for the rest of my life."

"They classified you as a predator?"

He nodded.

"That's ludicrous."

"Rape is considered a violent sexual act."

"But you just had sex with a minor. It was statutory rape."

"She was bruised. And I can't remember what happened."

"Predators are thought to be at risk of committing similar acts in the future."

"Again, I can't remember what happened. Who's to say I wouldn't do the same thing again?"

Chin slightly raised, she nodded. Then said, "So, what're you doing today?"

"I was just on my way to work," he said, content to give her an easy out. Mark didn't like everything about his life, but he was satisfied with most of it. He was free, after all.

"It's a holiday."

"I'm going to my sister's apartment complex for a cookout later—probably taking up my nephew on his usual challenge for a race in the Olympic-size pool outside their door."

Her smile was as lovely as her eyes. "Who wins?"

"I do, of course. That's why he keeps challenging me."

"You could let him win, and he'd stop."

"No way! It gives him something to work toward."

And a reason for him to look up to his uncle? Mark hoped he wasn't that shallow and needy.

"What about this weekend?"

"Sharon."

"Just meet me for coffee, down on campus. Like usual."

He didn't see the point.

"What time?"

"You name it, I'll be there."

"Ten. Saturday morning."

Her grin eased some of his tension and he chided her about the ragged state of her classic Mustang as he walked her to her car. Maybe he should offer to fix it up for her.

In exchange for coffee.

For a real friend.

He couldn't remember the last time he'd had one of those.

"HI."

Sara had waited a couple of seconds before answering the door, lest Ryan figure out that she'd been watching out the window for him.

"Hi." He looked her straight in the eye and gave her an easy grin—as if they'd known each other all their lives.

"Is that your Ranger?"

The little black pickup looked relatively new.

"Yeah."

"I like it," she said, and then realized that while she was filling her eyes with every aspect of him, she was still keeping him standing outside. "Sorry. Come in."

In his baggy jean shorts, clunky tennis shoes and T-shirt, he looked about seventeen. Except for the military haircut.

He walked past her and Sara had to consciously restrain herself from reaching out to touch him.

She ached to wrap her arms around him and hold him close to her heart. For real—not just as the ghost she'd been clinging to for so many years.

Whether he was simply a confident kid or because he felt immediately at home with her, Sara wasn't sure, but he walked into her kitchen, perched himself on a bar stool at the tiny island between the stove and the sink and started to munch on the veggies she'd set out as if he'd been doing it all his life.

"How're you doing?" he asked as she leaned back against the counter.

Shrugging, Sara grinned and said, "Finding out how nice it is to eat what I want for dinner."

How nice it was not to live with someone that she had to worry about disappointing.

And also how lonely.

He grabbed a handful of cucumber slices, eating them two at a time. "You never had any other kids."

The words were softly spoken. Sara couldn't tell whether they were a statement or question. Kind of disconcerting getting to know someone who already knew you so well.

"Nope."

"Why not?" The question was as direct as his gaze.

"He didn't want any."

Carrot midway to his mouth, he stopped. "But you did?"

Biting her lip to keep it from trembling, Sara bowed her head. "Very much."

Ryan nodded. And said no more on the subject.

HE ATE TWO HELPINGS of lasagna, drinking a quart of iced tea in the process.

"You don't eat much."

She'd finished her entire helping for once. "I stay alive."

"You should eat more."

Again, he sounded like his biological grandfather. They really should meet. Or…maybe not. Too much testosterone. If they had opposing viewpoints, they might hate each other.

Still, in some ways, it would be a great thing to see.

"Were you serious about wanting to help find out what happened the night I was conceived?"

Out of daydreams and into reality with a bang. Ryan was still working on his second plate of dinner, scooping up pasta and sauce with French bread.

"Yes."

He finished eating. Put his silverware in the middle of his plate. Carried it over to the sink, rinsed it and put it in the dishwasher before coming back to take his seat.

"I'm not sure what you can do, but I'd like a chance to run some things by your father. If you could ask him some questions for me, it'd help. You don't need to tell him I'm looking into this or anything—don't even tell him the questions are mine. There are just some things that weren't in any of the reports that are bugging me," he said, sliding his glass of iced tea in front of him.

The pleading look in Ryan's eyes nudged at her resistance. How could she refuse the first thing he'd asked of her in the twenty-one years he'd been alive?

"Tell me again why you think those bones that turned up across the lake have anything to do with that night."

"First off, the estimated time of death coincides. Maricopa's a small town. What are the chances of having a rape and a murder in the same month at the same out-of-the-way lake that aren't somehow connected?"

He was dressed like a boy, ate like a teenager and talked like a cop.

Regardless of the validity of his theories, Sara was a goner.

CHAPTER SIX

"YOU'RE RIGHT. Maricopa has grown a bit in the past twenty years, but it's still the smallest town in Montgomery County," Sara said, trying to ignore the longing in her heart and focus only on the topic at hand.

"One thing is for sure," Ryan continued, seemingly unaware of her emotional struggle. "In a town that size, everyone gets noticed. And that makes it hard to disappear without someone also noticing."

"But the body could have been brought in from someplace else. Someone could have buried it at night and no one would be the wiser. Have you been to the lake?"

"Yes." That gave her heart a jolt—picturing him there.

"Then you know that it can't be seen from the road."

"Especially the far side, which is where the bones were found."

"If someone from Dayton or even Cincinnati had a murder to hide, that lake would be a great place to dump the body."

"Possibly," Ryan said. Then he added, "After the flood exposed a couple of bones, diggers were sent to the area. They found a shallow grave, with the skull and the rest of a six-foot-tall skeleton. It had been buried well enough to be protected from animals, so whoever did it definitely made an effort. It's not as if someone was out and got lost or had a heart attack and fell over and died out there undiscovered." Ryan sat forward, his gaze, his voice, intense as he continued.

"But maybe death was from natural causes, and his loved ones just couldn't afford a funeral."

"There are graves for that kind of thing."

"So maybe he was someone on the run and his family didn't want his memory sullied with old sins. Or they didn't want media attention."

He shook his head, running a finger over the condensation on the outside of his glass.

"Following an inspection of the bones, the medical examiner reported that the man had been severely beaten shortly before he died."

"And I'm guessing you found no record of any reported bar brawls or fights that took place around that time."

He shook his head. "I checked police reports from the area, hospital records and newspaper clippings. There was nothing."

"And there weren't any other identifying marks on what was left of the body?"

"An old leg fracture that had healed."

"Shouldn't they be able to trace something from that?"

"Hospitals treat thousands of broken legs a year. Without a name…"

Even if they had access to all the X-rays taken in all the hospitals in Ohio over a span of several years, they'd probably be dead before they got through them.

"And without a dental record to check against the impression that was made, there's no chance there."

"Nope."

Sara went to the sink and rinsed the remaining dishes, intrigued in spite of herself. "Something's wrong, that someone could so easily go missing and be disposed of without any accountability."

"Thousands of missing persons go unidentified in the United States every year," Ryan said. He sounded like a teacher lecturing his class. "It's up to local police departments to do the paperwork and keep missing-persons files up to date with the FBI. But it doesn't happen as much as it should. A lot of counties don't even have medical examiners. And money for law enforcement doesn't often allow the kinds of investigations you see on television, even if there were forensic labs available."

She'd had no idea—and her father had been a cop for most of her life.

"In this case, we got lucky. An investigation was done and there was a report filed. Apparently, the bones were held for almost a year, waiting for possible identification. There was a dental impression taken and a piece of bone saved before the body was sent to the local mortician. Your father did his job, as far as all of that was concerned."

"So they can get DNA now."

"If someone authorizes it. But you'd have to have a good reason to spend the resources on a twenty-one-year-old set of bones, when the state doesn't have the manpower to keep up with current cases awaiting DNA results."

"My dad could arrange the authorization." Not that she was ready to ask him to. She'd need a lot more to go on than unexplained bones at the lake that year.

"Yes. But, would he?"

In the few hours she'd spent with Ryan, she'd recognized several aspects of his personality that were similar to her father's. And her father would never have been this hell-bent on something if he hadn't had good reason to be.

"You've got more than an unidentified, probably murdered man, don't you?"

Warmth spread through Sara at the glow of approval in her son's eyes. "I read through the trial transcripts," he said, somewhat apologetically.

She poured him more tea. "I expected as much." Filling her glass, as well, she left the pitcher on the table between them.

"One of the witnesses was a guy named Ralph Bonney. You ever hear of him?"

"The name's familiar." Sara frowned, trying to identify a time, a place. A face. "But not from that night."

"You're sure?"

She focused, repeating the name over and over, waiting for some spark, some connection. Thinking of what little she could remember, not from the point of view of a recalcitrant teenager, or a damaged one, but through the eyes of experience. "Positive. I know I know that name from someplace, but I'm certain it wasn't that night. It's before that. I was younger. And he's an older guy. More like my father's age."

Shaking his head, Ryan said, "It's not the same

guy, then. Ralph Bonney was one of the students at the party—he testified during the trial."

Panic gripped her stomach, tightened her chest, just as it always did at the mention of an event in which she'd been a central player, even if she couldn't remember being a participant. An event that had irrevocably changed so many lives.

"You're sure you want to do this?"

She was thirty-seven, not sixteen. And finally attempting to grow up. To be her own woman. Fully alive.

"I'm sure." She was trembling, though. Inside and out.

"According to the police report, Ralph was as hung over as the rest of the guys they arrested. But he remembered more than anyone else. He's the one who, later the next day, came forward with the names of the three guys."

Ryan's mouth tightened.

Bracing herself, Sara said, "Go on."

"He saw you with the three of them, describing exactly what they were wearing, what you were wearing—down to your underwear."

She hadn't had any on when they'd found her. She later overheard her father telling her mother that the undergarments had had to be admitted as evidence. There'd been semen on them.

She wanted to stop right then and there. Get up. Run the dishwasher. Wish him a good day, a good life.

Meeting her son's gaze, Sara sat in her chair. And heard herself voicing, out loud, the question she'd been asking herself for more than twenty-one years.

"Did I come on to them?"

He held her gaze as he nodded.

She swallowed bile, and nodded. She'd known. Someplace in her subconscious mind she'd buried the knowledge—but not deeply enough. It had lurked there, poking her with feelings of guilt. With shame.

"According to the testimony, you were drinking beer like water." Ryan's words were gentle, nonjudgmental. "And doing shots in between. You told them you were a girl who wanted to have fun."

She remembered thinking those very words on the way to the party. But her memories were only of alcohol. Cute boys. Spin the bottle. And maybe a midnight dip in the lake.

Clean fun. With just enough of a touch of naughtiness to show her father that she was grown up and able to do as she pleased.

"I can't even imagine that," she said, pulling

herself back to the present. "I hated beer. I'd snuck a sip of my dad's once at a backyard barbecue and nearly choked, which, of course, got his attention and I was caught."

"What'd he do?"

"Made me drink the whole bottle on the spot."

She'd hated him for that. Humiliating her in front of the other kids and families there.

"From what Ralph Bonney said, you got over the aversion that night."

"My hangover lasted three days." At least. Sometimes it seemed as if it would last a lifetime.

Ryan told her about the one and only time he'd gotten drunk. The night he graduated from high school. His dad was waiting up for him when he came stumbling in. Helped him to the bathroom to throw up, gave him a warm washcloth to wipe his face and put him to bed, all without saying a thing. It wasn't mentioned the next morning. Or anytime since.

"He sounds like a wonderful man," Sara said, overwhelmed by bittersweet emotions. A perfect father was what she'd wanted for her one and only child.

Ryan was quiet, watching her.

What did he see, this son of hers? What did she want him to see?

"What else did this Ralph Bonney have to say?" she asked.

"He saw the three guys taking turns kissing you. You didn't seem to be minding. The next thing he knew, they were leading you off to a patch of grass behind some trees. He tried to stop them, to get to you, but they told him to bug off. He tried to rally help from some of the other guys, but the few who were still sober enough to assess the situation said you weren't calling for help and to let you all have your fun."

So she'd gone willingly?

And then another thought struck Sara, draining the blood from her face. All these years, her father had known this about her. And probably her mother had, too. Known how she'd behaved.

No wonder they'd kept the details from her, refusing to allow her to testify at the trial.

If they thought she'd in any way deserved what had happened to her, they'd certainly never let on.

All that talk about not blaming herself, the counseling to overcome the shame and guilt of having been a victim of rape. She'd gone willingly.

"Anything else?" The voice hardly sounded like her own, but she managed to look her son in the eye.

"Not much." Head bent, he glanced up at her. "Ralph did as he was told and left you all alone. He was too drunk to drive, to go get your dad, and he knew that by the time he did it'd be too late, anyway. Besides, he didn't see where the guys had buried the can of keys. He climbed into the backseat of his car and passed out."

At least he'd tried. She'd like to thank him.

"Is he still alive?"

"He owns a car dealership in Cleveland now."

"Bonney Chevrolet?" She'd seen the ads.

"That's the one."

"Have you approached him?"

"Not yet." Ryan took a drink, emptying his glass of tea before setting it carefully on the table. "So far, everything I've done has been on my own. I don't have the authority to take on the case officially. Not only is it out of my jurisdiction, but I'm a beat cop, not a violent-crime detective. You're the first person I've told about it."

"I'm honored."

He bowed his head, and Sara wished she could retract her words. She'd embarrassed him.

"So what do you think?" he asked, glancing at her again.

"When I hear you talk about it all…" she said, and swallowed hard. "About that night… It's as if you're talking about somebody else. Someone I don't know at all."

He nodded. "I've never discovered anything else you've ever done, either before or since, that would give you the profile of the girl Bonney describes."

"I've lived a pretty boring life."

"I wouldn't call raising millions of dollars to educate teenagers and keep school-age kids safe boring."

"I meant personally." Except for the obvious drama of just having met the son she'd borne twenty-one years before, or finding out that her husband was sleeping with another woman.

"Doesn't it make you wonder?"

Focusing on the night she was raped, pondering it, was not something she allowed herself to do. And yet now...

"The facts are right there," she told him, wanting so desperately for things to be different. "Irrefutable."

"Unless someone lied."

"Ralph Bonney, you mean?"

Ryan just stared at her.

"You think my father lied."

"I'm not saying that. I honestly don't know. But did it ever occur to you that that was possible?"

It hadn't. Not once. "Why would he do that?" She frowned. "And what part of it would he have lied about? I went to the lake intentionally, to crash the fraternity party—planning to drink. No one asked me to go. No one even knew I was going.

"When I woke up the next morning I was naked underneath the coat my father had wrapped around me. And I had one hell of a hangover."

"I don't know what," Ryan quickly assured her. "Or why. But there are some things that don't make sense, and I'm open to all possibilities."

"What doesn't make sense?"

"If Ralph Bonney didn't see you after the four of you went into the trees, how did he know what your underwear looked like? You said yourself you didn't have anything on when you woke up."

"I don't know." It wasn't something she wanted to think about. "Maybe I had my jeans undone before I went off."

"Then why didn't he say so?"

"It wasn't important."

"If you saw the transcript from the trial, you'd know that this guy was on the stand for two days, being examined and cross-examined on everything from how many feet away he was when the kissing started down to how many bottles of beer he opened that night."

"So maybe he noticed my underwear on the ground the next morning."

"A deputy found your things buried in some leaves not too far from where you were discovered."

"You think Ralph was there while it was happening?"

"Possibly."

"From what I understood, the evidence they found on me pretty conclusively belonged to the three men they convicted."

"That's right. If he was there, he didn't touch you."

"So what difference does it make?"

"I don't know if it makes any difference. But it makes me wonder…"

"What?"

"It's probably safe to assume that there was no way your father was going to rest until those guys were sent to prison."

With a vision of her father's tense face those months following the rape, the memory of the many long weeks without seeing him smile even once, Sara agreed.

"They had forensic evidence, but conviction rests on there being no reasonable doubt. The defense claimed that the guys had never even been near you and that after you passed out someone had planted the semen inside you."

Sara blanched, and felt nauseous.

"How do you know that?"

There'd been nothing even remotely similar to that in the papers.

"It was in an early report. Ralph's testimony, putting the four of you in contact, took away any chance of that other motion holding up with the jury and the theory never made it to court."

Which could be why her father hadn't mentioned it the other night.

"It's kind of strange that, though he was as drunk as everyone else there, Ralph Bonney was the only one who could remember so many details. Including the color of your underwear."

"You think he was fed the information?"

"I think that if, say, he'd passed out in his car *before* you all went into the woods, and no one else was sober enough to be sure one way or the other, someone could have convinced him that it was the right thing to do to testify, with help, so that they could put away the guilty parties."

"Are you saying that my father somehow bribed this Ralph Bonney guy to lie in court?"

"I'm saying it's possible."

Sara shook her head, a rebuttal on her lips. But she couldn't quite get it out. She didn't think her father would do something like that. Ever. His unbending law-abiding attitude had been part of what had driven her to sneak away that night to begin with. If ever there was going to be a time when he'd be tempted to bend, though, it would have been then. How many times had she heard him promise, without a doubt, that they'd send those men away? That she'd be safe.

That justice would be done.

If he'd interfered with the system, however, justice hadn't been done at all. And three men might have been sent to prison unfairly.

Because of her.

RYAN WATCHED Sara's face, reading the flitting emotions, telling himself that while he felt compassion, her suffering and confusion weren't touching him on a deeper level.

There was some connection there. How could there not be? But while he knew a lot about her, he didn't really know her. And he wasn't looking for another mother.

He just had to find some answers.

"There might be no connection between the discrepancy in Bonney's testimony and the murdered body, but we have two highly questionable events happening in the same place at roughly the same time. Doesn't that make you wonder?" he asked Sara.

"Why is this so important to you?"

Ryan started, his head jerking back slightly as he realized that he hadn't been the only one interpreting expressions.

"Because my gut tells me there's more to that night than we understand."

"It happened a long time ago. Why does it matter?"

He'd asked himself that question a gazillion times.

"I'm sworn to uphold the law," he said at last, hoping the statement didn't sound as weak to someone else as it did to him. "I can't just close my eyes and pretend I don't see, when my instincts are telling me something is wrong."

"You sound like my father."

She was prettier when she smiled. And she didn't look like any mom he'd ever known. Ryan tried to control a surprising feeling of pride. He was here solving a mystery. His mother was Harriet Mercedes—as perfect a mom as a guy could hope for.

"Then you understand why I have to do this."

Breathing a little easier again as she nodded, he pressed on before she changed her mind. Or set up more roadblocks.

"I was hoping you were going to be able to give me some insight as to why Bonney might be willing to help your dad in court."

"That's why you wanted to know if I'd ever heard of him."

"Right."

She tried again to place the name, got the same nibble of some forgotten memory and then nothing.

"Maybe it's just the Chevy billboards I'm thinking of." But it felt more personal than that.

And more distant, too. From long ago. But... "I'm pretty sure I didn't know him."

"I'm going to do some more checking, go back to the newspaper archives for a couple of years preceding that night, and see if I can find any connection your father might have to Bonney."

"Something that would have earned him a payback, you mean?"

Sara obviously didn't like him casting aspersions on her father's character. Interesting, considering what a tough father the man had been. Still, there were many things he didn't yet understand.

For her sake he hoped to God that when he

found the answers, they didn't hang Sheriff Lindsay out to dry.

"I can't remember anything in conjunction with a college kid," she continued after a pause. "But I'll ask my dad about him."

And if the man had done something underhanded to secure a conviction against his daughter's attackers, he wasn't likely to admit it to her.

Ryan hoped he was wrong about his biological grandfather. But he'd read the complete file now and the man had been absolutely focused on vengeance for the damage done to his only child. His little girl.

His interview of an older couple who still lived alone in an ancient house half a mile from the lake had bordered on brutal. They'd gone to bed at eight that night—as they always did. They were hard of hearing, too, but Sheriff Lindsay had interrogated them for two hours, anyway, even bringing them into the station and splitting them up, to try to get them to tell him something.

Sara put away the iced tea. Rinsed the glasses.

There was something else she should know. "I'm going to trace the three men."

She turned, staring at him.

"If any of them are local, I intend to seek them out."

Her expression begged him not to, even as she nodded and turned her back.

"I thought you were concerned about the unidentified dead man, thinking the trial was used as a cover-up for a murder."

"I think it's a huge coincidence that two brutal crimes happened simultaneously in a town where there hadn't been a brutal crime in fifty years."

But now that he'd read the file, he wondered if maybe the sheriff of Maricopa had been so obsessed with tracking Sara's rapists that he'd just plain missed evidence of another major wrongdoing.

Perhaps the discrepancy he sensed was within the trial itself; perhaps there'd been a wrongful conviction. Or a dirty sheriff?

If so, Ryan knew one thing for sure. He'd tread lightly, proceed as the law required, but as quietly as possible.

He wasn't out to cause his biological mother any more pain.

She'd given him his life.

CHAPTER SEVEN

"I'M NOT GOING to have you closing the shop, Mark. You're too backed up, as it is."

"Why don't you let me be the judge of that?" Leaning forward on his plastic-ribbed pool chair, Mark spoke softly to his sister. "You have to go. You're thirty-six years old, and if you're ever going to run your own club, you need that management training. Two weeks isn't all that long."

Dana stood up to get them both a soda from the cooler. In trunks still wet from his swimming victory, Mark slid down in his chair. They'd had a pleasant evening. Their mom and her friend, Bea, had been over for the cookout. Dana's new male interest, Ken, a widowed doctor, had brought the steaks that he and Mark had grilled. Even the friend Dana had invited for Mark to meet—an ongoing battle between brother and sister that he'd been losing for the past four years—had been tolerable. They'd shared some good wine, lots of laughs and a clear view of the fireworks. Now, at nearly eleven, he was ready to head back to Columbus. If not for the fact that he'd promised a vintage Corvette to its new owner by the following day, he'd have taken Dana up on her invitation to crash in the third bedroom, which was unofficially his.

"It's not management training," Dana clarified, popping the lid on her can as she dropped back into the chair next to his, facing the pool. "It's training waitresses."

"For the new club opening up in Vancouver, I know." Mark took a long sip of his drink. "But the company is sending you because they think you're capable of managing others. You do this well, and there will be other opportunities. Show them you want this, make it happen, and they'll call on you the next time they need someone."

"My first loyalty is to Jordon, and not to my own personal goals."

Giving his nephew a thumbs-up, as Jordon finished another practice lap and glanced over to see if Mark was watching, Mark said, "Helping better yourself helps your son. You'll be happier, healthier. You're showing him that working hard for what you want pays off. You'll have more money to send him to college. And by the time he wants to leave home, you'll have a satisfying career, so you won't go crazy and he won't have to feel guilty as hell for leaving."

"I want to go, Mark. You don't have to convince me, and if it were only for a couple of days Jordon could stay with Kyle's family. But they're leaving on vacation. And Mom's not well enough to keep up with him. He's at that age, you know? Testing his weight."

"While his hormones test him," Mark said, understanding more fully than his sister ever could the wars waging inside his teenage nephew. "It's fine. I'll close the shop and camp out here for the duration."

"You'd have to register."

"Yeah." He couldn't be in any county, other than his own, for more than five days without checking in with the local authorities, which started the whole public-announcement process all over again. "But I'll be gone before anyone in the neighborhood gets wind of it and wants me gone."

"The complex is privately owned."

Shit. He'd assumed...

She'd never said anything before.

"They don't rent, or allow in, extended house guests who are..."

Dana had tears in her eyes as she nodded.

So much for the computer room being his.

"He can't stay at my place," Mark said emphatically, thinking of the audio pornography he was served up for free at night. "If you'd heard them, sis, you'd be as certain as I am that we don't want Jordon there. Especially not now."

His nephew had had a wet dream. He'd come to Mark the month before thinking there was something wrong with him, that he'd needed a doctor.

"Mom's place isn't big enough for both of you," Dana said, her face solemn.

Even at thirty-six, his sister was a looker. Slim, without being skinny. Long legs. And gorgeous hair. She wasn't so bold as to walk around the complex in only a swimsuit, but in the one-piece beneath her black cover-up she had nothing to be ashamed of.

She'd had a hard life. In spite of making great choices. And she deserved this chance.

"I'll get a hotel room in Franklin County."

He was already there. Already registered. And hotels didn't require disclosure, nor did they explicitly state that they wouldn't take ex-cons, registered or not. They'd have discrimination suits coming out the wazoo if they did.

"Only if you let me pay for it."

Mark didn't even attempt to hide his exasperation. "I can afford it." His new pecan floors could wait. "You can't. He's my family, too. And the problem is also mine."

"If my son is part yours to worry about, your issues are part mine."

Because she'd dropped the money thing, Mark allowed her that.

"I'll come for him tomorrow after work." And he'd call Sharon to cancel Saturday's coffee.

"That'd be four hours in the car, two days in a row," Dana told him, frowning again. "Just take him back tonight."

"I can't get a room tonight."

To her credit, Dana didn't argue any more.

SHE'D PLEADED, CAJOLED, EVEN CRIED. And John Lindsay would not budge. He was not going to rehash, talk about or in any way relive the incident that had changed the life of their family so drastically. He'd said what he had to say. Sara's mother and he had made the decision long ago that Sara's loss of memory of the events of the night she'd been so intimately abused was a silver lining inside a very dark cloud. A gift from God.

They'd vowed never to speak to her of that night, and that was that.

It didn't matter that she had a right to know.

That it was her life—her body, for God's sake. Nor did he seem to care that she was now an adult, attempting to face up to herself, meet her life head-on. He believed as strongly now as he had twenty years ago that she was better off not knowing.

Or so he said.

Slowing to consult the directions on the paper beside her, Sara verified the street sign one more time and turned. She'd never been in this part of Columbus before. Never been anywhere that boasted graffiti artwork on every single building.

Sweating, she set aside the mental rebuttals she had for every single thing her father had so emphatically told her when they'd met for dinner the weekend after the holiday.

If not for his stubborn, chauvinistic and, yes, demeaning attitude toward her, she wouldn't be in this neighborhood.

Professionally, Sara had been traveling alone for years. She could hold her own in front of a ballroom filled with hundreds of rich and influential people.

She just wasn't too sure how she'd do up against kids in the street.

Stopped at a light, it took her a second to realize that the yelling outside her Lexus was aimed at her. One teenager was gesturing for her to unroll her window.

Over my dead body, Sara thought, her hands shaking.

If the light hadn't turned green, Sara might have collapsed, arms over her head, and cried. It was what she wanted to do.

She was a woman, and she'd been a victim before.

She could be again.

She damn well should have taken the time to change out of her pink linen suit with the matching leather heels.

What in hell had she been thinking? Other than wanting to get down here before dark. Her meeting had run late, and if she didn't see the man tonight...

Focusing on the street sign, attempting to make out the white letters hidden by a blast of spray paint, she prayed that this was her turn and understood now why Ryan, when he'd called to tell her he'd located one of the three convicted men, had told her unequivocally not to come here.

Unfortunately, his order had been issued when she'd just had one too many *unequivocallys.*

And she wanted to get to this man before her biological son-turned-cop did.

She might be angry as hell with her father, but she still loved him. Had to protect him.

Lord knew what would happen if Ryan showed up here in his cop uniform and started spouting stuff about a possible mistrial. A fool could figure out that the man would stop at nothing to find out the truth—and seek prosecution of any guilty parties to the fullest extent of the law.

Not that she thought for one second that her father had broken any laws. He just wasn't the type.

The turn was not hers. And now the windows all had bars on them. And instead of sidewalks, there were broken curbs and patches of dirt bordering the street.

If not for the fact that she was afraid for her father, she would have pushed her foot to the floor and left the vicinity immediately—speeding ticket be damned. A cop at her side, even to deliver a citation, would be most welcome right now.

She wondered what kind of man she'd find at the end of this not-so-savvy journey. She thought she might be safer where she'd been than where she was heading, but even as fear held her back, it also egged her on.

With a sigh of something other than relief, she turned at the next corner. Looked for house numbers or building identification marks of any kind.

Halfway down the second block, she spotted a dirty brick building with enough letters attached to the broken-down sign above the door to let her know she'd found the right place. Other than one SUV parked across the street and down a little bit, there wasn't a car at the curb less than ten years old.

Rust was the in thing here.

Thanking God for all of her many, many blessings—sincerely—Sara also prayed hard for someone to watch over her safety now.

Only twenty minutes away from the comfort and safety of her office, and it seemed as if she hadn't been there in years.

Ryan was going to call her tonight, to find out how her meeting with her father had gone over the weekend. And tomorrow, his first day off after his three-day rotation, he was planning to find Mark Dalton.

Sara couldn't let that happen—at least not without getting to him first.

Like her, he was older now. And hopefully had some experience, a sense of logic, to appeal to.

A teenager in gang colors on a bike with no gears rolled by slowly, peering in at her. A skinny white woman with long, dark hair held back conservatively with a barrette probably wasn't a common sight. She couldn't sit here indefinitely.

Probably shouldn't stay another minute or two.

But inside that door, in number 2-B, if luck was with her, was one of the three men who'd raped her.

THERE WAS NO BELL. Just a new-looking plaster plate on the wall beside the apartment door.

No one answered her knock. Not even when she hurt her knuckles making an effort to be heard.

Sara jumped when the main door to the building opened downstairs. She was standing alone, unprotected other than by the pepper spray sliding around in her sweaty palm, in the second floor hallway.

Hold the spray in front of you. Three feet from your target, if at all possible. Aim at his eyes. Flip the safety and press hard with your thumb for two seconds, and only two seconds. Then flick your keys in his face, knee him, if you have to, and run. You'll have about forty-five seconds.

Her father's words, repeated so many times that Sara could give classes on the subject, echoed in her mind, and then she realized that whoever had entered the building had not come upstairs.

She knocked again.

And a little girl peeked around a stairwell farther down the hall—as if she'd been sitting there all along.

"You lookin' for Mr. Mark?"

She was looking for Mark Dalton. Taking a chance, Sara said, "Yeah."

The girl, who was not more than six, came out into the hall. Her ebony skin was such a beautiful color, and Sara couldn't help watching her approach.

"He ain't here."

"Do you know when he'll be back?"

The beaded braids on the child's head shook with the force of her nonverbal negative reply.

"Oh. Well, thank you."

Sara turned to go, her heels clacking loudly on the cracked tile floor.

"He's gone for days."

Though she wasn't sure why, Sara couldn't help turning around again. It was almost as if she wanted to spend as much time with the child as she could.

"Is he on vacation?" she asked, wondering what such a precious little girl had been doing sitting all alone in a hallway that was clearly not safe for grown men. And she didn't want to consider the various answers that occurred.

"He's at the castle."

Did she mean prison? That couldn't be right. Ryan would have known. Unless the man had just been arrested over the weekend.

"What castle?"

"You know, the one down beside the freeway…"

The way the child drew out the first half of the word charmed Sara. But she still had no idea.

"The one where people stay when they visitin' and got nobody to stay with but got lots of money instead."

If they were talking about the exit Sara had taken—a good five miles from where she now stood—the only building there had been one of those new suite hotels that served a full breakfast in the morning and hors d'oeuvres at night, all included in the price of a room.

She named it, just in case.

"Yep." The little girl's smile was as endearing as the rest of her. "He asked my ma if I could come and swim in the pool there."

"And what did your mom say?"

"She say I can go anywhere Mr. Mark goes, long as he's gonna stay there with me."

Sara's opinion of the white college dropout-turned-inmate moved up a notch. A very small, almost indiscernible notch.

The mother of this engaging child, she wasn't at all sure about, however. What kind of woman let her child go around with such a man?

Albeit one who'd been led on—and hadn't

known the twenty-one-year-old who'd been teasing him was really a cloistered sixteen-year-old sheriff's daughter.

But at least now she knew where she could find the man. She didn't doubt her son would get the information she'd just happened upon in no time. If he didn't have it already.

At least he'd promised to wait until after she told him what her father said before he pursued things any further.

"So did you go?" Sara asked as the little girl continued to stand there, her legs crossed and her fingers doing a spider climb in the air.

"Tomorrow." The urchin drew out that word, too. "Room 422. My ma's droppin' me in the mornin'."

"Well, have a good time," Sara said, backing up. She had to go. Had to get out of this neighborhood.

But she felt horrible leaving the little girl standing there alone in the dark, smelly hallway.

"GOTCHA!" Mark emphasized the word with a tough push of his thumb on the plastic control panel and watched as the colored tiles on his video screen disappeared, sending death to Jordon's similar, almost empty grid.

"Shit. I almost had you that time, Uncle Mark.

And if you weren't such a wuss, we'd be playing Master Commando."

Jordon's grinning face reminded Mark of a younger Jordon. One who'd laughed a lot and found good in everything. Apparently, other than spending time with Mark, the boy didn't find much to praise about anything else these days.

He nudged the kid's shoulder, wishing he could convince his nephew that the oversized jeans he wore hanging down so far made him look more foolish than cool. "You wish you almost had me, my man. *I* am the master."

He'd brought his electronic equipment to the hotel with them, including the newest version of the most popular video entertainment system on the market. To entertain Jordon, certainly. And also because he knew if he left anything of value in the apartment, he'd probably come back to find it gone.

Instead, he'd spread the word that he was taking everything with him, and consequently he wasn't all that worried about a break-in.

It wouldn't have been sensible to do otherwise. In his neighborhood, even his best friend would have to give in to such a temptation.

"Only because you always get to pick the damn games, otherwise I'd be kicking your ass."

"You'll please my ass a lot more if you stop

talking like that," he said now, but Jordon knew he was only saying the words because he felt he had to.

Jordon was a good kid. If he needed to use tough words sometimes to feel that he wasn't lacking in terms of manhood, Mark had no problem with that.

As long as he was never disrespectful enough to use them around his mom or his grandmother.

"I'm hungry," Jordon announced, attacking the next grid with a vengeance. "We ordering pizza again tonight?"

A fresh piece of broiled cod with a touch of lemon butter and garlic would be nice, Mark thought.

"We had that last night."

"Uh-uh. It was the night before. Last night we went for hamburgers—you said the fries were cold."

Oh, yeah. The meal he'd tried to forget. Pushing buttons with masterful precision, he landed a blue tile perfectly, sending a row of extra tiles over to Jordon.

"We could always go back to IHOP."

"We had pancakes for breakfast." The boy's negative response was probably tied more to the whammies Mark was sending him than to the restaurant choice. Jordon liked IHOP.

But he was right. Their cook-to-order hotel breakfasts were one of the nicer parts of this little stay.

He was getting used to falling asleep without nightly sound effects through his ceiling, too, but he knew better than to get too fond of that. No reason to set himself up for future dissatisfaction.

His winning tile presented itself. He flipped it, aimed, pushed to send it home and jerked as a knock sounded at the door.

"Aha!" Jordon cried. "Gotcha!"

Mark's shot had missed.

Jordon's hadn't.

The knock had cost him his game.

CHAPTER EIGHT

HE WAS NOTHING LIKE she'd expected. Tall, sandy blond hair, eyes that weren't bold enough to be one specific color—more like a cross between green and gold, with a little brown mixed in.

And a bit of curiosity mixed in as well.

In her mind, the men who'd raped her had never been endowed with curious eyes, character-lined faces or...muscled shoulders.

She'd always pictured them small.

Apparently, he didn't know who she was.

Drawing a breath, she tried to speak. Couldn't get beyond how tall he was.

"Can I help you?" the man asked a second time and his voice brought her back to reality.

Because she remembered it? God, she hoped not.

"You're Mark Dalton?" she asked, cursing the catch in her voice. Twenty years of training in "don't let it show," and here she was wearing her fear on her sleeve.

There wasn't even a spark of recognition.

"Yes." Curiosity turned to wariness in those interesting eyes.

"I'm Sara Calhoun."

The name was Brent's. Safe.

"What can I do for you, Sara Calhoun?" he asked politely, without the smile that might have made the line a come-on.

Dignity and class. That was the way to get through this.

"I was wondering if I could have a few minutes of your time." The words came just as she'd rehearsed them.

"Jeez, Uncle Mark, who's the babe?"

Stepping back, Sara stared at the longish-haired young man, perturbed and relieved at the same time.

He had a child with him. She was safe. But she could never say what she'd come to say in front of a child.

"I don't know yet, Jordon, but you can now apologize for being disrespectful. Ms. Calhoun is a woman, not a 'babe.'"

"Yeah, sorry," the boy said, grinning at Sara. "It was really a compliment, but my uncle here's a little stuffy when it comes to these things."

Mark Dalton actually turned red at that, confusing Sara. A rapist, even if he'd basically been a drunk partying college boy, bothering himself with respecting women?

"I didn't realize you weren't alone," she said, backtracking. If she didn't get this done tonight, Ryan would be on to him tomorrow. "I only need a few minutes of your time."

I need to get away from you, before I start imagining those hands causing the red welts that were around my wrists the morning after my first and only drunken binge.

Sara was trembling so hard inside she feared they'd both be able to see it.

"Sure," he said, though he didn't look all that pleased. "Play a game, Jordon. I'll be right outside."

He stood in the hall, right by the door to his room. Aware of the teenager still on the other side, Sara asked, "Do you mind if we go down there?" She pointed to a nicely furnished seating area by the elevators.

Seeing him nod, she headed that way, nerves growing tighter with every step they took.

"YOU LOOK LIKE a man who'd want things straight up," she said as soon as they were seated in the winged armchairs in the alcove. The house phone on the antique table between them was a comfort.

Again, his concurrence was nonverbal.

"I'm here to ask for your help." She looked at the man, and couldn't find even a hint of violence about him. "I think."

Those multicolored eyes were sizing her up. Still, he said nothing.

His jeans were new-looking. A name brand. The T-shirt, advertising a well-known brand of sporting equipment, was clean.

"Or maybe just to warn you..." Sara sat forward. And then back. Her hands on the arms of her chair, beside her thighs, and finally clasped in her lap.

Lounging beside her, Mark Dalton appeared to be willing to sit there all night, his face impassive.

She wondered if he was really as at home in the surroundings as he looked.

Judging by his address, she'd guess not.

Yet nothing about this man suggested he'd live in the dirty building she'd just come from.

"I'm Sara Lindsay."

He jerked forward, hands coming up to grip either side of the chair as he stared at her, horror in his eyes.

"I have a favor to ask you." She rushed ahead—away from his reaction. And the thing he was reacting to.

"Anything." The word was choked. "Whatever you need. Just name it."

With a feeling that she could ask him for the blood in his veins and he'd willingly drain it for her, something in Sara changed. She still felt the revulsion, the fear, certainly the shame, but...

"S-s-someone's looking into that night..."

His skin went absolutely white.

"H-he thinks that it was somehow tied to a murder."

Or at the very least that her father hadn't done his job—which was equally horrifying.

Still leaning forward, Mark's back straightened. "How do you know this? From your father?"

It took Sara a second to realize that Mark Dalton certainly would have known her father. John Lindsay had arrested him. And made it his life's goal to see him convicted.

Eventually, when she had herself under control again, she shook her head. "Someone else. Someone you...don't...know."

Oh, God, this was complicated. Getting more so by the second. She'd set out to protect her dad and had ended up in mire so deep she couldn't see beyond the carpet on the floor.

Ryan could be this man's son. Had her thinking really been so compartmentalized that she'd not allowed the thought to surface before then?

She certainly hadn't consciously acknowledged the fact. Had never separated the three men in her mind into individuals, only one of whom had fathered the child she'd loved and given away.

That boy back there in the hotel room, if he really was Mark's nephew, could also be Ryan's cousin.

When she looked up, Mark was watching her.

"I'm sorry." His words were thick, deep, as if he'd pulled them from his own personal hell.

Sara acknowledged the comment with a slight nod. She couldn't tell him it was okay.

Still, he looked at her intently, as if searching for something in particular. Not knowing what it was, she still knew he wouldn't find it.

"I—" he started.

"Please," Sara interrupted him. "I don't want… Can't rehash anything right now. I just…"

She stopped. She shouldn't have come. Wasn't ready. Hadn't found enough of herself to be able to show and tell.

And then she thought of Ryan, standing on her doorstep. Of Brent, with his young lover and her two kids.

"Have you ever heard of a guy named Ralph Bonney?"

"Yeah."

Of course he had. Mark had been at the trial. Everyone back then had been—except for her.

"Did you know him…before?"

"Just that year. He was in my fraternity."

When he talked, it wasn't as hard for Sara to remain seated. His voice was…calming. As if he'd found a way to live with himself. With life.

How did a rapist do that?

"Did he…have any business with my father?"

"Not that I know of."

"No previous brushes with the law?"

No reason he'd feel a debt of loyalty to Sheriff Lindsay?

"Not Ralph. He was almost stereotypically nerdy. He'd drink beers occasionally, but he was as straight as they came."

"But he went to the party."

"Of course. He was a brother. But before he'd let us open a single bottle, he insisted that we all bury our keys."

But…

"I thought he testified that he didn't know where they were." Sara frowned.

"Three beers put Ralph under the table," Mark said, his tone solemn, low, as if they were discussing a funeral, not a frat party at the lake. "He'd been known to get elevated opinions of himself—

think he was a superhero. We made sure he *never* knew where his keys were when he was drinking."

Didn't sound like the bunch of irresponsible animals they'd been in her mind.

And she wasn't getting anywhere.

"Other than that, I just need to know if you remember anything about that night."

"Bits and pieces from early on."

Do you remember me?

She couldn't ask. Didn't want to know.

"Such as?"

"The beer arriving. Grabbing a bottle out of the case of whiskey. The keys. Hot dogs. Fearing I was going to fail my chemical engineering final and intending to get drunk off my ass."

"Do you remember anyone you hadn't seen before? Anyone showing up unexpectedly?"

With his elbows on his knees, head bowed, he glanced up at her. "Other than you, you mean?"

The breath caught in her throat. He did remember her.

She nodded.

"Nope."

Her skin burned. Her whole body was a mass of heat, as if she'd slipped from earth to hell.

"You don't remember if Ralph was there when you... When..."

This was not going to work. She'd been a fool to think she'd recovered enough composure to move forward. To face her past so she could live the rest of her life fully, rather than hiding from it.

"Sara." He reached toward her and then stopped abruptly—but not before she'd blanched, jerked backward. "I don't remember anything about what happened," he said, his voice kind, in spite of the tightness in his face. "I wish to God I did."

That got her out of herself. "You do?"

"Hell, yes, I do."

"Why?"

"Because then I'd know that I hadn't been the one who hurt you."

She hiccuped. And started to sob.

HE COULDN'T TOUCH HER. And he couldn't leave her there all alone, suffering a hell he could only imagine in the darkness of her mind.

Mark's soul died another death. Now he had a face, a body—albeit twenty-one years older—to match to the scenarios that still plagued his mind and kept his gut churning late at night.

"Hey," he said, dropping to his knees in front of her chair. "Come on, it's going to be okay."

He was babbling, speaking nonsense. There were some things that would never be all right.

The elevator opened. A young couple emerged, arms about each other, their faces an inch apart—Tom and Elaine Buckle. They'd been married over the weekend, and Jordon had talked to them at the hot tub the night before.

Moving in front of Sara, Mark hid her from view, and touched her foot with his. "I'm so sorry." He said the words over and over again, his throat choked with regret. Self-hatred.

She shook her head, fists at either side of her face, and then covered her mouth. Her eyes, when she looked at him, were green. Luminous. Haunted. And still streaming with tears.

"I'd do anything to undo that night." He could manage little more than a whisper. Wasn't sure she could've heard him even if he'd been yelling.

Because she hadn't pulled her foot away, Mark continued to rest his own against it—the only human contact he dared to offer her. Ten minutes passed and he remained motionless, willing her whatever she needed, whatever it would take to help.

"I misjudged."

She opened the pretty pink purse that matched her shoes and the rest of her outfit, pulling out a packet of Kleenex as she spoke.

"Misjudged what?"

"Me." With a sad smile, she met his gaze before looking away again. "I thought I was stronger than I apparently am."

"How can you say that?" Mark moved slowly, sliding his foot away from hers before she noticed it, returning to his seat. "You're here, and though I'm still not sure why, I'm glad."

That earned him another glance. "Why?" she asked, holding his gaze this time.

He wasn't sure. But there was something. Forward motion in a still life. "Maybe it's a way to heal."

Not for him. But for her. If it was possible. Or was that just his conscience crying out for some cheap fix? For forgiveness.

"I'm really okay, most of the time," she said then, straightening, her tears all but gone. "All the time, until recently."

"What happened recently?"

"You wouldn't want to know," she said, shaking her head. "Besides, it doesn't matter."

More like, she didn't want to tell him. And why should she?

"What do you need from me?" She was going to leave and he wasn't ready, though he had nothing in mind for her. Nothing to give her. Or gain.

The elevator binged again. A family coming

back at the end of the day. They glanced over, looked away and moved down another hall.

It was almost seven.

Jordon must be getting hungry.

Damn. Jordon.

Yet thoughts of how he was going to explain this weren't a concern at the moment.

"I've agreed to help look into what happened," she said, her voice low and even, her eyes trained across the room. "I'm hoping you'll agree to answer any questions that might arise."

Going back was the last thing he wanted to do.

"Of course."

"Can I have your cell number, then? So I can call you?"

There was a note of desperation in her voice that bothered Mark, alerting him to the fact there was something she wasn't telling him.

He gave her his number, anyway.

"I work at High Import Mechanics."

"I know. You took a car-restoration course while you were in prison and already had an internship lined up when you were released."

She appeared to have a lot more information about him than he did about her. But then, he was registered. And she, above all people, would have access to that information.

He expected her to get up, turn her back and walk away. She held her purse on her lap, as if she didn't have the energy to walk to the elevator.

"Can I call someone for you? Your husband?"

"I'm divorced. And no, I don't need you to call anyone. I'm fine."

But still she didn't go. He wondered about that divorce. Had she been alone a long time, as well?

"So, what do you think happened that night that we don't already know about?" he asked, not upset that she wasn't ready to leave. Or even anxious to have her go.

Jordon had games to play. Snacks in the room. He'd be fine for a while longer.

"We're not sure...."

She told him about some unidentified bones that had been found. Questions they'd raised.

"Who'd be looking into all this, so many years later?"

The question was more curiosity than anything else.

Sara's stricken look made it much more.

"Who?"

Her father?

His entire being filled with horror. Was he going to be pegged for something else that had happened that night that he couldn't defend himself against because he couldn't remember a damned minute of it?

"Are they trying to say I murdered someone?"

That had her gaze flying back to his. "No!"

Relief had him sinking back in his chair, his arms and legs weak. He'd never forget how powerless he'd felt the day he'd been arrested, every day of the trial, every moment of his almost five years in prison. Powerless to defend himself, because he just didn't know. Powerless to change anything.

He'd rather die than ever feel that way again.

"It's a possibility that the…my stuff…took up so much of my father's attention that a murder just slid right past him."

"Your father thinks this?"

Sheriff Lindsay was not a man Mark ever wanted to face again.

He'd had nightmares about the guy for years— even after prison. Visions of him showing up on his doorstep, at home, at work, at his sister's, with a piece of paper that gave him the right to haul Mark away all over again.

Memories of the hatred in the man's eyes, the barely controlled anger that could have torn Mark apart limb by limb.

It took him a minute to figure out that Sara had answered him with a shake of the head.

"My father wants nothing to do with any of this," she said when he looked over at her.

"He doesn't know you're here, seeing me?"

She shook her head again.

Mark wasn't sure how he felt about that. The John Lindsay he'd known wouldn't hesitate to find some way to ruin Mark's life, even now, if he thought Mark was anywhere near his daughter.

He'd made that threat clear.

But Mark didn't owe John Lindsay, or even himself. He did, however, owe the beautiful, broken woman sitting beside him.

"He refuses to discuss the past and he's told me in no uncertain terms that nothing good will ever come of it. It's past, dead and buried to him."

"But not to you?"

Her chin lifted as she faced him. "I've spent the past twenty-one years running—and missing most of what's been on my path as a result. I find I'm out of breath and want to slow down. I want to live."

The smile that came surprised Mark, hurt the tense muscles in his face—and came from deep within him.

"Good for you," he said. Maybe, if she could do that, there'd be a small bit of peace for him, as well.

"So you never told me. How'd you find out about the bones?"

"Someone told me."

"Because you were asking?"

"No."

"Someone else is looking into it, too?"

"Yes."

"Who?" Who else would care? Ralph Bonney? She'd mentioned him.

Ralph was married to a pretty blond woman who reminded Mark of a modern Doris Day. He had two great kids and a lot of money. Why would he care about a college incident two decades ago?

Mark suspected that she wasn't going to tell him. And he had to know. "Who?" he asked again, more firmly.

"My son."

That took him a minute.

"You have a son old enough to be investigating all that? And your dad's allowing it?"

"My father doesn't know him. I only just met him myself." Her words were going somewhere, edging them both onto a precipice. He could feel it. And couldn't get down, get away.

"I gave him up for adoption."

Mark's ears burned. Roared.

"How old is he?" he asked, pinning her with a stare that he couldn't control, as he felt his life spiral down to hell once more.

"Twenty-one."

He did the math. Considered the source.

"You became pregnant that night."

Her nod was jerky at best.

"It never came up at the trial."

"My father wouldn't let anyone know until after the sentencing. I had no memory of that night, so I didn't have to testify, but the other…would have been seen as a hardship to me, an aggravating factor of the crime, and it would have come up at sentencing. I'd have had to appear."

"We would have been given more time."

"And my life would have been even more complicated than it already was."

As much as Mark detested Sheriff Lindsay, his opinion of the man underwent a slight alteration. He'd thought the man obsessed, beyond reason, with putting him and his buddies away. Had the man really let them off with a lighter sentence, just to protect his daughter?

Did Sara Lindsay—whatever she'd said her current last name was—have any reason to lie to him about it?

Certainly not for child support. The kid was full grown. And most certainly not for a piece of his reputation. No question about that.

Sheriff John Lindsay, the one man he honestly

couldn't help but hate, might actually have done him a favor.

Life never did turn out to be exactly as it seemed.

His stream of thoughts came to a screeching halt when Mark couldn't come up with anything else to use to hide from the real news here. When the shock started to wear off enough for him to acknowledge that life had just changed irrevocably. Forever.

As it had only once before in his life.

Swallowing hard, straightening his shoulders, he peered straight at her.

"You're telling me that I might have a twenty-one-year-old son?"

Mark felt as if he'd been hit by a truck, when Sara nodded her head back at him.

CHAPTER NINE

THE MAN SAT SO STIFFLY, for so long, it was almost as if rigor mortis had set in. Sara didn't know what to do with him—or with herself.

She was sitting face-to-face with one of the three men who'd raped her. There were no dignity-and-class rules to help in such a situation.

And rules had guided her life for so long, she didn't know how to live without them.

Though his face was unmoving, emotions flitted in and out of his golden-green eyes. They appeared to be on fire. And then grew moist, as if the pain inside him had begun to spill out.

"It's only a one-in-three chance."

Hearing the inane words come out of her, Sara hugged her purse. More than half her life had been spent serving—either the public, through her work, or her husband, at home. She was doing a lifetime of penance for her sins. And in spite of how ludicrous she knew her feelings to be, she still felt obligated to ease this stranger's distress.

"I want to meet him."

She sucked in a harsh breath. He and Ryan together, discussing an investigation her father was adamantly against reopening, one of them a grandson, the other a man he'd crucified. The idea of it put knots in her stomach.

"He wants to ask you some questions." And she had to be present. There was no way she was going to keep these two determined men apart. But she would do everything in her power to protect the father who'd stood by her throughout her life, loving her the best way he could, no matter what.

Mark Dalton's hands lay limply on the chair on either side of him. Mechanic's hands, according to her son. Without a speck of grease beneath the fingernails.

An unstereotypical man.

"How will I find him?" Mark's words, though softly spoken, were clipped. Firm.

"I can arrange a meeting," she said tentatively.

His eyes narrowed. "Fine. When?"

"Tomorrow?" Ryan was going to show up here alone, if she didn't find a way to stop him.

"What time? Where?"

Mouth dry, Sara had no way to wet lips that stuck together. And she was drawing a blank. Her office felt safe. But she couldn't have either of them there where people would see them, ask questions, talk.

Her house was just plain out. No way could she have Mark Dalton there. Not that she felt even an ounce of the fear she'd expected to associate with the man.

A restaurant was too public. She couldn't control what might happen between her son and this man.

"Here?"

The hotel was private, neutral. She could live the rest of her life without ever needing to be here again.

Mark glanced down the hall and then back. And she remembered the nephew who was waiting for him.

This wasn't going to be easy for any of them.

"We could meet at your place," she offered, though she wasn't sure if it was livable since he was staying here.

"Here's fine. There's a balcony off my room. We'll have privacy."

"What about your nephew?"

"He's thirteen, long past the time when he had to be entertained every moment."

She needed to stand, to be taller than he was. Even though she was also inclined to sit there forever, since she wasn't sure she was ever going to be strong enough to follow through on what she'd started.

What Ryan had started and she'd allowed.

What she'd started by rebelling against her father so foolishly, so long ago. What three college boys had done to themselves—and to her.

"I just thought… He might ask questions you'd rather not answer."

"Jordon knows about my past."

How did one explain something like that to a thirteen-year-old? And why? There were questions she wouldn't ask. His life was none of her business.

"I'd rather he not know about the boy…man… Our…your son."

"His name's Ryan." She purposely left off his last name, not wanting to take any chances this man would bypass her and get to Ryan alone. At least not until she knew that they weren't going to try to erroneously implicate her father out of some need for answers or revenge. Or until she knew the facts and could warn her father. "And I don't intend to tell your nephew anything," she said, adding, "Ryan won't, either. You can trust him on that."

"Ryan." Folding his hands in his lap, he faced the floor. "Did you name him?"

"No." She'd barely seen him, never touched him. Until six weeks ago. "His adoptive parents did."

Mark glanced sideways, giving her a glimpse of the intense emotions he was struggling to contain. "Do you like him?"

"Of course." He wanted to know more. She could read the need in his eyes. But could she do this? Discuss the baby who had been the heart of her heart for only minutes in a lifetime—with the man who might have fathered him?

As if Ryan was *their* son.

Did she have to?

"He's a cop."

He sat up, his brow raised. "With an attitude?"

Shaking her head, she pictured her son in her home that first day, telling her about Brent. With compassion, protectiveness. And telling her about not wanting to hurt his real mother.

"He's got a good heart." And then, though she wasn't sure she wanted to hear it, she added, "He reminds me a bit of my father, in that he views the world as black-and-white."

This meeting between Mark and her son was already fraught with perils. If she could prepare him, possibly make things go more smoothly, then she had to try.

"What does he look like?"

Does he look like me? She read the real question in Mark Dalton's eyes. And couldn't answer him.

"Tall. Athletic. Dark blond hair. Green eyes." None of which described the aura that seemed to surround the young man—at least as far as Sara was concerned. It was almost as if he was other-worldly in some sense, this child of hers who had appeared out of nowhere after so long and yet embodied parts of his biological heredity, anyway. She couldn't get enough of him.

Couldn't completely mourn the life she'd just lost because, at the same time, she'd met Ryan, and thoughts of him brought peace and a bitter-sweet joy that just as often consumed her.

Mark was staring at her. His hair was close to the same shade as Ryan's. Maybe a little darker. His eyes had some green in them. He was tall. But a lot of men were tall.

"The other two…" she found herself saying, and then she couldn't go on. Her parents had told her they were Caucasian and little else.

"None of us was short," Mark said, his eyes darkening as he spoke, almost as if he was wrapping her in safety and making it all okay. Which, of course, he could never do.

No one could. Least of all, him.

"Keith's hair was about like mine. Sam's was darker."

Keith and Sam. He said the names as if they were regular guys. She only thought of them in terms of their full names. Mark Dalton. Keith Gardner. Sam Hall. Just as their names had appeared in the articles she'd recently read.

"Ryan said that Keith Gardner was killed in a motorcycle accident a couple of years after he left prison." She had to go—not sit here speaking about the past with this man. This kind of talk could lead to nowhere good.

"He was drunk. Drove his bike into a tree."

She shivered. "You say that as if you think it was on purpose."

"I don't know that."

"But you think it." Why she was pushing this, she didn't know. Why she was sitting there at all, she didn't understand.

Something was driving her from the inside. Maybe the same pressure that had given her the courage to leave Brent, rather than turn a blind eye as both he and her father had expected her to do.

Wanted her to do.

Brent wanted Chloe, but he didn't want a divorce.

Mark lifted his hands upward and then let them fall. "If I had to guess, I'd say yes."

She wanted to ask why. But didn't.

"And you know about Sam Hall, too?"

"In prison for assault with a deadly weapon," Mark said, his voice expressionless. "He took a baseball bat to a man who accused him of stealing a carton of cigarettes."

That was more than Ryan had told her.

"Had he?"

"Probably. He'd been arrested a couple of times prior to that, but the charges didn't stick."

She felt sick again. "Charges of what?"

"Breaking and entering, and fondling a teenage boy."

I can't do this. Sara's mind raced. She didn't want to hear any more. To know.

"Did he do it?"

Frowning, Mark sat forward, elbows on his knees. "I'm not his keeper," he said, adding, "but I wouldn't put it past him. Sam was a pretty angry guy, even when I knew him."

But fondling a teenage boy? She followed the red-and-gold pattern of large flowers in the carpet, traced the black outline of a rose with her gaze.

The elevator opened and closed again without anyone getting out.

She studied the flowers some more, doing everything she could to keep the worst thoughts at bay.

Nausea welled as heat surrounded her, suffocating her. She was never going to be normal. Never going to escape.

And Ryan? Was Sam Hall her son's father?

Her dad had met all of them. Repeatedly. Interrogating them relentlessly, if she knew her father. Coming at them again and again, until they'd buckled and told him anything he wanted to know.

God, it was all such a mess.

"We'll need to do a paternity test."

She'd expected—and feared—that. And she didn't *want* a name to the father of the child she'd carried inside her most of her sixteenth year. That baby had been hers alone, or she'd never have been able to survive having it inside her month after month.

"You'll have to talk to Ryan about that," she said now, wishing he'd just leave her to breathe, to rest. She'd find the strength to go eventually. And if not, she was safe enough here. The hotel was nice, well-known, part of a respected chain.

"I'd think he'd want to know."

Maybe. Ryan seemed far more interested in finding out what really happened the night he was conceived, than in figuring out which of the three men had sired him. But that wasn't for her to worry about.

Whatever they decided, she could remain ignorant.

"You should probably be getting back to your nephew."

His presence was overpowering. And then he stood.

"I'll walk you to your car."

Because he expected her to, Sara stood—and managed to stay standing. She was stronger than she thought. "That's not necessary." She spoke over her shoulder as she headed for the elevator.

"Maybe not, but it's dark out, and I'd feel better if you'd humor me and let me do it, anyway."

The choice was hers.

Sara, clutching her purse, held his gaze for a long second. She couldn't remember this man hurting her.

"Thank you," she eventually conceded. Neither of them said another word as they rode down to the lobby and walked into the night.

The man was an enigma. Her worst nightmare.

And yet kind at the same time.

CHAPTER TEN

"DUDE, you're gonna pace a hole in the carpet."

With a grimace aimed at his outspoken nephew, Mark paced himself around the corner and into the bathroom he and Jordon were sharing, noticing that the dirty underwear Jordon had left on the floor was gone.

He leaned on the counter, staring in the wall-to-wall mirror.

You can do this, man.

Yeah. He looked himself straight in the eye.

You're a good man.

Not according to public opinion.

You live a decent life.

I try.

You have a right to meet this kid; to know if you have a son.

Do I want to know that I left a sixteen-year-old girl alone and pregnant?

You might even find out what happened that

night your life went from promising straight to hell.

"Uncle Mark?" Jordon's voice came from the bed, where he was reading the newest vintage Archie comic. "You fall in?"

Opening the door, Mark purposely did not check his hair to make sure it wasn't standing on end or curling at the edge. He didn't look for wrinkles in his khaki slacks or stains on the polo shirt. He was what he was.

He'd learned a long time ago, he might as well be good with that.

"I don't get who this woman is." Jordon wasn't lying on the bed now. Or reading the comic book. He was sitting on the edge of one of their two chairs, elbows resting on the arms, chewing on a paper clip.

The boy chewed incessantly. Pens were his favorite delicacy.

"I told you, she's someone from the past, from the party. She knows a cop who believes there was more to that night than what came out in court, and they want to ask me some questions."

"You were with her forty-five minutes last night. What more could there be to ask?" Jordon's serious face required Mark's complete attention. He'd underestimated the boy.

"Nothing more, but Ryan…" he stumbled over the name, "the cop, has some questions of his own. She's just coming along by way of introduction."

"Does she know what happened? Did she see?"

"No." Mark considered telling Jordon the whole truth—at least about Sara Calhoun. He'd considered it the night before, as he and his nephew sat at a table at a nearby café eating meat loaf and mashed potatoes. He wasn't sure why he hadn't—except out of some misplaced compulsion to protect her.

Even believing that his first loyalty must be to Jordon, he couldn't brush her with the darkness of that night which lived on in all of their lives, even decades later.

"What does she think happened?"

"This cop says an unidentified male skeleton was found nearby, and the estimated time of death fits."

"What would that have to do with the rest?"

"I have no idea."

"So what does she want from you?"

For the first time, Mark heard the fear in his nephew's voice. And then he understood.

"Hey, buddy," he said, sitting down close to Jordon, nudging him with his knee. "There's nothing to worry about here. I've already been tried, convicted and done my time. Statute of limitations is up."

Not technically, if a new crime was discovered, but he wasn't going to tell Jordon that. Or allow himself to think about it, either. He'd lose his sanity if he considered the possibility there could be another crime pinned on him that he couldn't possibly defend himself against.

He'd lain awake most of the night telling himself just that.

"So why do you need to talk to them?"

"Because if a crime was committed and I can help bring about justice, it's my duty to do so."

Jordon frowned. "How can you say that?" he asked, studying his uncle. "After what they did to you?"

Alarms went off in Mark's head. "Who's they?"

"Cops." There was no compliment in the word.

"The police didn't do anything to me that I didn't deserve," Mark said with finality. The tone in his voice spoke to himself as much as it was intended to speak to Jordon. The truth rang through. "Sheriff Lindsay was determined to see us pay for what we did to his daughter, it's true. But the evidence was clear, Jordon. Whether I remember what happened or not, there's no doubt that I was with that girl."

He hadn't seen tears in the boy's eyes in more than a year. "You wouldn't do that."

"My semen was inside her." He'd rather not have been so crude, but he couldn't have his sister's son mistrusting cops—or the legal system. That's how young boys went astray.

And it would be over his dead body that they lost another Dalton boy to prison.

"So? Maybe you liked her and she liked you, too."

Maybe. He'd like to think so. "The other two had been with her at the same time."

"So, *she* was loose."

"Uh-uh." Mark shook his head. "Doesn't matter who or what anyone else is or does, son," he said. "Your actions are your own. She could be naked on a table and offering herself to every guy there, and if I choose to take her, I become accountable, I become a man who would have sex irresponsibly, with others watching. I become a man who has disrespected not only the act of making love, but disrespected women, as well."

Jordon studied him and, reading his eyes, Mark relaxed just a tad.

"The fact that I'd been told the girl was twenty-one doesn't change the fact that I chose to get involved in an orgy with a woman I didn't know. Had I treated the act with appropriate dignity, I'd have known her. And I'd have had a good chance of figuring out that she was really only a kid."

"Stupid bitch."

Mark's first reaction was to wash the boy's mouth with soap for uttering the words. The second was to cut him to the quick with a verbal response.

But he'd said the same thing himself, repeatedly, during the weeks of the trial. And later, as he'd lain on a hard cot in his prison cell listening while next door, a couple of inmates got way too familiar with each other.

"She was a young girl whose sheriff father was hard on her. She rebelled. You ever done anything contrary to what your mother wanted, because you had to show her that you have a mind—and rights—of your own?"

He waited. Thinking of the previous month, when Jordon had been caught with a girlie magazine under his bed.

"Last year," Jordon finally mumbled. "I wanted to go out for football and mom said no, it was too dangerous. So I forged the permission slip."

Dana had failed to mention that to Mark. "What happened?"

Jordon shrugged, one of his endearing grins appearing on his face. "My handwriting's not so good. They called Mom as soon as I turned it in."

"And?"

"She told me to call you and see what you thought. If you said I could play, she'd sign the form."

"You didn't call me."

"Nah." Jordon stood up, flipped on the video game. "She was pretty shaken up when she got to school. I guess she thought I'd been hurt in tryouts. I didn't want to play badly enough to make it worth getting her all worked up like that."

God, he loved this kid.

"So." Mark stood, too, glancing at his watch. Still twenty minutes to go. "We're good? You're fine waiting to eat until they're gone?"

"Whatever," Jordon said. But his tone meant "sure," rather than "if you say so." Jordon took out the tile-game cartridge and slid one of his favorite good-guys-beat-villains into the machine.

Mark considered challenging the boy to a round, but feared his lack of concentration would alert his nephew to the fact that he wasn't anywhere near as calm as he was pretending to be.

"You might want to get some ice," Jordon said a couple of minutes later, in between the sound effects he was making as he alternately scored or lost points. "The sodas you bought are warm."

Mark did as he was bid.

"I NEVER WOULD HAVE TOLD YOU about him, if I thought you'd go meet him." Ryan was beginning to sound like a broken record—of an earlier time in her life.

"I know." Sara turned the Lexus onto the exit ramp, Mark Dalton's hotel visible in the distance.

"You actually went to that address?"

"Yes."

"It's the worst beat in the county."

"I can believe that."

"You might have been killed."

She stopped at the light at the end of the ramp and faced her son. "Ryan, I run a national organization—I'm a big girl. And I'm perfectly capable of taking care of myself."

"You're a beautiful woman who easily could be overpowered."

You're a beautiful young woman. You don't realize your own attractiveness. Or the superior strength of men you can't possibly defend yourself against.

"I was born female." Now she said what she wished she'd realized all those years ago. "That doesn't have to be a liability. I had my pepper spray and my cell phone. I took a risk, yes, but it was a calculated one, for what I deemed to be a good reason. I'm not sorry I did so."

And now she hoped to God she wasn't going to be sorry she was heading back to Mark Dalton's hotel, either, though not out of fear for her physical safety.

"I can't live my life afraid, Ryan, just because I'm a woman. Yes, bad things happen. I, more than a lot of people, know that firsthand. But I also know that I'd rather live—intelligently, of course—than wither away under the protection of men who worry about me. It makes me feel incapable, powerless, and before you know it I'm afraid to think for myself."

Where that came from, Sara had no idea. Certainly not from any conscious thought process. She was surprising herself by the moment, these days.

"I'm sorry."

Her son's wide-eyed look was more admiration than contrition and the bands around her heart loosened a little more.

That had been happening a lot lately, too— those ties that had been binding her, slipping. Sometimes replaced by fear.

But at least she was alive.

"Don't be sorry," she told him, thinking he looked far too old in his uniform. He said he'd worn it because he didn't know how long they'd be, or if he'd have time to change before he was due on shift. "I'm glad to know you care."

"And you don't need another father."

"You got it." The light turned and she pulled around the corner.

"Point taken."

Now, if only the rest of the evening went so well.

THEY WERE LATE. They'd said six o'clock and the red LED readout on the alarm between the queen-size beds rolled over to 6:00 with no knock on the door. He'd taken the day off so his young neighbor, Isabel, and Jordon could swim, and then he'd taken the little girl back to her home an hour ago. Ice was melting in the bucket on the patio beside the black wrought-iron table built for two—and the desk chair from the room. He'd called for two extra water glasses and they were out there, too, along with the soda.

"Maybe they decided to leave you alone," Jordon muttered, his eyes on the screen in front of him. The boy, dressed in his usual two-sizes-too-big shorts and a T-shirt that hung past his thighs, was sprawled on his stomach, propped up on his elbows.

At least he'd kicked off his tennis shoes before he'd settled in.

"Maybe," Mark said, his chest tight. He had a

right to meet the boy—he *had* to meet him. But how would he find him? Certainly not through Sara.

The knock sounded before 6:01.

RYAN WASN'T a nervous kind of guy. And he certainly had no hesitation about confronting criminals—ex or otherwise. But as he waited with his biological mother for one of her rapists to answer a hotel room door, he stepped back a notch, protectively in front of Sara Calhoun.

He'd have felt a lot better if she'd worn butt-sagging pants and a shapeless shirt, rather than the dark blue rich-looking slacks and figure-hugging jacket she had on.

No matter what she said, it made him sweat to think of her confronting this man on her own. And in his territory.

It wasn't by accident that Ryan's elbow rested on his weapon.

The door clicked, and Ryan looked impatiently past the clean-cut, well-dressed man who opened it, wanting to get this over with. And get his biological mother out of there. He'd done everything he could to talk her out of going, and only the suspicion that she'd still go and see the man alone again had finally prompted him to capitulate.

"We're looking for..." he addressed their greeter, stopping as Sara stepped forward.

"Mark Dalton, meet Ryan Mercedes."

With the rest of his sentence unspoken, Ryan stared.

The man regarding them with compassion and hesitation in his eyes was Mark Dalton? He didn't resemble the grainy trial photos—or his mug shot—at all. Or the mental picture Ryan had drawn of him.

"Thanks for coming," Dalton said.

The man didn't give Ryan the opportunity to refuse to shake his hand. Nor did he afford him the chance to be rude by failing to return a "nice to meet you" greeting.

"Mrs. Calhoun told you I have some questions?" He got right to the point.

And then watched uneasily as the man exchanged a look with the woman.

"Yes, she did." Dalton stepped back, indicating the nice, if generic-looking, hotel room behind him. "Come on in."

Not sure that was a good idea, Ryan considered having the anticipated conversation out in the hall, and then determined entering the room was the better of the two options.

Mark Dalton was tall and muscular, but Ryan could take him if the need arose.

And Sara was already moving forward. Ryan had to move quickly to stay one step ahead of her. Prepared to take charge as he stepped over the threshold, to conduct his interrogation as quickly and firmly as possible, he stopped so abruptly that Sara ran into him.

A young man was there on the bed. Playing one of Ryan's favorite games for unwinding after a tough shift. He was dressed a bit like a punk. And continued to play as if no one had entered the room.

"Jordon, this is Ryan Mercedes, and you remember Ms. Calhoun from yesterday."

"Hi, Jordon," Sara said, her smile appearing genuine, if a little shaky.

"Hey." He gave her a quick glance, and continued to ignore Ryan completely.

"Let's go out here." Dalton pulled open a sliding-glass door at the far end of the room. A bucket of ice, glasses and sodas were on the table.

The sodas looked inviting.

"Who's the kid?" he asked as he waited for the other two to sit down.

"My nephew."

"I didn't think he'd be here." Sara was addressing Mark. "When you said you didn't want him to know about—" She glanced at Ryan and stopped.

So the man didn't want his nephew to know that Ryan could be his kid. That was just fine with him. He wasn't any man's kid. Except his father's.

But he couldn't help taking another glance at the young guy on the bed. Not searching for resemblances. How could anyone ever really tell about something like that, anyway?

But wondering. His parents had never had children other than him. That kid in there, losing his game from what Ryan could see from this angle—could he be a blood relative? A cousin?

Before Ryan's emotions could engage, get the better of him, he turned away, focusing on an unopened can of cola.

He was here to clear up a mystery.

CHAPTER ELEVEN

MARK BUSIED HIMSELF with the drinks. His hands unsteady as he scooped ice, opened and poured, he forced himself not to stare at the young police officer sitting opposite him on obvious alert. For once, a lawman's suspicion didn't annoy him. Because the cop had obviously set himself up as Sara Calhoun's protector?

Or because he might be his son?

"Jordon's staying with me while his mother, my sister, is away on business." He filled the gap that had followed Sara's half-formed sentence.

"Something wrong with your place?" Ryan asked, more as a challenge than a question.

"Plenty," Mark replied, amazed that his hackles weren't sky-high at the young cop's tone. "But for now, the thin walls will do. A thirteen-year-old kid doesn't need to lie in bed at night listening to audio porn from other apartments."

"What about your sister's place?" Sara's expression was a lot more polite than her son's.

"It's in Cleveland."

"And you have to work."

That was good enough for him.

"He'd have to reregister," Ryan said, watching him.

The rookie officer expected an adverse reaction from him, but Mark was happy to disappoint him.

"That's right."

Sara's frown as she looked from one to the other caught Mark's attention. "Register?" She looked concerned. About a perfect stranger. Or almost stranger. If you could call the man who'd stolen your innocence a stranger.

"As a sex offender." Ryan seemed to take pleasure in saying the words—yet Mark didn't get the impression that the young man was deliberately trying to hurt him, merely remind them all that Mark was not just an ordinary guy here.

Or maybe he was only superimposing what he wanted to see on the man who could be his son.

"Oh," Sara said, her gaze dropping, leaving Mark to wonder if she'd known before that moment and forgotten, or if she'd just found out that she'd been alone last night with a man who was considered a potential danger to society by the U.S. and Ohio justice systems. "Right."

"Jordon knows you're here to talk about the past, but he doesn't know who you are." Mark served the drinks. "I'd appreciate it if we could keep it that way."

Ryan nodded. Sara's expression, as she met Mark's gaze, looked pained. Mark would have given much to be able to wipe that distress away. Permanently.

Seeing him was obviously difficult for her— and also for him, as he felt each ounce of her discomfort as a weight on his soul.

Officer Mercedes emptied the small glass in one gulp and Mark passed over the open can of pop. Mercedes accepted, poured, swallowed again and put down his glass with a steady clink, his chin stiff, as if holding back any emotion he might be tempted to feel.

Or fighting emotion he refused to acknowledge, Mark figured was more like it. He remembered being that age—in a very different place, of course, but still filled with the need to be all man, when he still felt at least half boy.

"Is there anything you remember about that night that wasn't brought out at the trial?" His tone, while not friendly, had dialed down a notch.

Mark didn't even have to think about it. He shook his head. "Most of what you would've read in the transcripts, I don't remember."

"You make a habit of that?" Ryan asked, adding, "Drinking to the point of oblivion?"

"It was the first—and only—time."

"You'd never passed out before?"

"No."

"But you'd partied?"

"Like any other college freshman away from home for the first time."

Leaning back in his chair, Mark crossed his arms at his waist, prepared to give Ryan whatever he wanted.

First, because he had to know where the kid was going with this out-of-nowhere investigation; had to know if he needed to find himself a good lawyer.

And second, because he intended to ask the young man for something pretty important, too. A DNA test.

"So it wasn't the first night you'd had a lot to drink."

"No, but it was the first time I'd mixed beer with whiskey."

"What about since? Any strong reactions to alcohol?"

"Haven't touched the stuff."

"Never."

"Never."

"Since that night?"

Mark held Ryan's gaze solidly.

"Since that night."

He wasn't a drunk—he'd just drunk too much. Once in his life. And he'd paid for it with his life.

Ryan seemed inordinately interested in the condensation forming on his glass. Sara, on the other hand, hadn't touched her soda. The expression on her face, as she peered from one to the other, was watchful—as if she was fully prepared to intervene, should hell break out.

"What can you tell me about Ralph Bonney?"

"He's married, has a nice wife, a couple of good kids. Built a two-bit used-car lot into a successful franchise dealership."

"On his own?"

"I imagine his father helped him. As you're probably aware, I was from Columbus, not Maricopa, and so I didn't know Ralph growing up, but it was pretty common knowledge that he was close to his parents—particularly his father. While most guys were kind of embarrassed by their parents, or at least a little resentful, Ralph hero-worshipped his old man. The guys used to rib him about it."

Ryan sat forward, his gaze intent. "Is the guy some kind of football hero or something?"

Not seeing how Ralph's childhood had anything to do with the night he had raped Sara Lindsay, Mark nevertheless listened quietly.

"Tim Bonney was a securities broker. He was also, by all accounts, a great guy. He spent a lot of time with Ralph, took him all over the world. Mostly, though, he was always praising the kid, making him feel good, I guess. Bonney was a scrawny guy, the kind girls want for a friend but would never consider dating. His dad never tried to get him to play sports, or put pressure on him. He just always supported whatever decisions Ralph made. I think half the guys were envious of him."

Mark might not have remembered so much, if not for the fact that his own story was so completely opposite to Ralph's. His father had hated having kids, to the point that, after Mark's birth, he'd run off, just hadn't come home from the grocery store one night after he'd gone out for a gallon of milk. Mark's mother had been a waitress at a diner and Mark could remember nights when he and Dana had slept in the back of her car while she closed the place.

In the Dalton family it had always just been the three of them, but they'd done all right. Better than all right. Dana had married the man of her dreams, a career firefighter, who'd adored her. Mark had been awarded a full scholarship to Wright State. They'd had their happily ever after, too.

Until Mark had consumed too much alcohol and broken all their lives.

And fire had robbed Dana of her husband.

"So what about the testimony regarding Ralph's character during the trial? Did you agree with it?"

Sitting up, Mark took a sip of his drink. His throat was getting dry again—as it always did when he pondered a time he couldn't accept, and couldn't change. Arms on the table, he faced Ryan.

"Yes." Where were all these questions going? And why? Trying to think like the prosecutor he'd never be now, Mark continued to try to get one step ahead of the game.

To figure out the name of the game.

"Ralph Bonney was your typical nerdy guy who was likable, funny and easygoing enough to get into one of the school's more elite frats."

Mark had made it in because he'd played a damn good game of baseball.

"So all that about the homeless man, that was true?"

"Yeah."

"What about a homeless man?" Sara sat forward, too, so that all three of them were now leaning on the small dark table, their faces close enough to see all the lines and shadows life had left there.

"I found out about him by reading the trial transcript," Ryan said. "He wasn't mentioned in the papers." Finishing, he looked to Mark, who continued the narrative.

"During the trial the prosecution brought in character witnesses to describe Bonney's relationship with this homeless guy who had been hanging around. The point was to show the jury what a great guy Ralph was, so that they'd trust his testimony."

"He had a relationship with a homeless guy?"

"Earlier that year this homeless guy suddenly appeared down by the lake where we all hung out. Most of the guys thought we should report him, have him hauled off. Some of us just wanted to leave him alone. Ralph brought him blankets. He couldn't stand the thought that the guy was freezing at night. The next thing we know, he's bringing him food, too. And later, he started hitting us all up for a buck or two to give him."

"Did you guys give it to him?" Her lips were moist. Thick and full. Mark couldn't imagine ever having touched them, let alone smashed them against her teeth hard enough to bruise them.

But they said he—or someone—had.

"Of course we did," he told her slowly, dragging his thoughts away from the trial and the closing arguments that had depicted him as someone he hated. "We allocated some frat funds to him, too. He was our charity project for the semester."

"Was he around…that…night?"

Slumping back in his chair, Mark shook his head. "The day before, when Ralph and some of the guys had taken the tubs down to hold the beer and dig a new fire pit for the party, Ralph and the guy got into some kind of tiff. It was the only time anyone ever saw Bonney get mad. He told the guy to take off. Said if he wasn't gone by the next day, he'd call the sheriff on him and have his ass hauled into jail for loitering. When we got to the lake the next afternoon, he—and the pile of stuff he'd kept in a little cave he'd rounded out of a hill—was gone."

"So what did he do to make Ralph so mad?"

"I never heard for sure," Mark said. "I was going to ask Ralph that night." He stopped, waited for the sick feeling to pass through him. "Maybe I did and just don't remember." How anyone ever survived real amnesia, Mark didn't know.

He'd always thought not remembering would be painful primarily because of the good memories lost. But he'd had no idea that lack of memory would also take away all your power to protect yourself—it put you at the mercy of anyone who wanted to point a finger at you.

Of course, in his case, there'd also been the undeniable physical evidence.

Dragging his thoughts back to the question at hand, Mark said, "According to trial transcripts, Ralph said the man had asked Ralph to introduce him to one of the girls who occasionally hung out with the guys at the lake."

"Was this forty-year-old homeless guy sexually interested in a college girl and he expected Ralph to fix them up?"

"Yeah. Ralph was furious. He felt like his trust in the guy had been betrayed and that's when he told him to get lost."

"Anyone ever find out what this homeless guy's name was?" Sara asked. Sitting with her arms on the table, most of her body was blocked from Mark's view, but he knew, from the few glances he'd allowed himself the night before, that she was a beautiful woman.

She'd been married, but had never had any more kids. Had that been because she'd been unable to live a normal life? Had something happened when she'd given birth at such a young age that prevented more children?

Had she had enough counseling to see her through, allow her healthy relationships?

"He called himself Dave," Mark finally said, when he realized the other two were waiting for him to answer the question. "No one ever knew if that was his real name or not. Frankly, I'm not sure Ralph knew for sure. The guy was kind of off."

"Off how?"

"He was always telling Ralph far-out stories. First, he was an astronaut. One day he said he'd worked for the CIA. And another time he claimed some beautiful rich woman was his wife."

"Do you think Ralph could have lied?" Ryan's gaze was open, interested. Focused. Without suspicion as he asked Mark the question.

"Why would he?"

"If, say, Sheriff Lindsay needed an eyewitness report to wipe out any reasonable doubt in the jury's minds that you and your two buddies raped his daughter?"

Mark noticed two things, as if from someplace outside himself.

His insides felt as if he'd jumped out of a plane.

And Sara Calhoun's face was pinched and white.

He had no idea what was going on here, but he sure as hell intended to find out.

CHAPTER TWELVE

SARA HELD HER BREATH. Here was where a convicted rapist, a man who had every reason to hate the sheriff who'd seen him sent to prison in the prime of his life—and labeled for the rest of it—had the chance to get his own back.

"Sheriff Lindsay didn't need an eyewitness to get that conviction." Mark Dalton's voice was deep, steady—and unequivocal. "The physical evidence convicted us beyond a reasonable doubt."

"What about the earlier theory that someone had planted evidence on Sara after she passed out?"

"Hall's lawyer threw that out there," Mark said, as if he'd never considered the idea a real possibility.

"It gave possible cause for doubt."

"That's a defense attorney's job."

"And if he's good enough at it, he gets even the guiltiest defendants off."

Sara watched the exchange. The two men, in

spite of their age differences, seemed to be evenly matched.

"It happens," Mark conceded.

"But Bonney's testimony left no doubt at all. From what I understand, the sheriff was obsessed with getting that guilty verdict."

"We'd abused his sixteen-year-old daughter." Mark's tone raised a notch. "Don't get me wrong, I still have nightmares about John Lindsay. If I had a list of people I would most want never to share air with again as long as I live, he'd be at the top." Mark stopped and took his first sip of soda.

Sara wished this whole thing would go away.

"But what I will tell you," Mark continued, "is that if I had been in his shoes and I'd found my daughter as he had, I, too, would have been determined to put the guys away."

"At what cost?" Ryan's question was soft.

"At any cost."

"My point exactly," Ryan said. "He'd be willing to do whatever it took to get a guilty verdict."

Sara's throat constricted with fear for her father, for herself. She almost lost the soda she'd just swallowed.

"Except that he wasn't prepared to tell the court that his daughter was pregnant, which would have been seen as further hardship to the victim and earned us more prison time." Mark's words surprised her again.

Who was this man? This perpetrator of evil, who'd done nothing in the few tension-filled hours she'd known him but show her a man whom, in normal circumstances, she'd admire and want to know better?

"His first thought was always Sara," Ryan said now, tapping his finger on the rim of his glass. "I'm not out to hang the man. I'm just being bothered by the sense that there was more to what went on there. I first had this feeling six years ago, when I was a kid sitting alone in my room surfing the Net for information about my birth mother."

The picture he painted brought tears to Sara's eyes. Thankfully, the men were too engrossed in each other at the moment to notice her sitting there, fighting for her self-control.

"I told myself to drop it a bunch of times over the years, but it keeps coming back. And now that I've seen the police reports, the trial transcripts, there are just too many unanswered questions for me to let it go." He paused, glanced down and then back up at Mark.

"Don't you want to know?"

In that moment, Sara could see a lost little boy

wanting a crazy world to make sense. And she understood, as maybe only a mother could, that inside her grown son, there still lived a small child who felt abandoned by the people who'd brought him into the world. The people who were supposed to love him because he was their flesh and blood—not because the law said, but because life said.

"Of course, I want to know." Mark Dalton's eyes brimmed with emotion. "I paid dearly, and I'm still paying every day of my life," he glanced in at Jordon, "for something against which I can't even defend myself. Because I don't know what happened."

The last words came out fast and sharp. And full of bone-deep frustration.

A feeling Sara identified with completely.

"Then we have to find out," she heard herself saying. Her real self. Not her father's daughter—though she would do all she could to protect him. Not Brent's wife. Not the woman who would be good, at all costs, to pay for her sins. But a woman who was alive, on earth, and wanted to live. A woman who scared her to death.

RYAN SCOOTED HIS CHAIR closer to the table. "What I know is this," he began, looking between Sara and Mark. The space engulfing them had changed in those past few seconds, forming a dreamlike bond between them in spite of who they were to each other.

In spite of the horrendous pain that hovered over them.

"We've got an unidentified male, somewhere between the ages of thirty-five and fifty, who died around the time of the party and was deliberately buried at the same lake."

"So if, say, our homeless guy had hung around, it's not possible that he just starved or died of natural causes out there on his own?" Mark's gaze was intent.

"No chance." Ryan shook his head. "There was a definite grave that protected the bones not only from the weather but from animal predators."

"Okay," Mark said. "What else?"

"In his testimony at the trial, Ralph identified the color of underwear Sara had been wearing that night."

"Yeah." Mark appeared to remember that.

And Sara had to think about what else he'd heard at the trial—that she hadn't heard—and still remembered.

There'd been medical testimony. Detailed medical testimony. She'd heard her father telling her mother that they'd failed to get it suppressed.

Sara remembered hearing her mother start to cry, and she'd been left to imagine the things that had been said about her most intimate parts.

"But according to Bonney, when the four of you went off, Sara was still dressed."

"That's right."

"And the next morning when she was found, she had no clothes on."

"So how did Bonney know the color of her underwear?" Mark asked now.

"And why didn't Sheriff Lindsay, who was reportedly an expert investigator, challenge this discrepancy?"

She couldn't let that go. "Maybe he saw it, but the prosecutor didn't find it relevant, so it didn't come up."

"The public defender didn't mention it, either," Ryan said now, looking at Mark as he referred to Mark's lawyer. The other two young men had come from families who'd had the ability to fork out the bucks required by expensive defense attorneys.

His frown was deep. "I don't remember anything being said about it," he noted. "The evidence was so clear-cut and condemning, it's possible that no one thought about anything Ralph said except what they needed to hear, to confirm what they already knew."

"Or maybe there was a cover-up for something else." Ryan's words were like a death knell, rung for her father. Sara hated them. But she had to know the truth.

"There's something else, too," Ryan said now, looking from one to the other. "Haven't either of you ever wondered why two people who'd never been so drunk before in their lives, both end up passing out and not remembering anything at the same party?"

"I was determined to show my father that I was my own person." Sara had to tell the truth. "I went to that party fully intending to get so drunk that my father couldn't possibly miss it."

"I was looking for oblivion," Mark added.

"But there's still a natural restraint in certain kinds of people, the point you reach that tells you it's time to stop. From what I know of Sara, she's one of those people."

She nodded. No doubt about that. That night aside, even when she'd tried to say to hell with the world and, safely in her own home, use alcohol to forget, it absolutely hadn't happened. Rational thought had prevailed and all she'd done was give herself a headache.

"I don't know about you," Ryan said to Mark, "but…"

"Neither do I, since I haven't taken a drink since, but before that night I'd say you pinned it pretty accurately."

"I find it disturbing that neither of you remembers drinking to that point. The most either of you remembers is taking those first few drinks."

"I remember four," Mark said, as Sara stared at Ryan.

"You think something was wrong with the alcohol?"

"But then why wasn't everyone affected?" Mark asked, shaking his head. "We were all drinking the same stuff and—"

"And most everyone there passed out and couldn't give relevant testimony about what happened to Sara," Ryan said, his voice gaining conviction as the conversation continued.

"Another thing I find odd is that of all those who did remember their own antics, no one was aware of what went on with Sara. I read the testimony of her injuries. Why didn't anyone hear her cry out?"

And why hadn't her father asked these questions, Sara wondered—but was afraid to ask. She was afraid of where it would lead.

"A couple of my buddies came to see me in jail," Mark said slowly. "I remember them talking about Sheriff Lindsay raking them over the coals to find out if they knew anything at all about his daughter's attack. But I also remember how relieved they were that once he was satisfied they didn't know anything about it, he let them slide. Didn't even ask about the amount of liquor they'd consumed—never mind that they'd been drinking whiskey at eighteen."

"Like I said," Ryan responded, "he was single-focused. Either because he had to get that conviction and didn't want anything to muddy the waters, or because he just didn't care about anything else enough to see it was there."

Neither choice showed her father in the best light.

But she hoped, if either was true, it was the latter.

Oh, Daddy, what did you do?

Please don't have risked your reputation, your own freedom, to avenge me.

"Was the alcohol tested?" she asked, grasping for anything that might put her heart at ease—even a bit.

"No." Ryan's expression showed his disappointment.

"None of us was tested, either," Mark added. "So many hours had passed, by the time we were identified and arrested, there'd have been no point in going for blood alcohol levels. It wasn't as if the three of us knew what we'd done and could turn ourselves in. We couldn't remember."

"No one knew who the three of you were until Ralph identified you," Ryan added.

Silence fell as the three of them digested that fact. And wondered what it meant.

"DO WE KNOW if Sheriff Lindsay gave Bonney any kind of payoff? Is there any way to find out if money was deposited in his bank account? Or maybe there was some other obvious windfall?" Mark wasn't out to crucify the guy, but he'd served his time, so justice could be done—he'd suffered far more than a loss of five years of his life during that endless stretch in prison—and if the man responsible for seeing him there had in any way seen that he was put there unfairly...

"He wouldn't do that." The pain in Sara's voice drew Mark's gaze to her. And the look on her face stopped him in his tracks. She'd already suffered far too much.

And even through her pain, he couldn't help but recognize how naturally beautiful she was.

He could see himself, at eighteen, mesmerized by her. He didn't doubt for a second that they'd had sex. But...

"There's no evidence of any further connection between the two of them, though records from back then are a little hard to trace."

"Speaking of which, how did you manage to get hold of trial transcripts and police records?" Mark asked.

"They have their ways," Sara said dryly. It was the first indication he'd had from her that she was part of a cop's family. Putting her in line with her father.

The reminder was unsettling.

"I'm taking a community college law-enforcement class, hoping to become a detective," Ryan said, impressing Mark with his humble attitude. "Sergeant Miller, the teacher, has kinda become my mentor, and when I told him I wanted to use the two cases to learn about the investigation process and see if I could find any connection that had been missed, he was willing to get the files for me. He's a violent-crimes detective. All he has to do is sign in with his name and password and he can get anything he wants—anything that's official and on file."

Mark didn't want to care about any of this. His life was bearable only because he'd learned what not to care about.

But if he could have one wish in life other than taking back that god-awful night, it would be to know, finally and for sure, what had happened to turn him from a man he knew into one he didn't recognize at all.

"And what about the trial transcripts?" Sara asked. "Can anyone just get those?"

"Sergeant Miller has a friend in the prosecutor's office. She was happy to provide them as part of my research."

Mark's radar went up. "Isn't that illegal?" He wasn't getting his ass anywhere near any place that smelled even a little bit like a prison cell.

"No," he said. "They're a matter of public record, just not easy to come by."

His head abuzz with possibility, questions, the need for answers, Mark pondered all that had been said, attempting to work out where he would go next. And he remembered something.

"You asked if Ralph had any reason to want to do the sheriff a favor," he said. And felt Sara tense next to him.

"Yeah." Ryan nodded.

"I don't. But I do remember something he said about that homeless guy."

"What's that?" Ryan sat forward, his young eyes eager, intelligent. The young man wanted the truth. Not blood.

Which made it harder for Mark to even consider walking away.

"One of the stories the guy told—it had to do with Sheriff Lindsay. I don't remember any details, but there was something in it about the sheriff being responsible for him being homeless."

"That's ridiculous." Sara didn't even hesitate. "Right along with him having a rich wife and flying to the moon," she added. "My father would give a homeless man the shirt off his back. Of that I am certain."

"Your mother volunteered at the local shelter, didn't she?" Ryan asked.

That was news to Mark. For twenty years he'd seen nothing but unanswered questions—in spite of all of his attempts to make sense of what had happened. Including investigations of his own while he was in law school and had access to libraries and case histories. Yet in one day, he'd learned more than in all that time.

"We all did," Sara told them. "And I don't remember anyone fitting this guy's description. Mostly it was abused women and kids. And an old drunk or two. Not that I went after the…incident."

"We need a plan." That was Ryan again.

Glancing in at Jordon, who was munching on a bag of stale popcorn, Mark knew they had to be winding down now. And he wasn't done yet. Couldn't be done yet. "I agree," he said.

"Let me try my father one more time," Sara said. "Once he sees that I know more than he thinks and that I'm not backing down, he might talk to me."

"And I'll give Ralph Bonney a call," Mark added.

"In the meantime, I'm going to see if I can find out more about any homeless shelters that might have been around during that time. See if we can come up with anyone who sounds like our guy. See if anyone ever heard of him, saw him, maybe even, if we get lucky, find someone who knows his name. He had to go somewhere when he left that lake."

"We're sure he existed at all, right?" Sara's question prompted a look between the two men that gave Mark an alarming feeling of belonging. He couldn't get too involved here.

He was who he was, a man forced to live on the outskirts. Not someone who could belong.

Ryan looked to Mark.

"Yeah," Mark said. "He existed. He was about six feet tall, had longish hair, some gray, but it was hard to tell because it was usually pretty dirty. Wore a trench coat a lot of the time."

"When they searched the site at the lake, what did they do with everything they found?" she asked.

"They'd have taken it in as evidence," Ryan

answered. "Depending on how diligent your father was, it could still all be locked up someplace. Normally, I wouldn't think so, since they got a conviction and the perpetrators—" Ryan paused, glanced awkwardly at Mark, who nodded for the young man to go on in spite of the tightening in his stomach "—all served their time..." Ryan added. "There wouldn't be a need to hold on to old evidence."

"Especially if the sheriff was aware of anything underhanded that took place to get the conviction," Mark added, unable to get that idea out of his head, as if he could still somehow be exonerated.

"Knowing my father, he'd keep evidence like that forever." Sara's expression had lightened a notch. "I'll ask him."

Mark guessed she'd feel better knowing that it was there, if only to show them they were on a false track suspecting her father of wrongdoing.

"Could it be possible, since he seems to have felt there was no importance in the homeless guy, that there'd be something in those personal effects that could help us identify him?" she asked.

"It's possible," Ryan answered. "And if we find him, maybe he could tell us something about that night that no one else knows."

"I'll call my dad tonight." Sara pushed her

chair back as if she was finished, ready to stand up and go.

"Uh." Mark coughed and glanced at her. She knew what this meeting was really about for him.

At least in part.

He glanced at Ryan. "I have a favor to ask of you. Apart from all of this."

"You want me to keep quiet around your nephew," Ryan finished for him and Mark was tempted to let it go at that. For now.

Until he looked in at Jordon. And thought about the boy's trust in him. The standards he held him up to. If Jordon knew that there'd been a child from that night, he'd expect Mark to find out if he was responsible. It was the right thing to do.

"I want you to submit a sample of DNA for a paternity test." The words were some of the most difficult he'd ever uttered.

His breath held in his lungs when the young man opposite him shook his head. "I'm sorry, I can't do that."

"Of course you can. It just takes a cotton swab in the mouth."

Ryan's lips tightened at that. "My father was a rapist." His teeth almost clicked, he spoke so sharply. "Do you have any idea how hard it is to come to terms with that?"

Mark said nothing. How could he?

"It's almost impossible to separate myself from the fact," Ryan went on, pounding more nails into Mark's coffin. "To know that there might be some latent tendency toward violence in me."

Because he could relate so clearly to that, Mark said nothing.

"As it is, I have to fight to remind myself that I had nothing to do with that. If I had a name, a history to relate to, it would be damned near impossible."

Mark looked at Jordon. Thought of Dana and his mother. The person he knew himself to be, one horrendous night notwithstanding. "Or it might make it easier," he said softly.

He knew, the minute Ryan met his gaze, that the rookie cop knew he was referring to himself. Asking Ryan to see him as the man he was, not as a young man who'd committed one act he couldn't even remember.

The other man glanced in at Jordon, and for a split second Mark thought he'd won. At least this one small round.

"I'll think about it," Ryan said.

Not what Mark had hoped for, but it felt like a small victory, anyway. Where there was hope, there was reason to continue.

CHAPTER THIRTEEN

SHE KNEW SHE SHOULD HAVE taken the home warranty. She'd been trying to conserve money those first weeks after she'd left Brent—hoarding her pennies, just in case.

Trying to ignore the sweat trickling down her back, Sara glared at her air-conditioning unit up on the roof Wednesday evening.

As though, if she looked at it long enough, she could shame it into working again.

She had to do something. She'd come home from work, lugging a briefcase full of information on computer servers, to find it was almost ninety degrees inside her house. Of course, the darn thing would choose to misbehave on one of the hottest days of the year.

What she knew about air conditioners could be summarized in two sentences. You turned them on. They blew cool air through the house. Oh, and a third, she thought, getting a crick in her neck as she looked up. They didn't use Freon anymore because it was bad for the environment.

The first thing to do was get up there for a closer look. But she didn't have a ladder.

Once she found a way up, she'd figure out how to figure out what might possibly be wrong.

She could call her father.

But she'd rather sweat for the rest of the summer than go to him all needy and helpless. Yet again.

The business she had with him—which they were going to discuss over lunch the next day, when he came to town to go over the revisions on his latest book—required that she appear strong, capable. Determined.

She had to get him to talk to her about the past.

Considering a cold shower, followed by a cool bath, an iceberg lettuce salad and then into bed with the fan blowing while she read over her paperwork, Sara heard her cell phone ring.

And worked up more sweat as she ran to answer it.

"I got hold of Ralph." Mark Dalton didn't introduce himself.

"And?" She dropped down to a chair at the table and started talking easily, as if they'd never left his patio the night before.

"He doesn't remember knowing the color of your underwear, but he said that if he said he did, then he did."

She *didn't* want to talk about her underwear. "Was he surprised to hear from you?"

"No. We've done business a few times over the years. He'll get a potential trade-in that's better suited for what I do, or I'll get someone who thinks he has something worth fixing, when what he really needs is a new car."

Right. She'd forgotten he owned a restoration shop.

"He was a bit taken aback when I brought up the past."

"Because he had something to hide?"

"Because I don't talk about it. We've had a mutual understanding about that from our first contact after I got out of prison."

Helping herself to a glass of ice water, Sara kicked off her shoes and sat down again.

"Does he think you blame him for turning you in?"

"We've never discussed it."

Sara couldn't even imagine calmly doing business with someone who'd played such a dramatic part in her past without first acknowledging the fact.

And that, she supposed, was one of the differences between men and women. Sometimes she envied men, their ability to file emotions away and get on with life.

But wasn't that exactly what she'd done these past twenty years? Filed away the blood of life and got on? And yet what was there to get on to when there was nothing inside you contributing to the journey?

Was Mark Dalton stuck in one place, the way she'd been all these years? Was his ability to do business with Ralph Bonney more the result of being partly shut down, than of being a man?

She didn't know why she cared. But finding the answer seemed important, anyway.

"Do you blame him?" she asked, when he seemed content to let the silence stretch between them.

"They'd have found us soon enough, anyway. They were in the process of getting court orders to make each one of us provide semen samples."

A logical, healthy conclusion? Or an escape from the feelings of betrayal that would seem more natural under the circumstances?

"So, besides being surprised, what was his reaction to your inquiry?"

"He said he was happy to help in any way he could."

Her neck itched where sweat was forming. Wiping at it, she asked, "Because he feels guilty?"

"Maybe. He was a friend once, and he's been a good business acquaintance for a long time now."

She peeled off her panty hose. Unbuttoned the silk blouse that had been cool against her skin when she'd put it on that morning.

"But he couldn't give you anything substantial to go on?"

"Actually, he said that when those bones were found, he remembered a guy he'd seen hanging around on campus. He'd first noticed him because he was dressed like a student—jeans, long hair, backpack—but he was older and his clothes looked expensive. Ralph particularly remembered him because he'd later seen the same guy with a woman he'd never seen before at the diner in town. She was about his age, and dressed expensively. He was wearing slacks, but still had that backpack. And then Ralph had seen him a third time, driving in a shiny red Jeep, on the road out to the lake."

Condensation dripped off her glass. Sara held it up to her face.

"He just remembered that today?"

"No." Mark's tone was resolute. "He remembered back then. He says he told your father all about it."

"Ryan told me the police reports indicated no one had come forward regarding that skeleton."

"I know."

She got up. Grabbed a towel from the drawer by the sink. Wet it down and patted her forehead, her cheeks, wrapped it around her neck.

And sat once more with her feet tucked upon the chair.

"You think my father fudged the report."

"I think Ryan's right. *Something*'s fishy."

Sara was at a loss. All her life, her father's approach had been too black-and-white. There was right and there was wrong, and the Calhouns lived on the right side. Period.

How did she connect that with this?

Her father wouldn't have done anything that wasn't completely legitimate, would he?

And what about her? Was her part in all of this going to get him into trouble? When he'd only been thinking of her?

"Have you told Ryan?"

"No. I wanted you to know first."

The momentousness of that choice was not lost on her. Mark had declared his loyalties.

The man who'd played a part in hurting her

so horribly was now doing what he could to protect her.

"I'm having lunch with him tomorrow. Would you mind waiting to say anything until I have a chance to ask him about this?"

"Of course not."

"Thank you." She not only said the words, she felt them. Felt gratitude toward a man she'd feared and hated—and she agonized over having played a part in ruining his life.

He'd been found guilty of statutory rape. She'd lied about her age.

"You sound tired."

His words startled her. They were personal.

"I'm more hot than anything else." She unsettled herself further with her reply. And "it's been a long day" would have sufficed. Or even, "I am." Either would have kept him firmly beyond her private boundaries.

"Did I interrupt a workout?"

"Only a mental one." She actually chuckled. "My air conditioner's out and I don't have the first idea what to do about it. I called every service place in the Yellow Pages, but the soonest anyone can come out is Friday."

"I'd be happy to take a look at it."

She almost jumped at the offer. Until she remembered who he was. Who she was.

"You don't have to do that."

"I know I don't. But I'd like to. I'm pretty good with that kind of thing."

"That's okay," she said, a little more quickly than she'd meant to. "I'll be fine."

The pause on the other end of the line was too long to be comfortable.

"You don't feel safe with me in your home."

"Of course I do!"

"I just want you to know that it's okay." His voice was neither cajoling nor compassionate. It was simply matter-of-fact. "I do understand."

"I... It's not like you think."

"Sara, you of all people don't have to tap dance around the issue. I'd feel the same way if I were you."

Tempted to leave it at that—the gracious out he'd given her—Sara heard honesty win out instead. She was her father's daughter, after all.

"I'm not afraid you're going to hurt me," she told him. "I know you won't." Which made no sense at all, either.

"What, then?"

"I'm afraid I'm going to like you too much."

She cursed the day she decided she wanted to

quit hiding and live. She had no idea what she was doing; what she was getting herself into.

"How about I bring Jordon with me? We'll take a look and be gone before you even know we've been there," he suggested after another long pause.

Before she could chicken out, change her mind, Sara rattled off her brand-new address, went in to change from her half-dressed state into a multicolored sundress and sandals, and worried about her sanity during the entire thirty minutes he'd said it would take for him to get there.

She had a son who was as black-and-white as her father—and bent on exposing the truth.

And a man who'd spent five years in prison as a result of her father's investigation.

How could she hope to protect her father against that?

How could she turn her back on the truth, no matter what it was? Her entire life had been shaped, hurt, by that one night. She had to know.

Mark's entire life had been shaped, hurt, by that night, as well. Was still profoundly affected by the results.

And Ryan. Struggling with his own issues, fearing his own heredity. He had a right to know the truth.

Most particularly if something pointed to the fact that the rape hadn't just been a random act of alcohol-induced violence.

"IT WAS A FROZEN COIL," Jordon announced, coming through Sara's back door an hour and a half later.

She'd just heard her unit come on and had done a little jig as the cool breeze hit her in the face. Stepping back from the air vent, she faced the smooth-faced boy whose voice squeaked on his final words—and the man appearing just behind him.

"Uncle Mark put the blow-dryer on it and now it's working great," Jordon said.

Mark was unlike any other man she'd ever known. He was tall, and his body definitely commanded attention. But he stood back at the same time, reminding Sara of herself, all those years; hosting events at Brent's side, but ever so slightly in his shadow, not wanting anyone to think that she expected anything from them.

As her husband definitely had. Everything Brent did was for a purpose. There was an ulterior motive to every outing, party, golf event he attended. Every person he associated with was chosen because of something he—or she—could do for him.

"What caused it to freeze?" she asked now, meeting Mark's gaze and realizing that it felt good. He didn't have that wary look—or a resigned one. Mark Dalton was apparently feeling good about himself.

It suited him.

"The filter was way dirty," Jordon piped up.

"You need to change them every three months or so," Mark added.

"I just moved in!"

"By the looks of it, the previous owner hadn't changed it yet this year."

He smiled at her. She smiled back.

"I'm glad it was something simple," she said, wishing she had some fresh-baked cookies to offer Jordon.

"You do know how to change them, don't you?" Mark still stood just inside the door, a small toolbox in his hand. "Because if you don't, it's going to freeze right back up again."

"I'm sure I can figure it out."

"You gotta climb up on the roof to do it," Jordon said. "Me and Uncle Mark are going to get a new one and change it before we take the ladder back."

Mark's grin grew wider and Sara realized she'd been figured out—because he knew that even though she didn't have a clue what to do, she would have been reluctant to ask him for help with it.

"Thank you." She directed her appreciation to Mark's nephew, all the dignity and class of her twenty years of self-discipline evident in the two words.

The uncle got a brief look, too. One filled with more questions than answers, but at least no rejection.

Maybe life wasn't completely bad.

JORDON WAS INVOLVED in a game of water basketball with a couple of teenage hotel guests when Mark's cell phone vibrated in the pocket of his swim trunks Thursday night. He hadn't gotten wet yet.

"Hi," he said, answering as soon as he saw Sara Calhoun's number on the screen. It wasn't that he'd been waiting for her call, not exactly.

But she'd had lunch with her dad that day. And she'd said she'd call.

"Is this a bad time?"

"Nope," he told her, settling back on the folding chair, his arm on the table beside him. They had business to discuss, an issue to resolve. There was no other reason to feel relieved because of her call.

No other reason to welcome it.

He'd long since left high school.

"How was lunch?" he asked. Her day, the state of her air conditioner, whether or not her dinner had been better than his fast-food sandwich, were not his concerns.

"The Oriental chicken salad was good." It was almost as if he could feel her pushing the cheer into her lighthearted response.

"That bad, huh?"

"Not really."

He wondered where she was, if she was sitting at her ornate expensive-looking table in that quaint, homey kitchen of hers.

"Your father was open to the conversation, then?"

"Not really," she said a second time. Mark might have felt frustrated, except that there were certain undertones to the conversation. As if she wanted to say more. Longed to say more, as much as he longed to hear more.

But there were boundaries between them that neither could scale—or thought they *should* scale.

Or maybe he'd just been alone so long he was seeing things that didn't exist, overanalyzing, projecting his own reality onto a situation that was entirely different.

He tried that one on, tried to convince himself of its truth.

And failed completely.

So he did what felt right, down beneath the fear. He went with his instincts.

"Does he know if the evidence collected at the party scene is still around?"

"It isn't."

"What did he say about the unidentified skeleton?"

"After months of searching with no leads, he assumed the guy was probably the homeless man that Ralph had testified about at the trial, but that was only his personal assumption. As far as the official report went, the case is still unsolved."

"What about Ralph's report regarding the rich guy with the backpack?"

"Ralph did approach him about that. He followed up, even had a sketch done with Ralph's input, but he couldn't find a single thing to substantiate the claim. No one at the diner remembered seeing a stranger in there who matched the description or recognized the sketch. My father pinned it up around town, on campus, and not one person besides Ralph came forward as ever having seen the man. He asked about the Jeep at the local filling station and no one could remember either it or the man."

"So why wasn't this in the report that Ryan read?"

Sara's sigh gave the first hint that she was starting to wonder about her father's role in all of this. Doubts were beginning to surface.

"Three reasons," she said, as though considering the validity of each of them in turn. Still trying to convince herself they were completely logical, ethical and proper procedure? "First, because there was so obviously no truth in what Ralph said, it wouldn't help the investigation to have the report included, but rather it could slow down the process if others looked at it later and wasted time following a false lead."

He could accept that. Jordon scored a shot. High-fived one of the brothers he was opposing and swam down court to defend against the other brother's approach to the basket.

"Second, because Ralph had been such a help to him on the…other…issue, he didn't want to embarrass him with a public recording of false information. He didn't want to make Ralph look stupid—or make a laughingstock out of him."

Okay. Maybe.

"Third." She took another deep breath, and Mark listened intently. "He was afraid that exposing Ralph's false information would lead others to discount the other testimony he had given during the trial."

"Lead the defense attorneys or defendants to think that," Mark clarified.

"He didn't say so."

"But you know that's what he meant." He didn't push to be hard on her, but to make certain that they weren't going to play around with the truth this time. They were here, sharing this time and space, to find out, if they could, what had really happened the night both of their lives had changed so dramatically.

"Yes."

"Do you think he was afraid there'd have been an appeal?"

Her pause was all the answer he needed. And still, his respect for her grew when she said, "He didn't say so outright, but yes, I'm sure he was."

She sounded tired. And alone.

But not as if she was in any way backing down. Or out.

"What did you say?"

"Nothing. And I won't. Not until I'm sure of what I know. Or don't know. My father is a good man, and he deserves my trust and loyalty. He deserves the benefit of the doubt."

For her sake, he wanted to believe that.

"I'm not out to get him, Sara. I'm not going to spare him, if the truth shows that he robbed me of my right to justice, but I'm not on some personal vendetta here. I just want to know the truth."

"I think I realize that," she said slowly. And then she added, "I have to know, too."

CHAPTER FOURTEEN

SARA'S FATHER HAD WARNED HER to leave the past alone the first time she'd raised the subject. At Thursday's lunch, he'd ordered her to do so, and now she couldn't talk to him about the thoughts and images that refused to go away, the questions that filled her mind at all hours of the day and kept her awake at night.

She couldn't talk to him about the man she'd met and was getting to know, who was the least likely candidate for rape she could imagine.

But she had to talk to someone.

Ryan was young—and idealistic. She didn't completely trust him to come to her first, if he had suspicions about her father. Didn't trust him to give her a chance to save her father's name before he tarnished it.

Which left her only one other individual on the face of the earth to turn to.

And so she did. Every day, over the next several

days, if Mark Dalton didn't phone Sara, Sara phoned him. And if, on those days when they'd already spoken, he called again, she still took his call immediately.

He called on Friday to tell her he'd spoken to Ryan, filling him in on what Ralph had had to say on Wednesday. Ryan was going to try to find anyone who'd been around Maricopa then who was still there now, to see if he could get anyone to remember the man Ralph said he'd seen.

Or at least find someone who remembered the sheriff asking around about such a man.

Sara had to be satisfied with that. And prayed that her father didn't get wind of the inquisition.

On Sunday, Mark called to say he was on his way to Cleveland to take his nephew back a couple of days sooner than they'd planned. His sister had finished and taken an earlier flight home because she missed her son. He'd be returning to his place that night.

Sara missed her son, too. She'd left a message for him regarding her lunch with her father, but he hadn't returned her call so far.

On Monday, she called Mark to say that she'd be out of town for two days, first flying to New York to meet with the agent and publisher who handled her father's books for NOISE. They wanted specific rights for this book, in order to be able to supply extended excerpts on Internet safety without the need for special permission. And then she was on to Washington, D.C., to meet with lobbyists regarding strengthened legislation to deal with predators on the Net.

That Wednesday, a week and two days after she'd met him, she sat on the plane coming home, looking forward to telling Mark she was home safely as she'd promised she'd do. And she had to admit to herself that Mark Dalton was more than just a cohort in a search for truth.

Up in the sky, miles above reality, trapped in a manufactured cocoon of air and engine noise, she considered the fact that she liked him. That he made her smile; made her think. She respected him—and she trusted his judgment.

In a world where everything was changing, she actually felt safe with Mark Dalton—in some kind of elemental way that had been missing since her one night of rebellion all those years ago.

After she'd gotten home and unpacked, she called to tell him she was back and invited him over for dinner.

"ARE YOU SURE you want to do that?" Mark's response was an acknowledgment of the oddity of their situation.

"If you can be here because you want to be and not just because I asked you," she answered with complete honesty.

"I..."

Sitting on the side of her new bed, Sara felt her skin go hot with embarrassment. "Hey," she interrupted. "Don't worry about it. I overstepped and I'm sorry. It's no big deal. I'm supposed to hear from Ryan tomorrow. I'll call you after that."

"Wait!"

She caught his call to her before the cell phone had completely folded shut.

"I'm here," she told him, phone back open and to her ear.

"You didn't overstep." The words were firm. Clear. "I just want both of us to be completely aware of what we might be opening up with every step we take here."

"I'm offering dinner, Mark. Nothing more."

"At your home. Alone. The two of us, right?"

She got hot again. "Yes. But I trust you not to expect anything more than food."

"Of course I wouldn't." His answer was so immediate she might have been insulted, had the circumstances between them been at all normal. "I just want us both to understand that it's more of a friend thing to have someone over for dinner, than it is two people with a project."

Relaxing back on the bed, Sara's entire being softened. "You don't take any chances, do you?"

"Sure I do. But not in certain areas."

"Okay, it's understood. I'd like us to be friends."

"And how will you explain me to your friends? Or to your father?"

She rubbed the back of her neck. Traveling always made her tense. "I'm not in the habit of explaining myself to other people."

"And if someone stops by or calls? If, tomorrow, someone asked you what you did last night?"

"No one stops by." She told him the sad truth. "For years, my social life has been entirely Brent's—surface relationships meant to promote business. Those people I considered my friends are now all his friends.

"My father still lives in Maricopa, and you don't make that drive without calling first, to be certain it won't be in vain.

"And tomorrow, when the people I work with and care about ask me what I did last night, I'll tell them I had dinner with a friend. I'm the boss and they're going to be respectful enough not to ask further questions."

She could see what he was getting at, though. Everything to do with him was complicated.

Feeling vulnerable, Sara stood, facing the window opposite her bed. "I've got chicken breasts and broccoli in the freezer and rice in the cupboard. I'm planning to make a casserole," she said before he could make a comment or ask questions about any conclusions he was drawing. "Should I make enough for one or two?"

"Two, please."

And just like that, some of the tension drained away.

MARK HAD A CALL from Sharon on the way across town. It was the day Jordon was supposed to have returned home.

"How was the visit?" she asked, while he shifted immediately into "keep your distance" mode. Purely out of habit.

And yet the need to remind himself to do so was not habit. It called for a deliberate choice, as if the normal pattern had been broken.

"Good," he said. "Jordon was a great help at the shop. I'm going to miss him."

He was also missing having someone around to share dinner with every night. To think about and provide for, watch television with and laugh with.

"So what's up with you?" he asked before she could question him any further, and he listened with honest interest as she told him about her first days on the new job, a class she was taking to prepare for the bar exam and a conversation she'd had with her teenage daughter about tattoos.

Sharon was intelligent, entertaining. They shared some of the same interests, especially where public law was concerned. And yet he felt none of the eagerness to be with her that he felt as he grew closer to Sara Calhoun's modest home.

"How about that coffee?" Her question came as their conversation was coming to an end.

Mark arranged to meet her Saturday morning. And immediately wished he hadn't.

THERE WAS SOMETHING about coming out of a dark hole—everything seemed brighter, newer, more exciting. Having dinner alone with a woman who was not a relative for the first time in more than twenty years was like emerging from a pit of darkness.

At least that's what Mark told himself as he

relaxed in one of Sara's fancy chairs, very well fed and still not wanting dinner to end.

"That was excellent, thank you," he said.

"You're welcome." Her smile had to be genuine. Its warmth enfolded him.

He could rise from his chair, clear his dishes, help her clean up. And go.

"I have to ask," he said instead. "Why this table in this room?"

"There's no dining room in the house." She stated the obvious.

"And you just loved the table so much you had to have it?" He liked the freedom inherent in that. The ability to do what one wanted in spite of convention.

"I am fond of the table," she told him. "I had it custom built. But not for this house. And the only reason I still have it is because my ex got the kitchen set."

"Is your divorce recent, then?" He'd wondered, after the air-conditioning episode. She said she'd just moved in.

Sara's nod was more jerky than smooth. "This summer."

More recent than he'd thought. Sara Calhoun was obviously an expert at hiding pain.

Something else they had in common.

"I can't imagine any man letting you go." The dinner, their strange connection, coming after twenty years of having to watch every word he said, loosened his tongue.

Pulling a strand of hair over her shoulder, tickling the ends against her fingers, Sara said, "He didn't."

"You left him."

"Yeah."

Her eyes were sad, her mouth not quite steady—nothing like a woman celebrating freedom.

Mark told himself not to care. Sara's life, her upheavals and challenges, were none of his business.

But they felt as if they were.

"You sound as though you wish you hadn't," he said, after watching the emotions flit across her face.

"No." She released the strand of hair as she shook her head. "I'm glad I did. Just coping with the residuals."

"Was he a drinker?"

"No. A womanizer."

"Then he was a first-class fool." Mark hadn't been in the market since he was eighteen, but he still lived in the world. There couldn't be a whole lot of other women out there who were any more beautiful than Sara.

Smiling, she set her silverware in the middle of her plate. "Thank you for saying so."

He reached out to cover the hand that was crumpling her napkin. And barely stopped himself. "I meant it."

Her gaze met his and Mark was content to let the moment go on. And on. He wasn't touching her—hadn't touched her since they'd met—and yet he felt as if he was. And as if she was touching him.

"Yeah, well, maybe he had reason."

"No man has the right to step out on his wife. Period. I don't care what's right or wrong with her. If he's going to seek that kind of intimacy somewhere else, he needs to end the marriage first."

Her smile hit him just as his words replayed themselves in his head.

"You don't have strong feelings on the subject, or anything, do you?"

Grinning back at her, he shrugged. "I guess it comes from wanting what you can't have." His candid conversation surprised him. "You tend to be critical of those who throw it away."

"What can't you have?"

"A wife. I came to terms with the fact that I'd never get married years ago, but that doesn't mean I don't still envy the guys who do."

"Why can't you marry?"

With anyone else, he'd have given another shrug and been done. In any other situation, he'd never have made the comment to begin with.

"I could never ask a woman to live as I live, where I live. Or ask her to deal with the kinds of looks and comments and actions she'd face, attached to a sex offender."

"If she loved you, she wouldn't care about any of that."

"And if I loved her, I would. It's not just the ostracism," he told her. "When it comes to sex crimes and those who appear to condone them by aligning with an offender, there's always the threat of violence. Especially in today's world."

He didn't really understand why he was telling it like it was. But then, he couldn't understand all that much about his association with Sara.

"I had no idea." Her eyes were clouded, and he wished he knew what she was thinking.

"It's one of those things you don't learn unless you have to."

"I lied to you about my age. What if I consented, that night..."

Mark leaned forward, bringing his face close enough to hers that she couldn't escape him.

"Please, don't ever blame yourself for what happened. You were a young girl…"

"And you deserved to know that."

"There were three of us. And one of you. No matter what your age, we were wrong to come at you, someone we didn't even know, three at once."

"You went to prison for statutory rape."

"Only because it was the easiest, most efficient win. But even if you'd been of age, they had us."

The only difference would have been his own self-loathing—maybe. The fact that he'd done it at all sickened him. But that he'd had sex with a minor…

"Brent wanted to stay married to me. He just wanted my permission to find his sexual gratification elsewhere, since I wasn't capable of providing it."

Hitting him like a punch in the solar plexus, Sara's words just hung there. Mark's mouth was dry.

"What do you mean, not capable?" He'd heard about her bruising, but there'd been nothing about internal or permanent damage.

"His words, not mine," she said, unusually interested in the salt and pepper shakers in front of her plate. "That night apparently shocked any wild tendencies out of me for good."

Not sure what Sara was saying, Mark chose his words carefully. "But you feel…things…in that area."

What he knew about a woman's body, he'd learned mostly during the first six months of his freshman year of college—a lot of it from magazines and guy talk.

"Do I get turned on, you mean?" He thought her face was turning red, but he couldn't be sure, since she wouldn't look at him.

"Yeah." He couldn't feel bad about this conversation. He understood now that they needed to have it—that maybe this was the reason why they'd been compelled to dine together. To find absolution.

"I think so." Her answer wasn't quite the unequivocal affirmation he'd been hoping for. "I used to think about Brent, like that, a lot. And enjoy when he touched me. But then, I don't know, I never seemed to please him, and I felt so much pressure. And as if I was a failure."

"Sounds more to me like your ex-husband was the failure."

Her green eyes were large, luminous, as she glanced at him. But she didn't say a word.

ON THURSDAY, Sara finally made it into her desk chair hours after she'd arrived at NOISE headquarters, following a meeting with her assistant and her office manager to disperse tasks resulting from her recent trip. They were going to market her father's latest work as a series of pamphlets and also as a complete book. And they would release it as an e-book, as well. It was up to Donna to get all the appropriate information to all concerned parties.

And Matty, Mathilda Johnson, the office manager, was going to follow up on several pieces of correspondence to be distributed to their entire mailing list regarding the new legislation. They would urge all educators, parents and ordinary citizens to write to the nation's capital.

The light on her phone was blinking with three messages. And then her cell phone rang.

Mark Dalton. He'd left immediately following their discussion of her sex life the night before.

Sara took that call first, getting up to close the door separating her office from Donna's.

"Is this a bad time?"

"No. I'm getting ready to have the peanut butter and crackers I brought for lunch." She glanced at her gold watch. Noon. Unless she was in a meeting or had a business lunch, she always broke at noon.

"I won't keep you." The familiarity of his voice

sent a frisson of some undefinable something through her. A good something. "I just wanted to make sure you were doing okay after our conversation last night."

"Yes. Fine." She was at work. She reminded herself that dignity and class were her mantras. In spite of the somewhat unpredictable woman emerging from inside.

"Good."

She didn't want him to hang up, but she couldn't think of any reason to hold on to him. She couldn't invite him for dinner—she'd done that last night. She wasn't going to have him thinking that she was coming on to him, or chasing him.

She simply enjoyed the way she felt when she was with him.

"Tomorrow's Friday. Do you have plans?" For a split second she wondered if he'd read her mind.

"No."

"Would you like to go out for dinner?"

"Yes."

She glanced out her window, then looked at the pile of papers on her desk, crossing her legs as a nip of completely inappropriate excitement raced through her.

"Can I pick you up?"

"Yes."

He named the time and rang off. And Sara, choosing to think of the man she knew, rather than the thing she knew he'd done, smiled all the way through lunch.

Ryan called late that afternoon. He had a list of names of men ranging in age from thirty-five to fifty who'd been visitors at homeless shelters in Ohio the year before and the year after her night at the lake. He was going to be spending his free time over the next few days following up on all of them.

She invited him over for dinner that night, but he had other plans.

Or else he just didn't want to spend time with her.

Ever since their meeting with Mark at his hotel, Ryan had avoided all personal contact with Sara, and she wasn't sure why.

But it hurt.

CHAPTER FIFTEEN

BE CAREFUL, MAN. The whispered warning crossed Mark's mind as he ran a comb through his freshly washed hair, tucked the brown polo shirt into off-white cotton slacks and slid his feet into a pair of brown sandals late Friday afternoon.

He had an acceptable life, one that brought a level of satisfaction. Was finding answers about the past worth all the risk of losing a hard-won peaceful existence?

What about dinner with a woman who had every reason to detest him?

If Mark was listening to himself, he'd stay home.

He pocketed some cash, his wallet. Grabbed his sunglasses and keys and locked the door behind him as he left.

HE TOOK HER to a new steak house on Highway 161. He'd caught Sara watching him with curiosity as she slid into the booth opposite him.

"What?"

"I don't know," she said softly, as though weighing whether or not to share her thoughts with him.

"Go ahead with whatever it is," he told her, unfolding his napkin and dropping it in his lap.

Her hair was pulled back in a clip, leaving the sides cascading around her face. She'd put on lipstick, too. Mark glanced away before he started to do more than just appreciate how nice she looked.

"I was glad to see that you were treated with respect when we arrived, that's all." Her tank top and denim skirt made her look about seventeen.

Or would have, if he didn't already have a clear awareness of Sara Lindsay at just about that age.

"You don't have to register to eat out." He tried to make light of her compassionate comments.

And when she didn't respond with a similar quip, he added, "It's not as if my picture's in the paper every week or anything."

How could it be so easy for him to speak with *her* about things he could hardly think about around other people? "For the most part, as long as I don't make changes, I come and go as I please."

"By make changes, you mean move?"

"Right. Then the notices would go out again

and, for me, it starts all over. The letters, protests, signs in the yard, vandalism to my car."

"You've had that happen?"

He'd had people spit on him, too, but he wasn't about to tell her that—most particularly while they were sitting in a nice restaurant about to enjoy a delicious dinner.

"Yes." He gave her the respect of an edited version of the truth. "Multiple times" would have been more accurate.

"What about when new people move into your neighborhood?"

"It's up to them to check the registered offenders list."

"That's why you live where you do, isn't it?" she said, eyes focused on him instead of studying the menu. "Because people come and go so often there that no one even knows anymore…"

"Some know," Mark said. His super certainly did. "But most don't care. I'm not the only offender in the area. And not the only convict, by far."

Not exactly the type of neighborhood for picket fences and nice girls like her.

SHE ORDERED A FILLET of beef, rice and a salad, and couldn't remember when any meal had tasted so good.

Mark entertained her with stories about older guys and their sports cars, their midlife crises, he called them, and the money they'd pay to restore them to their original condition. He told her about things Jordon said. And about a judge doodling while on the bench in court, unaware that a press camera in the back of the room had zoomed in and caught a picture of the car he'd drawn.

"How do you know that?" she asked, laughing out loud.

"I know the judge. He told me the story."

"He's a client?"

"No. I met him in court."

She stopped short. Remembering.

"Do you still have to go?" she asked softly, wishing that life could be different. For both of them. "To appear, I mean?"

"Not as long as I abide by the terms of my release," he told her. "I haven't been in a courtroom as a defendant since I got out of prison."

"Then...?"

Mark's expression stopped her from finishing her questions. It was an odd combination of humility and pride, and she hated to see this evidence of the war that must constantly be going on within him.

"I met Judge Early when I was in law school," he finally said, putting down his silverware.

"You went to law school?" She couldn't keep the astonishment out of her voice. He was a mechanic. Apparently a great one, but...

He just nodded.

"When?"

"I graduated a couple of months ago."

"So you're waiting to take the bar," she said, figuring out that there wasn't a happy ending to the story even before he shook his head a second time.

"You can't take the bar—or practice law," she guessed. It made sense, considering what she knew about the criminal justice system from living with a sheriff, and then an attorney, all those years.

"That would be correct."

He didn't sound bitter—or even angry.

"I'm impressed." Sara voiced the first thing she'd felt.

"Why?"

"Most people go through life doing what they have to do to get ahead. I can't honestly think of one person who'd put himself out to the extent it would take to get through three grueling years of law school, all the while knowing he could never use the degree. That's what I call bettering oneself in the truest sense."

Picking up his knife and fork, Mark cut off another hunk of the New York strip he'd ordered. "I wouldn't take it that far," he said, looking somewhat agitated. "I won't ever be a lawyer, but I use what I learned all the time. Everyone should know about the laws they're bound to live by."

She supposed. But not many people had a sense of that quite like Mark Dalton did. Or the conviction to follow through on it, if they did.

Regardless of what he'd been in his past—and Sara wasn't convinced, in spite of the evidence against him, that he'd been all bad back then—she really believed that today, Mark Dalton was a good man.

And today was all anyone really had.

MARK WAS PAYING THE BILL when Sara noticed Bill Harmon arriving with his wife. The Harmons were clients of Brent's—the kind they'd paid attention to because of the amount of time Brent's firm billed them. Sara bent for her purse, taking as long as she thought she could to retrieve it from the banquette next to her.

And then she looked at the dessert menu, ignoring the fact that she'd already declined anything more.

"Sara? Is that you?" Denise Harmon came to a halt beside her. "I told you it was Sara, Bill," she said to her husband. "I'd know that hair anywhere."

Sara should have cut it off when she'd left Brent—and her old self—behind.

"Hi, Denise, Bill," she said, smiling politely at the couple. "How've you been?"

"Good!" Denise said. "We just got back from the Mediterranean. It was everything you said it would be," she gushed. "When you said the water was bluer than anything you'd ever seen I thought you were exaggerating, but—"

"Good to see you, Sara," Bill Harmon interrupted his wife, something Sara had seen him do many times in the past. It was almost as if, as far as he was concerned, Denise's thoughts were irrelevant to him.

"I'm glad you had a good time," Sara responded. "And pleased I didn't steer you wrong."

"Oh, no, you never do, Sara. I know that if you tell me something's going to be good, it always is."

She'd made it her business to know. An effective hostess always did. And while Sara had had a lot of responsibility in her own job, as well, her real role had always been understood. She was the hostess for a rainmaker.

While her husband took her arm, avoiding Sara's gaze entirely, Denise's attention turned to Mark, who'd been sitting there watching the entire exchange.

"Who's this?" Denise asked Sara, while studying Mark with an approving smile. "You certainly didn't waste any time!"

"Denise, Bill, meet Mark Dalton. A…friend of mine."

They thought she and Mark were on a date. And there wasn't much she could do to set them straight. Not without embarrassing all of them.

Bill Harmon's handshake was as brief as politeness would allow. Denise gushed and, interrupting her once again, Bill pulled her away.

"Nice couple." Mark's words were dry.

"Clients of my… Of Brent's. Bill's in shipping."

Mark didn't say anything more about them. Or about anything else as they left the restaurant and he turned the car toward Sara's new home.

"YOU'RE AWFULLY QUIET."

Sara's words drew Mark back from the darkness that was threatening to suck him back in.

"Just relaxed."

"It doesn't seem that way."

How could she say that? She'd only known him a couple of weeks. He took the next turn, pulling to a stop in front of her house with a sense of relief.

Sara didn't get out.

"I wish you'd tell me what you're thinking."

How had he led her to believe she had a right to his thoughts? And yet...

"It's like I was saying the other night on the phone," he told her. "You, me, being anything other than victim and perpetrator... It's not possible."

"Who says?"

"The world will say."

"And you've always lived your life according to what other people tell you to do?"

"Of course not." He'd sure as hell never have attended law school if that had been the case. He didn't know of one person, other than Sharon, maybe, who didn't think he was crazy for shelling out thirty-six thousand, plus books and fees, to earn a degree he'd never use.

"Are you trying not to tell me that now that you've actually gone out with me, spent an evening in my company, you find I bore you to tears?"

He turned in her direction and stared at her. "Where'd you come up with that?"

"I'm superfluous," she said, as if stating the obvious. "Bill looked right through me. And

Denise made it clear that I'm only there to dole out generic opinions on superficial topics."

"On the contrary, she made it clear that she values your opinion—no matter what the topic."

"It never even occurred to her to ask how I was doing. Or to offer any sympathy." Sara didn't have the least hint of self-pity in her tone. "Don't get me wrong, I don't blame them. I've spent the past twenty or so years trying to stay in the background. It's ingrained at this point."

"I thought Denise was just being polite because of the situation. You out with another man, and all."

He was surprised when Sara shook her head. "That's how it always was. With everyone. We talked about their lives. Or what Brent and I were doing together. Rarely did anyone ask about me. And frankly, I wanted it that way.

"I've come to realize that while I have people I care about—mostly through work—no one's all that close to the real me. Other than Brent, of course. Otherwise, I might have had to expose too much of myself."

Her words resonated so loudly with him he could barely stand the noise. Didn't want to deal with the fact that his actions in the past had consigned her to a life as lonely as his had been.

"You ever get into conversations with yourself, then?" he asked with a tentative smile.

"Doesn't everyone?" She smiled back, suddenly looking tired.

"You ever start jabbering in there just when you're about to fall asleep at night?"

"Oh, yeah." Her voice was soft in the darkness of his SUV. "And sometimes I wake myself up for another round at three in the morning, too."

"I hate it when that happens."

"I wake you up, too?"

Mark chuckled. "No, I take care of that myself."

The silence wasn't as threatening as it had been on the drive home.

"We're a pair, aren't we?" Sara finally said.

He liked the sound of that—too much.

"We're just two people looking for truth before we move on." He forced himself to say what he knew was right.

"You really don't have any interest in a friendship, then?" Her eyes were little more than glistening lights in the shadows, but he felt them penetrate.

"Ah, Sara." He couldn't stand the disappointment in her voice. Couldn't be responsible for putting it there. "I'd love that more than you can possibly know, but it's not going to work."

"It will, if we let it."

He wanted to go with that; to pretend that he believed her, that she believed herself. The idea was more tempting than anything he'd ever considered before.

But he couldn't get past the panicked look in her eyes as her friends had walked up to the table. Or the way the other man's rudeness to him had bothered her.

"What's going to happen the next time we're out and someone wants to know who I am? How are you going to explain—to anyone—that you're hanging out with the man who once raped you?"

The words scraped his throat. And he thought that now was the moment when he really began to pay for his actions all those years ago.

Prison life was nothing compared to facing this beautiful woman who'd touched him so completely; this woman who made him feel peaceful and excited at the same time. He felt elementally connected to her, and yet he knew that being with her was impossible.

His presence in her life, even as a friend, could only hurt her.

"No one in Columbus knows about my past."

"I'm assuming your ex does."

Her nod was abrupt.

"And he knows my name."

"I don't know that he remembers it."

"The man would have to be dead not to remember the name of the men who violated his wife when she was little more than a child."

He could tell by her silence that she knew he was right. He waited for the click of the car door. And considered stopping at a carryout for a six-pack of beer on his way home.

He'd lock himself in. Throw away the key.

He'd spent twenty years running from his past, proving to himself that he wasn't the guy who'd committed a horrendous crime. Maybe it was time to face up to the fact that he was who he was.

There was no escaping.

"I DON'T CARE, Mark." Sara reached deep inside herself for the truth of those words before she dared to say them. The thought wasn't something she'd ever be able to take back.

His face turned toward her slowly and she wished she could read what was hidden in those golden-green eyes, which had shown her only kindness, compassion, respect—and a hint of his own pain.

"I don't care if they know. It's not against the law for us to be friends."

"You'll care when they start talking about you behind your back."

She shook her head. "No, I won't," she said, completely sure of herself. "Six months ago, maybe you'd have been right. Even three months ago. But I'm a different person now."

"You're on the rebound, raw. You don't know how you'll feel when everything settles down."

"That's just it." She looked at him, wishing she had the courage to grab his hand, hold it, beg him to hold her. "I don't want to ever settle down, not if it means going back to that state of being half alive."

He didn't say anything and she searched desperately for a way to convince him, afraid he would drive away and never talk to her again.

"They're all talking behind my back now, and I'm still standing."

Still nothing.

"Do you know how many of those people that I'm supposed to worry about even called me after Brent and I split up?"

"How many?"

"Zero. Not one. I spent every holiday partying with them, and most of my free nights entertaining them. I went to concerts and on cruises with them, and no one sent so much as a card. My staff cared—they've been great. A few people I know around the country, educators I've become friends with, have called or sent e-mails, but none of them would turn their backs on me for knowing you, either. In the first place, they have no way of recognizing your name, and in the second, they don't judge my life. They're my friends."

"And what about your father?"

Her insides tightened, but she couldn't let fear paralyze her. Not any more. This was too important—even if she still had no clear idea why. She just knew that it was; that she had to follow her heart. Trust it to lead her where she was meant to be.

"I'd *rather* he not know—at least until we clear up whatever happened back then—but I'm willing to take the chance that he'll find out. And I'm prepared to face him when he does."

"Why?" Mark asked, leaning his back against the driver's door.

"I don't know."

"That's not good enough."

He was challenging her, she knew that—but it felt like tough love. He'd stopped saying no, but it was almost as if he was forcing her to make certain she was fully aware of what she was saying.

"I can only tell you what I feel," she said slowly, searching for the complete truth. He deserved it. They both did.

"I'm listening."

She began, then faltered, feeling vulnerable in a way she'd never experienced before. Nothing was being taken from her here. She was giving.

"All my life, since that night, I've been marked." She tried again, the words slow in coming as she worked them through in her mind. "I'm different, you know. I walk in the same world as everyone else, eat the same food, hear the same jokes, but I don't experience them like others do. It's as if I've got this invisible brand on my forehead. Even those who can't see it, sense that it's there. And the few people who know it's there, see it every time they look at me. It's this big *V*. For victim."

Pausing, Sara wished Mark would say something to stop her—or finish for her. But he didn't move.

"When I'm with you, I feel normal." Maybe those words weren't an answer to his question, but she felt as if they'd set her free. Tears filled her eyes and trickled down her cheeks.

"I never realized that before," she said, both wonder and pain evident in her voice.

Mark reached forward, and then pulled back. "Don't cry."

"I can't help it," she said. "I've got twenty-one years of dry eyes to make up for." She wasn't sobbing, though; wasn't consumed with grief. She just sat there, weeping quietly.

"I'm crazy, huh?" she asked after a time.

"Not at all." Mark sat up straighter.

"Tell me what you're thinking."

He took a long time. She was afraid that he wasn't going to be as candid. And she still wasn't sorry that she'd said what she'd said.

"I'm thinking what I've been thinking since the first time we met—again."

"What's that?"

"That you understand things about me I didn't even know about myself. You share much of what I thought I would have to endure alone for the rest of my life."

"You're marked, too, huh?" Her smile was small, but she felt it clear to her toes.

"Yeah, I'm marked, too."

CHAPTER SIXTEEN

MARK HAD COFFEE with Sharon. And felt as if he was in a completely different world, one where people were little more than paper cutouts, there to look at and listen to and think about, but never to wrap his arms around. She was a fine-looking woman. In any other situation, he could be attracted to her.

He laughed at her jokes.

And as he'd done every waking second since he'd left Sara at her doorstep the night before, he thought about the woman who, in two short weeks, had changed his life.

He hadn't touched her, and yet he felt fully alive. He'd lay down his life for her without hesitation.

As he drove away from the coffee shop at OSU, where he'd met with his study group regularly over the past three years, Mark picked up his cell phone to call Sara and see if they could get together.

And then he put it back down. She was going

to be there tomorrow. And with all of the tensions and hurts and challenges stacked against them, taking things slowly was mandatory.

Feeling as if he belonged, with someone other than his sister, mother and nephew, was a new experience for him. A heady one. He couldn't let it carry him away from what he otherwise knew and thought.

He made it until six, but when he called her then, because he didn't want her to think he was regretting the previous night's conversation, a man answered her phone.

Mark hung up without saying a word.

"CAN I TALK TO YOU GUYS?" Ryan Mercedes faced the two people he loved and trusted most in the world. They were sitting in the family room of their modest home in south Columbus.

"Sure, son." His father, Glen, reached for the remote and turned off the golf game he'd previously been half-watching, half-snoozing over. His mother put down the afghan she'd been crocheting, in spite of the summer heat that was topping ninety outside.

Ryan sat on one end of the tattered couch, elbows on his knees, trying to figure out how to say what he'd come to tell them.

His parents watched expectantly, their eyes filled with acceptance, anticipation—and the love that had always been there for him, every single day of his life.

"I met her."

He could tell by the blink of his mother's eyes that she knew immediately what he meant. Her shoulders dropped, as if a weight she'd been carrying for a long time had suddenly grown even heavier.

"Met who, son?" Glen, a mail carrier who initially took everything at face value, asked.

"His biological mother," Harriet told her husband before returning her attention to Ryan. "Right?"

He nodded slowly. Continuing to look down at the floor. Waiting.

Nothing happened. His mother didn't start to cry; his father didn't sigh as if he was disappointed. When Ryan looked up again, they were both watching him. With anticipation and love.

A bit of wariness, too. And it occurred to him that for the first time in his life, he was the one who had the power to fix a family situation. For just that second, it was almost as if he was the parent and they were the kids needing reassurance.

He didn't like the feeling much; wasn't ready to stop being their kid. But then, there'd been a lot about growing up these past couple of years that he hadn't enjoyed all that much.

And still, he wanted to be the man he'd been born to be. A good man. A serving man.

"She's nice."

They exchanged a glance and his father nodded. Ryan had the feeling he was screwing this whole thing up.

"She's not you," he said to his mom, leaning over to grab her hand. "She'll never be you."

Harriet patted his hand, tears in her eyes. "I know, Ryan. It's okay. I've always known this day would come."

"You're my mother."

"Yes."

"You're the one who was always there for me."

She smiled. "That's right."

"So why do I feel compelled to take care of her, too?"

Harriet blinked and the first of her tears fell. "Because you have a particular bond with her that no one else will ever be able to break," she said softly. "You knew her first. She cared for you first."

He scoffed, shook his head. "I don't remember any of that."

"Maybe not in your head, but the heart's a funny thing, Ryan. It leads us down all kinds of strange paths. The one thing I can tell you is that no matter where it leads, you'll only be happy if you listen to it. And follow it."

If only it were that easy, that clear.

"It's never going to lead me away from you," he said, including his father in the glance. "Either of you."

"We know that, Ryan," Glen said. "You're our son. Nothing will ever change that. Love isn't just a feeling, it's action, and we've got twenty-one years of that already banked."

He took one breath, and then another. More frightened in that moment than he'd been facing two gunmen outside a bar the night before.

"I'd like you to meet her."

"That would be nice."

Staring at his mother, Ryan felt tears prick the backs of his eyes. Tears he'd never acknowledge or let fall. "You sound as if you mean that."

"I do," Harriet said. "You can't imagine how many times I've wondered about her. She was a baby herself when she had you. She could have terminated the pregnancy, but she chose to have you instead. And give you to us. I've always hoped that she grew up and found happiness."

"She's recently divorced." Ryan felt a twinge of guilt when he thought of the part he'd played in that. At the moment, he was too ashamed to tell his parents about it.

But he didn't see what else he could have done, either. He'd have wanted to know. Sara seemed to have wanted to know.

At the moment, he had something more pressing on his mind than his own absolution.

"There's something else," he said, glancing down again. He told them about the research he'd done, his growing conviction that something was wrong about that night, the trial, the skeleton. "Sara and I have been in touch with one of the three men who…were with her that night."

His mother's indrawn breath didn't help the knot in his stomach.

"Was that wise, son? You don't know this man. He committed an awful crime. And what about her? Shouldn't she stay as far away from him as humanly possible?"

"I agree with you about that," Ryan said, with a grimace. "I had no idea she'd look him up herself or I would never have told her about him."

It was a mistake he was still kicking himself for making. At least he wasn't in the habit of making them a lot.

"In any case, the guy actually seems more decent

than you'd expect. I've done a thorough check on him and he's probably cleaner than we are."

Which, considering Glen Mercedes, was saying a lot. "Not even an overdrawn bank account or a balance on a credit card."

"He has credit cards?"

"Several. And an A-plus credit rating. He owns his business free and clear. He's never had a single complaint filed against him. He's got a law degree. His probation officer said it was a waste having the state pay money to keep track of him, but he enjoyed their visits tremendously. And I can't find a single person who has a beef with the guy."

"Maybe prison scared him straight."

"Maybe. But added to everything else I find questionable about what we know of that night, it kind of makes you wonder, doesn't it?"

"From what we were told, the evidence was irrefutable," Glen said.

"It was."

That was a point he couldn't work his way around. No matter how he looked at it.

"He's helping with the investigation." Ryan told his parents the easier part. "I think it drives him crazy that he can't remember anything about that night."

"He's paying for a crime he can't remember," Glen said.

And Ryan couldn't procrastinate any longer.

"He wants me to submit to a paternity test."

Neither of his parents moved. "How do you feel about that, son?" Glen finally asked.

"I'm not sure. I certainly have no interest in knowing which of the three jerks had fish that swam faster." He bowed his head. "Sorry, Mom."

Lips in a straight line, she nodded her acceptance.

"But he seems to need to know in the worst way and, I mean, what would it hurt? On the one hand, I don't owe him anything. But on the other, am I being selfish denying him some possible peace of mind, when to provide it wouldn't really hurt?"

"Won't it?" Glen asked, his look intent. "If it's true that you won't be affected one way or the other, then I say do it," he continued. "But you make darn certain, son, that you aren't going to start seeing things in yourself that aren't there, negative things, if you put a name and face to the biological part of you that you aren't so proud of."

His dad knew him well. "It won't change anything here." Ryan pointed between the two of them.

"Wouldn't matter to your answer if it did," Glen said, certainty giving weight to his words. "This isn't about you and me, Ryan. This is something you have to figure out inside you."

"Yes, sir."

"IT'S NOT WORKING OUT with me and Chloe."

Brent's legs looked skinnier than she remembered, and longer, too—they went on forever in his golf shorts. He really should stick to long pants.

"I'm sorry to hear that," she said, working hard to maintain her newfound self before old habits overpowered her and returned her to the woman this man thought he was talking to.

After she'd opened her door, he'd come in without even asking if he could. She'd watched, feeling helpless and angry inside, as he'd answered her phone.

Thank God it had been a hang-up.

Unless it had been Mark, in which case their situation just got more complicated, when it was already stretched beyond the limit.

"It's partly the kids," Brent said, pulling out a chair and dropping down so that his knees were touching Sara's. "We were right to choose not to have them," he said. "They get in the way of everything you and I were hoping to accomplish."

He was hoping to accomplish, Sara corrected

silently. And "they" hadn't decided not to have kids. How could he have forgotten that? All the talks and plans and hurt feelings, when he'd refused to consider her needs in relation to his own.

How had she missed the point that while Brent always said he was acting in her best interests, he'd only viewed her from the perspective of his own needs. He'd always been so convincing.

"The thing is," he continued when she maintained her usual silence as he worked through whatever was on his mind, "I know I screwed up, Sara. Badly. I feel horrible about it."

Judging by the shadows beneath his eyes—and his consternation when she'd pulled out of the hug he'd tried to bestow—she believed him.

"But I've learned," he continued, enclosing her knees with his and squeezing them gently together. "I need you, Sara. More than I ever knew."

As much as she once could have found satisfaction in his groveling, Sara was afraid to allow her old self to hear much more now. "We're divorced."

"That's just a formality," he said, leaning forward to bring his face level with hers. His eyes were wide open, sincere as he gazed at her, taking her hands in his.

"I didn't want the divorce, Sara. You know that. I've always loved you, and now I know how much I *need* you, too. We can be married again within the week. You can sell this place or keep it for an investment if you want and move all our stuff back home."

She considered what he was saying. She had to. The man she'd loved and served for fifteen years, the man who'd stood by her as she learned to stand up with dignity and class in spite of her own self-doubt, the man who'd held her up to the world as a person of value and worth, was asking for her support and love.

"Please, Sara," he said, rubbing a thumb against the back of her hand. "Come home with me tonight. I'll help you get everything moved back tomorrow."

Instead of his Sunday afternoon golf game? That said a lot. Sara couldn't remember the last time he'd put her before work.

"Does Chloe know you're here?"

"No. But I'm sure she's guessed that I'd be coming, eventually. I was honest with her. I told her that I wanted you."

"Or do you just want the life we had?"

"Isn't that the same thing?" His tone was soft, filled with honest question.

And Sara understood that for Brent it was the same thing.

"If Chloe hadn't had the kids, would you still be with her?"

Shaking her hand, Brent raised their interlocked fingers to touch her chin. "Ifs and onlys don't matter, Sara. What matters is that I've come to my senses. I apologize for the pain I've caused you, the disrespect I've shown you. And I'm ready to give you my word that it won't happen again. Nothing is worth losing you."

She couldn't keep the tears from welling up in her eyes, but she didn't let them fall.

Ah, Brent, why couldn't you have said these things, known them, two months ago?

But would she really have wanted him to?

If he had, she'd never have found herself. She'd have spent her whole life with him and died only half alive.

"I appreciate that," she told him now, squeezing his hand. "So much."

Humility was hard for him; she'd have said impossible before right now. "But I'm not coming back, Brent." Her smile was sad, her heart filled with sorrow—and compassion. "I can't."

Frowning, he only held her closer. "What do you mean, you can't?"

"I'm not the same woman you were married to." She searched for a way to help him understand something she still didn't fully comprehend herself.

"I can't go back, Brent. I don't want to be your hostess, when it means having to play all those social games. I don't care about climbing the ladder so much as I care about knowing which step I'm on. When I'm angry, I want to be able to say so. When I want something, I'm going to ask."

Pulling back slightly, Brent stared at her. And she nearly started to panic. Took a deep breath. Thought of how she'd felt the night before in Mark's car, the hope and exhilaration and zest for life that had overcome her as she'd realized that she didn't have to hide with him.

"I don't mean to sound selfish," she continued. "And I certainly don't intend to spend my whole life spouting whatever I feel whenever I feel it, or always putting my needs above anyone else's. But I do intend to express my desires. And one of them is to get off the merry-go-round of who's who and who knows whom and says what about whom. I don't want to worry about what I'm wearing so much as about what I'm doing while I'm wearing it. I don't want to spend the majority of my time socializing and schmoozing with people I don't even have anything in common with."

And I want a child.

It wasn't unheard-of for single women to adopt these days.

Brent stood up, helped himself to a bottle of water from the refrigerator and sat back down, studying her.

Tensing, Sara withstood the perusal, guarding herself against whatever manipulation he might try to use. Brent was a master rainmaker. He could convince people to donate their feet to charity if there was some way to get charity to take them.

But she knew that about him—which gave her an edge. She hoped.

"I'm worried about you."

She didn't need the unfeigned regard in his eyes to convince her he was telling her the truth.

"I know." She grimaced. "I am, too."

"You've been through a lot, Sara," he reminded her. "You're fragile."

She'd always thought so. But was that because she was? Or just because she'd been told she was?

"I'm stronger than you think."

I've stood by my conviction to leave you. I've met my son. One of my rapists. I'm sleeping in a house all by myself every single night.

"I run a nationally recognized agency," she told him. "I fly all over the country and face influential businessmen and lawmakers and educators with success."

"You've always been great at what you do," he told her. "Professionally there's no one better. But I'm not talking about the *working* you, Sara. I'm talking about the woman inside." He made her sound damaged.

"All I'm saying is that I know you. I understand you. And I'm here for you."

The words any woman she'd ever known would want to hear, long to hear—die to hear.

"How can you know me, when I'm only just getting acquainted with myself?" she said, scared to death that he might be right about everything he was saying.

And more frightened still at going back to the life she'd had.

"I've known you since your first year in college," he reminded her. "From the time you still walked with your head down, didn't socialize and were afraid to be alone in the dark."

"And you've tried to keep me there, haven't you?" She had no idea where the words came from. But the force with which they just sprang up was not to be denied. "Throughout our entire marriage, any time I was really upset with you, any time I might have stood up for myself at the risk of you not getting what you needed, you'd remind me that I had every reason to be emotionally distraught after all that I'd been through, implying that I was being irrational because I'd been raped. Implying that I'm emotionally fragile."

"You are."

"No, Brent, I'm not." This time Sara stood, left the kitchen table, the place that was safe for all family discussions. "I'm doing just fine."

"You call having dinner with your *rapist* just fine?" The words were softly spoken. Brent stayed seated, but his tone cut through her completely.

CHAPTER SEVENTEEN

"Is THAT WHAT THIS is about?" Sara asked, arms crossed as she faced Brent. "The fact that Bill and Denise saw me out with another man last night?"

Now that she was standing, she didn't know what to do with herself. Walking out wasn't an option.

It was rude. And a little low on dignity.

She couldn't sit back down, either. Couldn't risk falling under the power of his convincing tone.

"It's so shocking it's sad, Sara," he said now, hands clasped between his knees. "What are you thinking? Out in public where all the world can see, where anyone you know might happen upon you with the man who molested you?"

"In the first place, no one in this city, with the exception of you, would know who he is." But she gained strength from his telling statement. As always, Brent put the most importance on what others thought. "In the second, Mark paid for his crime. He's not the same man anymore."

If he'd ever been. The more time she spent with Mark Dalton, the more Sara felt compelled to learn the truth about that night. Because the man she saw and felt him to be, just like the girl she'd known herself to be, would not have acted as they'd been said to have acted that night.

"I can't believe I'm hearing this." His voice rising with disbelief, Brent leaned his head against the back of the chair.

Sara's limbs tightened. Brent could derail her; he could cut her down and have a chance of her accepting it. But he wasn't going to tear down a man who'd already been at life's lowest and then fought his way back up.

Brent had gone to law school in order to get rich.

Mark went to law school because he wanted to live his life right.

"I'm not any of the things you describe me as when I'm with Mark Dalton," Sara said, pretty sure she'd regret giving him that much information. "I don't feel abnormal or branded. I'm just a person who's lived life with all of its ups and downs. That night by the lake, it's just one of my downs, when I'm with him. It's not a character- or life-defining event."

Brent shook his head, his gaze filled with regret. "It breaks my heart to think of you so low that you'd put yourself in the same class as that criminal," he said. "That you think you have to go so low to feel normal."

Is that what she'd done? Was she really not thinking clearly, but rather finding a way to justify her changed existence? All in the name of finding herself?

"I don't feel low," she said, sinking back into her chair, nonetheless.

And truth be told, neither did Mark feel that way to her.

"The mind does what it has to do to cope, Sara, you know that. You'll convince yourself you're okay because you see no other option but to accept where you currently find yourself. But it doesn't have to be this way. Come home with me—we'll get married again. And this time, I won't fail you. I promise."

By his definition or hers?

"Are you trying to tell me you've discovered you're in love with me?"

Brent leaned forward again, taking both of her hands, before touching his forehead to hers. "Ah, come on, honey. You don't need to hide behind words that are meaningless. I'm here for you, ready to pull you up from where you've sunk. I'm promising to forego my earlier activities and devote myself fully to you and our future, for as long as we live. Call it by whatever name you like."

"And what about sex?" She had to ask, though she had no desire at all to be naked with this man ever again.

"We'll work it out."

He sounded so confident that she almost wanted to believe him. Life would sure be one hell of a lot easier, and safer, if she just gave in.

But in that moment, she knew. Fearlessly, she sat back, pulling her hands from his grasp. "I don't want to work it out," she said.

The fear would return, she had no doubt of that. But she also knew that this was the end of the line for her, the crowning moment. This was the time she either trusted herself or lost herself forever.

"I don't want to marry you again, Brent. And this is my home."

It must have been something in her tone that got to him, or maybe it was in her expression. Pushing back from his chair so hard it hit the wall, Brent stood and faced her.

"You're leaving me no choice, but to call your father."

Keeping her seat at the handmade wooden table, Sara watched Brent pace back and forth across the small kitchen.

"Then call him." She'd face him, too. If she had to.

Studying her face for a painfully long time, Brent finally turned away. "I'm not coming back, Sara."

"I know."

Glancing back, he held her gaze one last time, nodded, and left.

CLICKING JEWELS, blue faces and orange spacemen back and forth, erasing them, avoiding killer squares until he could manipulate their disappearance, Mark cleared level after level on his computer screen. Delving deeper into the ancient ruins of some make-believe land.

Zoning. Removing his mind from his body long enough to let emotion simmer and then cool.

He clicked his mouse. Three, four or five at a time, the faces and jewels would disappear. And then new combinations appeared. Sometimes he'd have to line them up two or three times before they'd show themselves and then disappear. Much like life. Sometimes you could size things up with one glance and get it completely right. And other times you had to look at people, at situations, repeatedly before they really made sense.

Another black square fell. Mark tried to superimpose Sara Calhoun's face on it, but he couldn't. She was that diamond over there. The gold medallion.

Being friends didn't preclude her from having a male companion. To the contrary, it would be better for her—for both of them—if she did.

But why hadn't she told him? Was all that talk about trust and confidence and being open and honest just more of the social niceness by which she'd said she'd lived her life the past twenty years?

The thought made him sick. Not of her, but of his own brief journey into the halcyon world of being whole. When he knew that his life was cracked and would *always* be cracked. But pain came with fighting what was, and acceptance brought peace and satisfaction. Contentment.

Congratulations!

The word appeared on his screen. He'd turned the last square to gold—clearing another level. That made thirty and counting, for the evening. A box popped up, requesting his presence farther back in the cave.

He agreed to go. And watched as another level emerged with nooks and crannies that had diamonds and blue faces and medallions and orange spacemen to rescue. The pieces fell into place. The timer set. And Mark began to click.

SOMETIME AFTER MIDNIGHT, his phone rang. Leaving the forty-fifth level, an evening record for him, Mark grabbed his cell phone. Calls this late weren't social. They were bad news.

Which meant Dana, Jordon or his mother.

"Hello," he said before the phone was fully open and against his ear, not bothering to wait to see the caller ID. He was two hours from Cleveland and didn't have a minute to waste. He slid one foot into a sandal by the door.

"Mark?"

The voice was feminine—and not a relative. Mark took off his sandal.

"Yeah?"

"Were you asleep?"

"No." He sank down into the middle of his leather sectional, not bothering to turn on any lights.

"I'm sorry to call so late, I just…"

"It's okay." Maybe it shouldn't be. But it was.

"I…did you call here tonight?"

He contemplated lying. "Yes."

Her sigh didn't sound happy. "I was afraid of that."

For a second, he was gratified. And then remembered himself. "Hey, there's absolutely no reason you shouldn't have a guy answering your phone. You're young, beautiful, single. It's natural. A necessary part of life."

He shut up before he overdid it.

"It wasn't just a guy."

She didn't have to tell him that. "That's why I didn't say anything," he told her. "I didn't want to cause problems."

"I wish you had." Her answer was dry. And forgiving him nothing. "It would have been good to talk to you."

He had no idea how to respond to that.

Pushing himself down in the seat, Mark straightened out, his head resting against the top of the back of the couch. He'd long since stripped to boxers, and the leather was cool against his skin. For the moment.

He'd be sweating shortly, in spite of the seventy-four degrees his thermostat was set at.

Leather looked great and was easy to clean. It didn't breathe.

He was having a little trouble doing that himself.

"I heard from Ryan tonight."

That had been Ryan's voice? It sure hadn't sounded like her son.

"He was over?"

"No. He called and said he's got some new information and asked if we could meet him tomorrow. I invited him here for dinner. If you're free, you should come, too."

Disappointment was a bitter thing when it came twice. The call was a courtesy. Business. He should never have thought it anything else.

"I'll be there."

He should get up. Head into bed. He couldn't find the energy to move.

"It was Brent."

Mark clenched the phone. "Answering your phone?"

"Yeah."

"You getting back with him?" He didn't see how that would make her happy, but maybe it was for the best.

At least for the best that he accept she didn't belong as a part of his life. And be thankful that he'd had the chance to know her, however briefly.

"He asked me to." Her voice was sleepy, husky, drawing out sentences. "It was weird, Mark. Two months ago, if I could have written a script for what I'd most like to hear from him, it wouldn't have been as good as what he said tonight."

Good for her. He hoped. If she was happy, he'd be at peace.

"And you know what the most amazing thing was?"

He didn't. Wasn't sure he wanted to. And then it hit him. She'd been with her ex-husband that night. So why was she calling him at, he glanced at the LED screen on his cable box, 12:23 on a Saturday night?

"What?" he asked, settling into the couch's softness.

"I saw through it immediately. I mean, it was hard, and I had to really think about how I was feeling and what I was thinking, so I didn't get lost in what he wanted me to think, but I didn't lose me. Not for a second. I didn't waver or have any compulsion to go running back."

"He wants you back?"

"Not now, he doesn't."

Light-headed, Mark tried to pretend he was just overtired, dizzy from so much video-game artifact hunting that night. But relief was a palpable thing—and not to be denied.

"He asked me to marry him," she continued while he wrestled with the hope that was beginning to emerge. "He said he needed me and loved me and he promised not to step out on me ever again."

"And you weren't the least bit tempted?" She'd had a secure life with Brent Calhoun. Financially and otherwise.

"Not for me," she said, her voice lowering. "He was a safe harbor for a lot of years, and while I now see that he used my past to keep me feeling weak enough to favor his needs over my own, he's not all bad. We were good companions and we managed life well together. I loved him for a long time."

God, what he'd give to have someone say that about him at some point before he died. To know that part of life firsthand.

But this was a fruitless game to play. Nothing good or positive came from yearning for what didn't exist. Great good and happiness *could* come from keeping his gaze firmly fixed on the successes that he'd already reached and those within his reach.

"So, for him, I was tempted. I could make him happy."

"At what cost?" She'd called him a friend. He could be one.

"Yeah, that's what I came up with, too," she said. "If making Brent happy costs me my life, then it's not right. And as soon as I'm fully out of the picture, there'll probably be someone else who comes along, who can make him even happier—and be happy herself."

"In a perfect world."

"You don't think that will happen?"

"I expect it probably will." For the Brents of the world.

Life could be good for anyone if they had a mind to find it so.

"It didn't work out with Chloe."

Mark grinned at the satisfaction in Sara's voice. "Vindication feels good every now and then, huh?"

"Yeah, though I don't want to make a habit of seeking out that particular feeling."

"Me, either. I saw enough of that mind-set while I was in prison and once it takes hold, it's like a disease that eats away every legitimately good feeling you might have had."

Silence fell for a moment, and he wished he hadn't brought the conversation back to their challenges. Even inadvertently.

"I hate to think of you there."

"Me, too."

"Was it horrible?"

He couldn't lie to her. Nor make light of that time, not without being untrue to himself.

"I was housed with other sex offenders," he said, skirting the surface of memories he still prayed he'd one day forget. "A bunch of perverted, horny guys whose moral character is mostly nonexistent. A lot of them because they'd been abused themselves at such young ages, often by family members, so that the development of their consciences didn't take a normal course. To them, society's got it wrong."

"You know them well."

"I had a lot of time to think about them, to figure out what went wrong that there were so many grown men who thought nothing of raping young children. Or new inmates."

She had to know. If he was going to open himself up to a real friendship, he was going to have to bring his whole self to the table. No more being ashamed or hiding.

He couldn't honor her courage in facing life with his own cowardice.

When the silence went on too long, he figured she'd hung on up him. He held the phone to his ear, anyway, as he went into his bedroom, pulled back the covers, climbed in and pulled the sheet up over his chest.

"If…if…if we find out that I'm to blame… That my father is to blame…"

Her words broke on a sob.

He thought she'd been repulsed. Instead, she was crying for him.

"I got him off me before anything happened," he told her. "And when I was through with him, no one came near me that way again."

"And then you got in trouble for beating him up, right?"

"No." Mark grinned. "Funny thing about prison. The rules there are made up as you go. In his case, the guard on duty pretended not to see, while he stood right there watching me beat the guy to a pulp. When I was done, the guard told me that I was going to be all right, and walked away. I believed him. And he was right."

Mark had tried to find that guard once he'd gotten out. To thank him, maybe offer to fix his car for life. But he'd never been able to track him down.

"Thank God for him."

"I did. And do," Mark said, hearing a motorcycle outside his window and cringing—little Isabel's mama was entertaining again tonight. Mark hoped to that same God, as he did every time he heard that motorcycle, that the man would be content with the mother's favors and leave the child completely alone. Isabel was one of the special ones—a child destined for greatness. If she could just grow up intact.

"Other guys aren't so lucky, though." Mark returned to the conversation he'd been having, telling Sara things he'd never been able to discuss with anyone else before. Isabel was beyond his control. "And a lot of those inmates don't seem to want to be as lucky as I was. I guess they'd rather get it from each other than not get it at all."

The idea was beyond him, even after years of living in such a society, but he'd seen enough of it to know that it was true. Sure made him wonder how a system that allowed such behavior expected those same men to behave rationally and appropriately when they got back on the outside.

"Life's confusing, huh?"

At that moment, hearing the slightly lost, yet strangely hopeful tone in her voice, Mark wanted to be with her. As he'd never wanted to be with a woman before. Just to be near her. To breathe in her scent. To relax and fall asleep and know that she wouldn't be gone in the cold light of day.

He wanted other things, too. Intimate touching that he hadn't allowed himself to consider with another human being in too many years to count. His self-control was rock-solid—he'd depended on it to win back his self-respect. But in opening himself up to all of life, he'd apparently loosened the constraints he'd placed on his dreams and desires.

Either that or Sara Calhoun had sent out signals to him that he was not superhuman enough to resist.

"Did Brent tell you what went wrong with

Chloe?" he asked, fumbling for anything that would get his mind off more explosive topics.

"Not completely. But I know her kids were a part of it."

Staring at the ceiling, Mark closed his eyes. "They didn't accept him?"

"He didn't accept them." Sara sounded sleepy, too. "To Brent's way of thinking, kids get in the way."

That surprised him. Seeing Sara with Ryan, catching a look or two of longing on her face, noting her instant compassion for Jordon, her sensitivity to the boy's needs, he'd just assumed…

"You'd rather live in a quiet house than a noisy one, I take it?" he said, wanting to know everything about her.

Whether he agreed with her ways or not.

"Brent needs to be free to call all the shots all the time. If a client, or a potential client, needs attention at a moment's notice, that has to be able to come first."

"And you were happy with that." It wasn't a question, but a clarification.

"No, I wasn't." The unequivocal answer had Mark's blood pumping harder again. She'd given the exact answer he'd have given.

"I don't know how it is for other women, but

when I gave up Ryan, I knew I was never going to be at peace again unless I carried another baby under my heart, felt its feet kicking me from the inside, talked to him in the wee hours of the morning when it was just me and him alone in the world, went through labor pains and the hard work of birthing him and then had the joy of touching him. Nursing him. Watching him grow.

"I gave away a part of my heart when I let them take that baby away from me. At the time, I made the best choice, the right choice, for him and for me. I still believe that. But I've paid the price every day since."

Mark swallowed. Understanding so well. He'd wanted kids of his own, too. Ached sometimes when he was with Jordon and knew that he'd never really have a son—or daughter—of his own.

And it would always be that way. No matter what. No matter who he was friends with—or not. He could never bring into this world innocent little children who would, merely by product of their birth, live underneath his stigma. He'd be condemning them to hell before they breathed their first breath.

"When I married Brent I was perfectly clear with him about my need for a family," Sara went on, her words painful for Mark to listen to. "He didn't deter me in any way. Instead, he assured me that he understood and wanted the same thing. Within the past couple of years I've found out that he never even considered having children. He was confident that he'd change my mind—that after living with him, I'd see the light."

"Did you?"

"Not for one second."

"And now? You're what, thirty-seven?"

"I still want that family."

CHAPTER EIGHTEEN

SARA WAS A MASS of nerves, but feeling more peaceful than she could ever remember feeling as she prepared dinner on Sunday. Her father had called, offering to grill steaks for her or drive to Columbus for dinner, and she'd had a hard time telling him she'd rather make it one night that week. She loved him. Hated to picture him home alone—especially on a Sunday afternoon. And yet her life had new dimension, new priorities and loyalties that were equally pressing.

It had only been a short time since she'd taken Ryan to that first meeting with Mark, but it seemed like a lifetime ago.

And like she had a lot more at stake. Mark was fragile, where Ryan was concerned. And she didn't want him hurt.

On the other hand, Ryan was her son. The child she'd carried beneath her heart when she'd still been a child herself. In some ways, she owed him more than anyone else on earth.

Three men. All of them precious to her in different ways. All of them trying to do their best.

And in coming together, in their dealings with her, all capable of exploding or being badly hurt.

For a woman who'd done nothing but ride the waves for more than twenty years, going against the current was completely foreign to her.

Yet she didn't hesitate, didn't look back. She knew she was making the best choices for herself, at this place and time. If challenged, and she'd had her father's voice in her head challenging her on an hourly basis these past few days, she couldn't explain how she knew. She just did.

But she wasn't all that sure how she was going to face so many things that meant so much with so little experience.

Mark arrived first. Dressed in cotton shorts, a deep green polo shirt that matched his eyes, and sandals. He smiled at her. And she knew she'd make it through the afternoon—no matter what news Ryan had to bring.

He was there before Mark had even fully come through the door. Complimenting her on how nice she looked—she had on comfort clothes, an old flowery skirt, tank top and bare feet—he gave her a tentative hug.

And her heart melted.

THEY TALKED about the weather—hot and muggy and mostly overcast—a relatively normal Columbus summer. And about Ryan's job. A bar arrest he'd handled had been in the papers for a couple of days. The arresting officer hadn't been named.

Sara felt cold all over as Ryan talked about the case. And she realized that her newfound son was in grave danger every single day he went to work. It was different with him than it had been with her father. The city was bigger, the world harsher and Sara much less naive.

"You've got that same look my mom gets when I talk about my job," he said, his mouth full of barbecued spareribs.

She wanted to tell him not to talk with his mouth full.

But she wasn't his mom. Harriet Mercedes was.

"I'm going to be fine." Ryan, who had finished chewing, was looking at her. "I promise."

"You don't know that."

"More people die in car accidents in this city than cops do on the job."

There were a lot more people driving than there were cops. Sara met Mark's gaze across the table and knew he'd read her mind—or at least shared the thought she'd been thinking.

"Does your mother buy that?" he asked the young man.

Ryan shrugged, grinned kind of sheepishly. "She's nice enough to pretend to," he said. And then, looking at Sara, he added, "She wants to meet you."

Immediate fear for her son's safety was overtaken by anxious thoughts and feelings tied to the thought of meeting Ryan's adoptive mother.

Invitation into the private circle. Acceptance. Judgment. Rejection. Staking of claims—or sharing love for a boy?

"I'd love that." She spoke the truth.

"Is it okay if I give her your number to set something up?" He took a huge bite of au gratin potatoes, completely ignoring the coleslaw.

"Of course."

Mark, helping himself to another spoonful of coleslaw, seemed not to have heard the conversation at all.

"WHAT NEWS HAVE YOU GOT for us?"

They'd cleared away the dishes and were sitting at Sara's table with glasses of iced tea. Mark seemed in a hurry to get on with things.

"As I was asking around for anyone who might have known Ralph Bonney twenty years ago, anyone who might have been aware of his story of a man with a backpack driving a shiny, new jeep and hanging around campus, I found a guy you all knew in college." Ryan was looking at Mark. "A Wayne Rollins. You ever heard of him?"

"Yeah. A doctor's son." Mark named a rival fraternity, one composed mostly of rich men's sons, that the man had belonged to.

"Apparently, he's had a bit of a hard life," Ryan said. "Lost his wife to cancer and then his little girl to a car crash. His dad has Alzheimer's and he's got him at home, caring for him himself."

Sara couldn't imagine. And yet didn't that just prove what she'd said to Mark, and had been unable to ever get Brent to see? Everyone had challenges. Making them different but equal.

"He's convinced that a lot of his bad fortune was caused by the choices he made as a young man—that he's reaping what he sowed, so to speak."

Ryan's tone was skeptical.

"Don't dismiss the idea out of hand," Mark told him. "But I can't imagine anything Wayne would've done that would have brought so much tragedy."

"He sold drugs," Ryan informed them both. "Mostly prescription stuff that he stole from his father, or got by forging his father's name on his prescription pad. And then he also got into selling street drugs. It's how he paid for the Corvette he drove, among other things."

"I'm assuming this has something to do with us?" Mark asked, sitting forward. He looked focused, but not optimistic.

Sara's insides were churning like a whirlpool. She wished she had an ounce of Mark's control as her mind sped into possible scenarios, looking for ways to offset any potential implications for her father.

John Lindsay had never been involved with drugs. That much she knew for certain.

"He'd been selling street drugs to Ralph Bonney since the beginning of the fall semester."

The party had been in the spring—just before the end-of-May finals.

"That's hard to believe," Mark said, frowning. "He certainly never appeared to be high. Or zoned, either, for that matter. What'd he do, sell them? And Sheriff Lindsay caught him? Is that the hold he had on him?"

Ryan shook his head, his shoulders looking massive in the tight navy T-shirt he had on.

"They were sex enhancers—what's known on the street as ecstasy, but mixed with PCP," he said, glancing briefly at Sara before giving his attention fully to Mark. "Ralph had never been able to hold an erection and once he joined the fraternity and knew he'd have easier access to girls, he panicked at the thought of anyone finding out about his…problem."

"I still don't see what this has to do with us," Sara told him.

"I'm not saying it does," Ryan answered her. "But doesn't it make you just a bit suspicious, knowing that neither of you were apt to join an orgy, neither of you remember a thing about that night after your first few drinks, and Ralph Bonney—the only person who remembered anything at all—was in possession of medication that not only enhanced sex drive but suppressed memory, as well?"

"You think he put something in our drinks?" Sara wanted to weep at the waste of it all. So many lives changed forever.

And she wanted to dance at the possibilities. If she'd been drugged, she couldn't be blamed for all the things that had come about as a result of her behavior that night. At least, not completely.

Her eyes met Mark's. And her heart started beating triple time.

If Mark had been drugged, everything changed.

He'd been a young man pushed beyond his own control by a substance that was completely out of his control.

Or was she creating reality to suit her own needs?

"I see you're considering the possibilities," Ryan said.

"There's only one problem," Mark observed. "Or two." He had both Sara's and Ryan's attention. "What possible reason could Bonney have had for drugging us? And how does this explain him knowing the color of Sara's underwear? Or Sheriff Lindsay's miss on that fact? Or his failing to report Ralph's misinformation when the skeleton was found?"

"And how does it explain the skeleton?" Sara asked.

Holding up his hands, Ryan smiled. "Slow down, I'm not the enemy here. Nor do I have all the answers. I'm just passing along information as I find it, in case either of you has an explanation. Or even a possible theory."

Sara wanted there to be some kind of huge truth to uncover, a tie-in to the illegal drugs. And she was afraid they were grasping at straws. That Ralph Bonney's sexual issues were separate from anything to do with anyone but himself.

THE SUN HAD MOVED, leaving Sara's kitchen in the gloom of near dusk, and still the three of them sat at the table, throwing out possibilities, one or the other finding holes in every theory.

"I have one other piece of information that probably amounts to nothing," Ryan said, as they were beginning to repeat themselves. "I wasn't even going to mention it, but if we're going to consider Keith Gardner and Sam Hall as possible blackmailers, paying Ralph to get you in the mood and then implicating Mark to take the rap, I guess everything is worth a mention."

"What've you got?" Mark asked, slumped back in his chair, seeming as much at ease as if he sat there every night. Sometime during the couple of hours they'd been together, the two men had become more of a crime-solving team than potential adversaries—strengthening the apparent truce they'd reached the previous time they'd sat around a table together.

"I went to or called every homeless shelter in the state over the past week, asking for anyone who'd been around twenty years ago—who might remember anything about any of the people they'd serviced."

Sara really wanted this over. She wanted answers. "And?"

"Out of all of it, I found a handful of people still alive and in the area who'd worked at any of them. Of those, every person remembered particular visitors to the shelters, someone whose story had touched their lives or whose hopelessness they'd never forgotten. All of them remembered more than one client who could fit the description of our homeless guy."

"Our homeless guy." There was a peculiar warmth to that statement. As if they were all in this together, in spite of the separate and dichotic roles they played.

"One woman remembered a name. Mostly because it was also her late husband's name—James Danielson. And interestingly enough, this woman was somewhere else when your father might have been asking around. She'd retired to Florida with a sister and just moved back north to live with her daughter when her sister died last year."

"Did you find anything on a James Danielson in the system?" Mark's gaze was intent again.

Ryan shook his head. At least, Sara thought he did. She couldn't be sure over the static in her mind, the cotton that seemed to be enveloping her.

"Public records show that he was born in Toledo in 1944. As far as I can tell, he's still alive, but there's no known address for him."

"I know that name," she said aloud. Shaking her head, hoping to clear her thoughts, she sought Mark's face, focusing until she felt safe again. "I just can't remember why."

Ryan leaned into her. "Think," he said. "Is he someone you knew? Someone who threatened you?"

She shook her head. But couldn't be sure.

"I get a feeling, scared, confused, but I can't tell you why. It's almost like it's not personal."

"You and your folks volunteered at the shelter closest to you. Maybe he'd been there."

"Maybe." Sara didn't think so.

"Was he in your home? A friend of your parents?"

"No." But she couldn't be completely sure of that, either. "It's right there, teasing me, but I can't seem to..."

She closed her eyes, trying to will the knowledge back.

"Hey." Mark's voice was close, too. Closer than Ryan's. His face filled her gaze as she opened her eyes. His hazel eyes kind, reassuring.

"It's okay," he told her. "Let it go for now. It's been twenty-one years. It's not like we need to solve the problems of the world tonight."

Nodding, she gave him a grateful smile, and still tried to remember whatever was there, in the back of her mind.

"Maybe I just heard the name on the news," she said.

Ryan opened his mouth, but before he could speak, Sara intercepted a look between him and Mark.

"I gotta be going." Sara was fairly certain those hadn't been the words Ryan had been about to say. If she'd had her guess, he'd been about to push her again.

And she wondered if that was what they taught them in cop school.

He stood, slid his chair back beneath the table, took his glass to the sink and stood there.

"Oh, there's one other thing," he said, turning slowly to face Mark and Sara, who were also standing.

"What?" she was almost afraid to hear.

"I'm good with the paternity test." He made the announcement as if he'd just said that he had hamburgers for lunch.

Mark didn't seem to be all that moved by the statement, either, unless you were close enough to see the pulse beating in his upper lip.

"You're sure?" His voice was calm enough.

"Yeah." Ryan looked him straight in the eye.

"I'll call tomorrow to set it up."

Ryan nodded. "Great. Well…I've really got to

be going. I've only got an hour to get home and change before work."

His words brought Sara right back to the fears she'd suppressed while trying to find the connection between James Danielson and her past.

She didn't like the fear any better than memories that wouldn't surface. "You be careful," she told him.

"I will."

Sara saw him to the door, promising to call if anything came to her and nodding when he said he'd be in touch the next day. Her heart filled with fear as she watched him walk away. She wondered if she'd just had her first taste of real motherhood.

She was scared to death to let him go out into the cold, cruel world. And blowing off her concern as though completely unaware of the harm that could befall him, he went, anyway.

"IT'S GOOD TO SEE YOU." Sara turned to Mark as soon as Ryan's car had rounded the corner, closing the door behind her.

He had to leave. The intimate warmth in Sara's eyes, the soft tone in her voice made him want things he wasn't going to have. Absolutely couldn't want from her.

"It's good to see you, too." His mouth had a mind of its own. But it wasn't the boss. He had to get out of there.

"I think that went well." She stood there, six inches from him, acting as if it was perfectly natural for them to be alone, rehashing an evening spent together after everyone else was gone.

"Yes."

"You're getting your paternity test."

He was thankful for that. And dreaded it, too. "I just hope to God it comes up negative."

A cloud passed over her expression. "You don't want to be the father of my child?"

"I—" He stopped, hearing her words, seeing the situation as she might see it. And cursed himself for his insensitivity. "I never thought of it like that," he told her. "I just didn't want to be the one who'd put you through the agony of a teenage pregnancy on top of everything else."

She stepped closer. "And I think I could bear the memory of those months enough to actually acknowledge them, if I knew you were the father of the child I'd carried."

Her gaze was open. Sincere.

"Do you have any idea how hard it was to be falling in love with the baby I could feel growing inside me, the little being who went with me everywhere, who depended on me for life itself, and hating it at the same time, because of how he'd been created?"

He wanted to hold her. And to start running and never stop.

"I hope you are Ryan's father, Mark." She stepped closer to him. "He'd be lucky to have your blood in his veins."

Mark's skin seared with heat, and yet he felt cold, as well.

"What?" she asked, peering up at him. "Did I say something wrong?"

Sliding his hands into his pockets, he looked down at her. At a total loss for words. "You're… I can't believe you're real."

"Why?" She was frowning and he was afraid he'd hurt her. The absolute last thing he wanted to do—ever again. Which made this all so difficult. What was right? Or for the best?

What did she need from him? Not in the moment, but in the long run? Logic told him it was far better for her if he walked away.

And something else, something far beyond reason or even physical feeling held him there.

"When I'm with you, it's like I'm dreaming— and finally living the life I lost. You see me as the man I could have been, not the man I am. It's as if I've died and somehow ended up in heaven with the sins that should have condemned me magically forgiven."

He saw her hand raise, tried to pull away, and braced himself instead. Not to ward off a blow, but to resist any reaction he might have to her touch. Her fingers were soft, silky against his face.

And they nearly brought him to his knees.

"I see the man you are, Mark. What you've made of your personality, your soul and your circumstances. That night left devastation in its wake…and it also honed your compassion, your sense of goodness. It opened your heart to let you see people, really see them, where most people just look through them."

"Or maybe I'm just determined not to go back to prison."

Her fingers slid down onto his neck, the heel of her hand resting against his pulse, which pounded.

"Go back? It seems to me you're still there." Her words shocked him.

He moved only enough to see her eyes. "What do you mean?"

"I'm touching you. I can feel your heartbeat pounding wildly. And yet you stand there as stiff as a man who's died."

"I have to go." He could barely get the words out.

"No, you don't."

She didn't understand, had no idea. But he did. It was up to him to take control and prevent disaster.

"It's not that I'm not gratified. Because I am," he said, his jaw aching from the effort it took him to speak. Hands clenched in his pockets, Mark prayed his legs would carry him past her, two feet forward and out that door. "But this isn't right, Sara. You'll get through this time, wonder what you were thinking and hate yourself. I ruined your life. You don't want to…"

Her fingers were crawling down his chest, rubbing against a nipple.

"You talk too much," she said, licking her lips, her eyes half closed. "And you worry too much. And you better stop now, because you're starting to sound like my father and my ex-husband and even Ryan, thinking you know better than I what I want, what's best for me, who I am inside. Don't do that to me, Mark. You of all people. Let me be me."

"I—"

"Don't disrespect me like they do."

Her hand had reached his waist and stopped there, while the other joined it, holding him.

"Sara…" Even he could hear the strain in his

voice. And it didn't take a scientist to notice the bulge inside the fly of his jeans.

"I've never consciously come on to a guy before, you know," she said, her smile slow, and knowing, and a little sad, too. "You aren't going to make my first attempt a flop, are you?"

God help him. "I'm only human." He was begging—for what, he no longer knew.

"It's about time you realized that."

He was on a precipice, teetering and about to fall.

"I haven't been with a woman in more than ten years."

"And I'm guessing you haven't crossed over, either."

"Of course not."

"Well, I have a secret to tell you, too," she whispered, her gaze vulnerable as she stared up at him. "I haven't ever felt this way before in my life. My…down there…is doing things I don't recognize, but damn, it feels good."

He couldn't reject that look, those words, her. Couldn't leave her here feeling broken all over again. Even if it meant that ultimately he burned for his choice.

Neither was he quite sure what to do. Oh, he knew the body parts all right. Had had his share of relations without commitment those first years after prison, when he'd been trying to work his way through his own sexuality.

What he was feeling now bore no resemblance to any of that.

"I can't make any promises."

"I'm not asking for any."

"I'd rather die than hurt you."

"I know."

His hands were trembling so fiercely he was afraid to use them. There were so many reasons why he had to go. The history between them that would never be accepted and could never be erased.

Her hand touched his crotch. "I'm sorry," she nearly choked. "But I really need this, Mark. From you. Only you."

One minute he was a man alone; completely, horribly, irrevocably alone. And the next, he had the only woman who could ever offer him absolution in his arms.

CHAPTER NINETEEN

AT FIRST, SARA WAS in a hurry, wanting to be out of her clothes, have him out of his and making love. As if she had to make this happen fast before something went wrong. And then, the second Mark touched her, just his hand holding hers, she wanted the experience to last the rest of her life.

"I don't know how much longer I can stand here," she confessed, a little afraid he'd find something wrong with her for saying so.

Or for any number of other things that she might not do right that night.

"Where would you like to go?" Mark's voice was thick, his hands shaky as they held on to hers.

"My bedroom?" She hated to be so direct, but she needed to lie down. Wanted to lie there with him, his whole body touching hers—knee to knee, thigh to thigh, chest to chest. It was either her bed or the floor.

"You're sure?" His gaze was penetrating, but he hadn't dropped her hands. Thank God he hadn't dropped her hands.

"Completely."

The walk to her room was so natural, she wondered what she'd worried about. Side by side, hand in hand, they could have been making the trip for years.

She turned on a small Tiffany lamp, sending soft colored light through the room, and when she turned Mark was right behind her, his gaze running over her face, her lips, back to her eyes.

"I'm sure, Mark," she whispered. "I've never been more sure of anything in my life."

No matter what happened, there'd be no regret for tonight. She was following her heart. Her instincts. And wherever they led was where she was meant to be. Which was far better than wasting the precious years she'd been given to experience life. She could be at peace with that.

His eyes glistened and she suspected there were tears mingling with passion when he slowly bent his head. Lifting her chin, Sara kept her eyes open as his mouth descended. She wanted to be fully cognizant of every nuance of Mark's touch. His lovemaking.

His lips were thick and full, soft and strong all at

the same time. He touched her so briefly that first time that she barely felt kissed. And yet the coil of desire that shot through her body was fully inflamed. His lips barely rose before they were back, with soft pressure, opening, coaxing her response.

A moan filtered out between them. Her breathing, the sounds she made, the feel of the carpet beneath her feet all served as aphrodisiacs, sending her further into a world she wanted to know everything about.

When she could stand the tension no longer, Sara touched her tongue to Mark's, and she would have fallen had he not held her up. Lifting her, he got them both to the bed, placing her sideways across it before lying down beside her.

"You're so beautiful, I'm afraid to touch." His voice was ragged.

She peered into his eyes, only inches from hers. "Please, please touch." Sliding her hand beneath the bottom edge of his shirt, she shivered at the first contact with his bare stomach. "Everything. Everywhere," she added. "I need this so badly, Mark. I need you."

On a journey someplace she didn't understand, Sara gave herself up to whatever might happen without question. Someplace within this man's arms was her salvation. She didn't know why or how. She just knew she'd find it there, and she helped him as he began to undress her.

MARK'S BREATH WAS LABORED, his hands unsteady as they trailed slowly beneath Sara's tank top, sliding it upward. He'd been touching and kissing her for more than an hour and he knew that there was no going back. He was going to see her naked, touch all of her, make love to her in every way he knew how.

As he bared her bra, she reached up and with a quick click, loosened the front closure, her breasts springing into view. They were lovely. Larger than he'd thought, firm and perfectly rounded. He touched one, then the other, lightly. And when she arched upward, he lowered his head to pure joy—and extreme discomfort at the same time. He wanted her so badly that controlling himself was painful.

He kissed, caressed with his lips and when he could stand it no longer he found one nipple with his mouth, suckling it, almost crying out with pure joy. A sense that he belonged there.

From that moment on, Mark was aware only of the feelings overwhelming him and his partner. They moved as though choreographed, finding the most sensitive points, allowing access. He'd meant to use his fingers to prepare her, to assure himself that she wanted him—this—as desperately as she said she did, but in the end, he had no chance. Sara spread her legs and he was inside her, without a single conscious thought.

And when, far too soon, they were done, he lay still half on top of her, still within her, breathing and laughing and perhaps crying a bit, too. Not tears. Nothing so overt, but releasing years of self-denial, of insecurity and loneliness up to the powers that were stronger than he. No matter if he spent every other hour of his life completely alone from then on, he'd left the isolation behind.

FOR MOST OF THAT NIGHT Sara and Mark lay together, healing and being healed. Far more gentle than Brent had ever been, Mark managed to coax responses from her, desires out of her, that changed her forever. No longer could she ever think of herself as a dry, unresponsive woman. She was passionate. Eager. As wild as her ex-husband had always claimed she was not.

She knew they needed to sleep. They both had to work in the morning, and she hoped they might hear more from Ryan regarding their single-named homeless man from twenty years ago. They had life to live. And yet she couldn't give up one second of the night to unconsciousness.

"I'm afraid to go to sleep," she finally said, her head on his chest, listening to his heartbeat. "What if I wake up tomorrow and don't remember?"

He chuckled. "You think I'm that forgettable?"

But they both knew the anguish of the inability to remember one of the most critical events of their lives.

"I know not many of the actual details came out in the trial." Her voice fell into the darkness, daring to bring to light demons that had been too private to ever mention before. "But I also know that guys talk."

His fingers stilled on her arm as he gathered her closer to him, sliding one leg around hers, as though warding off whatever nightmares might be haunting her.

"I have to know what happened that night, Mark. I was so bruised afterward, worse than after I had Ryan. I want to know what they did and who did it first. What happened to me?"

She'd thought herself immune, in that unreal moment, to the agony, but she found she wasn't at all as tears choked her, blurred her vision, slid down her face.

"You'd think we'd remember, wouldn't you?" Mark's tone was bitter. "You're right, guys do talk, Sara, and I can tell you, honest to God, none of us knew the answers to those questions. Believe me, I've asked myself a million times over the years for any kind of hint, a dream, some brief flash of awareness. But there's nothing."

She swallowed. And gave herself the right to travel back over that road again. To get it all out. 'I used to lie in bed at night, picturing things. Imagining myself as some toy that the three of you would do things to. I'd get so filled with rage I'd scare myself."

His hands were completely still. But he didn't let her go.

"And then what would you do?"

"I'd remember that I'd chosen to go to that party. That I'd expressly disobeyed orders. That I'd lied about my age. I'd think about you all thinking you were with an experienced older woman. And when I couldn't stand to think anymore, I'd fall asleep."

Not a peaceful or restful existence, by any means.

"I've been afraid of myself, of things I might not know about myself ever since," Mark said. 'Anytime I'd start to feel healthy or whole, I'd remember and shut down. Part of my withdrawal from certain things is reality," he said, and the words hurt her far too much. "I'll never be a normal man, free to move about the country without fear and hate coming at me. But I'm beginning to see, thanks to you, that I don't have to fear myself. I know who I am. I can trust that."

Sara smiled. Kissed him. "I trust you implicitly," she said and made love to him all over again. This time, she stayed on top.

PUTTING THE CLIP IN HER HAIR the next morning, smiling at her face in the mirror as she thought about the man who'd left to go home and shower less than an hour before, Sara stopped, hands still on top of her head, and stared.

The smile faltered. Fell. And her eyes seemed vacant, even to her.

Without bothering with lipstick, she grabbed her watch and slipped it on as she moved slowly toward her bedroom, and picked up her cell phone.

"I remember why I know that name," she said as soon as Mark picked up. "James Danielson."

Talking on the way to her car, she grabbed her purse and briefcase and went outside. She didn't want to be late for work. To risk questions.

The interior of her Lexus, even parked in the protective shade of her garage, was sweltering.

"He worked for my dad," she said, letting the memories flow over her. "My mom was doing my hair one day when my dad came in and started talking about him. I remember like it was yesterday, because she pulled my hair so tightly it made me cry. And then she told me that she hadn't hurt me. It was so unlike her…"

"Do you remember what was being said?"

"I was about four at the time," she told him, backing down the driveway. "But it had something to do with my mom. And also…" Pieces were falling into place—and leaving her with more questions. "With Ralph Bonney's mother. I remember the Bonney name now. I have no idea what the connection was. But I know there was one. And whatever it was, it upset my mother, who, as I remember it, never made waves. Not ever."

"You going to call Ryan or do you want me to?"

"You can," she said, not because she didn't want to speak with her son, but because she knew how badly Mark needed to connect to him. And she knew, too, that Mark would never approach Ryan with anything other than business. And DNA testing.

"I'm going to give Bonney another call, too," he said. "See if the name sparks anything."

"My father's coming to town for lunch

tomorrow," Sara told Mark, moving onto the freeway for the short drive to NOISE. "We're going over some revisions on the most recent safety manual he's written. I think I'll wait and ask him about this when I see him."

She had a feeling that whatever was happening wasn't something her father would want to discuss with her over the phone. She also knew that this time, she wasn't taking no for an answer.

"And Mark?" she said when she'd meant to ring off.

"Yeah?"

"Thank you for last night."

"No regrets in the cold light of day?"

"Only that you had to leave to go to work. Can I see you again soon?"

"Is tonight soon enough?"

"No, but it will have to do."

She did hang up then. And worried about how much better she felt just knowing that it was only a matter of hours until she'd be with him again.

He'd sleep with her, but he'd made it very plain he was never going to subject her—or any woman—to the challenges of a permanent relationship with him. Nor was he going to sire children who would always have to live under a cloud.

On the surface, she couldn't blame him. Underneath, however, where her heart lay tender and healing, she couldn't bear the thought.

RYAN RETURNED Mark's call at three that afternoon. "I have no idea what any of this has to do with the night Sara was raped," the young man started, "but what I know isn't good. Not for Sara."

Wiping greasy hands on a chamois, Mark grabbed the phone from between his shoulder and ear, gripping it tightly.

"You found something on James Danielson," he said.

"I'll say I did."

"Who is he?"

"Sara's father."

"AND THAT'S NOT ALL." Ryan's words continued to play themselves through Mark's mind as he finished the project he'd promised by that evening—an old Model T that was being driven in a parade over the weekend. "He's Ralph Bonney's father, too."

Ryan had asked him to wait to contact Ralph, thinking maybe they needed to see him together. Waiting wasn't easy. Mark couldn't get the sick feeling out of his stomach, no longer able to deny that there was something very wrong about the story they'd all been told about the night Sara had been raped. He didn't know what. Couldn't figure out how the homeless man Ralph had befriended fit in with another homeless man who happened to have fathered him, while his mother had been supposedly happily married to Mr. Bonney. If he fit in.

Nor did he know how any of that connected to the rest. But one glaring fact could not be ignored.

Ralph Bonney was the only eyewitness to the night his half sister had been raped.

This was going to bring Sara to her knees again. He just knew it. Her entire perception of herself was going to change once more. And he was damned well going to be there while she picked up the pieces.

Then he'd get on with his solitary life.

SARA'S HEART LEAPED when she pulled around the corner of her block to see Mark's SUV already parked out front. She'd been trying to warn herself that he probably wasn't as eager as she was to continue where they'd left off the night before.

He worried about the past's effect on the future far more than she did.

Her spirits took a dive, however, the second she saw his face.

"What's wrong?"

"We need to talk."

She didn't want to talk. She wanted that doomed expression to leave his face and never come back. "Let's go inside," she said, thinking ahead to the tea in the refrigerator, the glasses in the cupboard, ice in the freezer. She had them all in place, on the table, before she took a seat and gave Mark her attention.

Whatever was coming, she needed to sit down.

"Ryan found a woman from your hometown who knew James Danielson. It didn't take long, once he knew the man had once worked for the sheriff's office."

"He worked for my father?"

"Yes."

"Why didn't any other records show that?"

"My guess is that your father destroyed his file when he ran him out of town, making certain, through careful word-of-mouth, that Danielson wouldn't find a job anywhere in Ohio law enforcement."

"How can you just wipe out the entire record of a police deputy?"

"He didn't." The look on Mark's face scared her. Badly. "They weren't on computers back then, and for someone as well-known and highly thought of as your father it was easy enough to fire the guy and spread whatever truths he had to, to make everyone want him gone. The state has financial records, pension stuff, but you'd have to know where to look to find that."

"And today Ryan knew where to look."

"Correct."

But this wasn't about Danielson's job. Right?

"So what did the woman in Maricopa have to say?" she asked, trying to rein in thoughts that were running haywire; trying to land on some explanation she could live with.

Mark took her hand, pulled her up and into the living room, and then sat with her on the couch, holding her close.

Sara was shaking so hard she couldn't think.

"Danielson was a womanizer," he said succinctly. "A charmer. He was also young and movie-star gorgeous. And he used all three characteristics, plus that added allure of the uniform, to convince women they were meant for him. Married women. It was perfect, really. He had women besotted, but not pressuring him to make the relationship public because he'd arranged things so that *they* had to keep things quiet. He'd play on them, telling them how much it hurt him to not be acknowledged, begging them to leave their husbands and yet placing doubts in their minds about how much it would hurt these good men to be left. How much it hurt the women, themselves, to do something so painful to someone who'd been loyal and loving to them. Each one thought she was the only woman for him."

"How many were there?"

"Four that we know of."

No wonder her father had wanted the man out of town. A moral, decent man such as John Lindsay would see it as a personal affront if one of his men, someone he'd put in charge of the public's safety, was using that power to hurt the women in his care.

"So my father found out and ran the guy out of town."

"Eventually."

She glanced back, catching the grim look in Mark's eyes, and knew she hadn't heard the worst of it.

"How did my dad find out?" She was grasping at straws. Maybe John Lindsay had walked in on his deputy with one of the women in town.

"He found out when your mother got pregnant."

That made no sense at all. She shook her head. "What did that have to do with anything?"

"Sara, apparently your father's sterile."

SHE JUMPED UP. Choked. Turned horrified eyes on Mark. And ran from the room. Sara had no idea where she was going. She just knew she had to get out of there. The backyard beckoned, but its fence was a barrier. The driveway was too exposed. People could look at her.

Her car was in the garage. The street was too full of people.

Back in the house, she dropped down to one of her dining chairs, staring blankly. It was all she knew to do. Sit there at the kitchen table until everything worked itself out.

MARK GAVE HER SEVERAL MINUTES alone, and then went in to join her, fully prepared to deflect any rage she might throw his way.

Instead, what he saw was worse than anything he'd feared. Her gaze, as she stared at him, was completely dead.

"James Danielson is my father," she said the words without expression. Coldly.

"Yes."

"I'm assuming there are records to prove that?"

"I don't know."

"But…this woman…she was certain."

Mark nodded. "She was one of the four of them. Danielson told them about each other on his way out of town, with some bizarre thought that they'd band together and come to his aid against the sheriff."

"Even though one of them was the sheriff's wife."

She spoke of her mother as if the woman was a stranger.

"Yes."

"Who were the other women?"

Mark named two of them. Sara showed no signs of recognition. And then he named the last.

"Sue Bonney?" she repeated the name.

He nodded; saw the questions flit across her expression. It was almost as though she was bracing herself for what was still to come. Her shoulders straightened, stiffened.

"How long did this go on?"

"Several years."

"Were there any other children as a result?"

"Just the one that I know of."

And as quickly as she'd sat upright, Sara's entire body drooped.

"Ralph Bonney is my half brother."

Mark held her as the horrified awareness filled her eyes.

CHAPTER TWENTY

ON TUESDAY, after more than fifteen hours of self-enforced seclusion, Sara showered, dressed in a sedate navy suit, donned matching jewelry, clipped back her hair, put on lipstick and her watch and went in to set out glasses, a pitcher of water and napkins.

She didn't jump when the first knock sounded at her door. Nor did she say a word as she opened it and the first man came in. The second and third entered as wordlessly, two exchanging wary glances, two completely ignoring each other.

Her father was seeing her son for the first time in his life. They were nothing to each other. Completely unrelated ships that were passing in a very dark night.

She led them into her kitchen, the three of them, the youngest in uniform, the other two wearing slacks and shirts, following behind her in single file. It didn't seem to matter that they dwarfed the room. She felt suspended above all of them—even above herself.

When she sat, they sat. She poured. They sipped.

And then she faced the man who'd shaped every minute of her entire life.

"You stand for truth, and yet everything about me is a lie." The words had been repeating themselves in her mind for hours.

"What are you talking about? We're here to discuss the discrepancies this young man here thinks he found in my case reports," Sheriff Lindsay said, his tone brooking no argument. He didn't acknowledge Mark Dalton's presence across the table.

Neither had Sara, other than a brief meeting of the eyes when she'd let him in her house. She couldn't afford to feel anything right now.

Maybe not ever.

"I know about James Danielson." Twenty years of dignity and class got the words out of her.

She watched with a distanced eye as John Lindsay's face aged ten years. The entire man seemed to shrink in on himself, until he appeared to have lost not only his credibility, but stature and weight, as well.

"You thought it better that my life be a complete lie, than tell me that my mother had been taken advantage of by a con man? Did you think I wouldn't have loved her, anyway?"

"I loved her too much to do that to her." John Lindsay's tone was lower than she'd ever heard it. "No one knew. No one would have known if not for the bastard's last shot, letting all four women know about each other."

"He was hoping to get back at you."

"And them, I'm sure. They made a pact, the four of them, never to speak of what had happened, to learn from their indiscretions and live the rest of their lives making up for them. They became friends, of a sort, the kind who talked in tears in the middle of the night, but never socialized with each other in the light of day."

"Did all four of them stay married?" It didn't matter. She was just curious.

"No." John's eyes were wide open as he submitted to her interrogation. "Only your mother and Sue Bonney. When the other husbands found out, they filed for divorce."

She nodded, impatient with herself for drawing this out.

"What I want to know now, what the three of us want to know, is what the connection is between all of this and the night I was raped."

"Absolutely nothing."

"I don't believe you." She didn't even flinch as she faced down the man she'd alternately feared and adored her entire life.

"That's your choice," he said, his gaze sadder than she could ever remember seeing it, other than the week her mother died. "It's also your mistake," he added so softly she barely heard him.

Thank God for a lifetime of preparation for this moment. She was holding up just fine. Feeling nothing.

Or almost nothing.

"Excuse me, sir, but if you don't mind my asking, how do you explain the fact that not only was Ralph Bonney's testimony inconsistent, but you, a fine detective by all accounts, didn't catch the discrepancy?"

"I caught it."

Mark's jerk upright was too blatant for her to miss. But she tried. If she felt him over there, connected in any way, she'd be lost.

And for what gain? He was going to go on with his life without her, no matter what they'd shared. She'd always known that.

Her brief foray into believing there was more for her in life than what she'd known had been exhilarating. Excruciating. And now it was over.

She had a business to run.

And maybe, some day, a child to adopt.

"Then why didn't you say anything?" Ryan asked when no one else said a word.

"Ralph was a good kid. I...felt...a kinship toward him."

"Because he was my half brother." There were going to be no more hedged truths between them.

"Yes." He nodded at Sara and looked back at Ryan, his head high. "He'd done a hard thing, coming forward like he had, implicating himself in the drinking, in having turned his back when he'd realized it was three against one. I was grateful to him. And because it didn't matter one whit to the case that he'd turned his back after my daughter's underwear had been exposed rather than before, I saw no point in dragging him through the examination and cross-examination such a detail would have brought out."

"The prosecutors didn't know—"

"Or they chose not to use it."

"You left it in your report."

"I was bound by law to do that. It was buried, but it was there. If they'd looked hard enough, both sides had access to it."

"But your testimony led them away from looking."

"It wasn't going to help prove their case."

"And it wouldn't have helped the defense, either," Mark added. "It would only have dragged out the entire thing, with the only result being Bonney's public humiliation."

John Lindsay bowed his head, as though he'd never heard the remark.

"What about later?" Ryan asked, his badge reflecting off the chandelier above them. "When the skeleton turned up and Bonney told you he'd seen a man around town."

Sara's father told her son the same thing he'd told her. Verbatim. "There was absolutely no evidence to substantiate a single thing he said," John finished.

"So you didn't know that James Danielson was back in the area, hanging out in various homeless shelters?"

"My family and I worked in the local shelter," the retired sheriff said, including Sara in a brief glance before once again turning his full attention to the officer across the table. "You can believe that if I'd ever seen him there, or anywhere in my county, I'd have had him removed."

There was much Sara didn't believe anymore. But this, she did.

IT TOOK EVERYTHING Mark had to remain seated at the same table he and Sara had sat at nearly naked the morning before. Now he was sitting across from the man who'd made it his life's quest to put Mark away forever.

Or for as long as his laws would allow.

The demon in his nightmares. And a major player in his waking fears, as well. To have his freedom completely in the hands of another, to be rendered completely incapable of defending himself against anything the man might say, was, to him, a horror worse than death.

"Do you have any idea where Danielson is now?" Ryan's question was different from any he'd asked before. His voice had gone up a notch. Mark focused on the young police officer.

"None," Lindsay said. "I've neither heard from, nor laid eyes on, the man since I saw his ass out of town."

"It might interest you to know, then, that through some special favors to a mentor of mine, we got the dental records you saved from the skeleton, and just this morning received a positive match for one James Danielson."

"He's dead?" Sara's voice squeaked. It was the first crack Mark had seen in her armor since she'd asked him to leave the night before.

Ryan stared at John Lindsay. "Someone buried him across the lake from where Sara was raped.

And based on positive IDs we have for him at a shelter in Dayton, and personal things he left there, but never returned to collect, we've narrowed the time of his death down to within a week or two of that party."

"Could it have been the night of the party?" Sara asked.

"Yes."

"So you think the rape was used as a cover-up for James Danielson's murder?"

Mark's gaze ping-ponged back and forth between the other three at the table.

"I don't know, Sheriff," Ryan said. "What do you think?"

SARA HAD NEVER KNOWN horror as she did in that second, looking at the man she'd turned to for safety and security her entire life, and considered the fact that he could have murdered a man.

And used her to cover up the fact.

He met her gaze head-on, holding it for as long as it took her to know.

"He might have wanted to kill that man," she said, real conviction not only in her voice but in her heart, too. "But he would never have risked my health, happiness or safety for anything. He'd have given up his own life, first."

The frost encompassing her almost started to thaw when John Lindsay's eyes swelled with tears.

"What I think—" he turned to Ryan, blinking once, before focusing on her son, all cop now "—is that someone ought to be bringing Ralph Bonney in for questioning. This is one coincidence too many, and as all good cops know…"

"Coincidences usually aren't."

WITH ONE PHONE CALL, Ryan arranged to have the car dealer picked up and brought into the precinct in Westerville for questioning. John Lindsay slid a hand behind Sara's back as they all headed out to their cars, guiding her toward his. "Why don't you ride with us, young man?" he said to Ryan.

"Thank you, sir, I'd like that." Ryan looked as pleased as he sounded at the invitation.

The retired sheriff didn't even acknowledge the presence of the third man who, by himself, climbed into his own car and followed them across town.

SITTING WITH MARK and a couple of police detectives on the blind side of a one-way mirror, listening as Ryan, his mentor Sergeant Miller, and John Lindsay subjected the small bespectacled man to an interrogation he would never forget, Sara wondered if she'd ever know a life that was free of tension.

For twenty years she'd fought the tightness she was feeling now. She'd tried to escape it, determined to risk everything for the chance to be free.

And here she was, right back at the beginning.

"We know what you did, Ralph," John Lindsay said, his voice infused with disappointment. "What we don't know is why."

Another lie. They had no idea what Ralph had done. How many lies had her father told while Sara had been trying to live up to his picture of perfection? And failing so miserably she hadn't even liked herself half the time.

"There's no way you could know…"

The man's head locked into place, terror written all over him as he realized he'd just given himself up on the first round.

"What do you know?" He tried to backtrack.

"All of it."

The man had been Mirandized. He knew his rights. He could stop things right there—for now.

"I stood by you before. You were good to me," Sheriff Lindsay said. "You helped me. And now I want to help you. Just tell us why you did what you did, and we'll find a way to make things easier on you."

"I want my lawyer."

"Okay." All three men stood, though only John had spoken so far. "But you have to know that once he comes in here, the chance I have of doing anything for you is gone."

Ralph was trembling so hard Sara could see his shoelaces shake. His eyes were glazed with fear as he looked back and forth between the other men, his head jerking with each motion of his eyes, resting for the longest time on John Lindsay.

"What can you do?" The screamed question made Sara jump. Mark was beside her. She saw him glance over. Felt his hand move up against hers—but she wouldn't take hold of it.

Wouldn't even think about it.

"You're the whole reason I had to do anything!" The little man was practically squealing at the top of his lungs, his voice high, face red. "You had to go and run Danielson out of town. And make damn certain he'd never get another decent job, too."

"Just in law enforcement in Ohio," John Lindsay's voice was low, and Bonney didn't even appear to hear it. "I had no jurisdiction beyond that."

"And all because he'd slept with *your* wife," Bonney was spitting as he hollered. Flecks of saliva sprayed the Formica table in front of him.

"You didn't do anything when you'd caught him in the office with my mother on his desk."

Oh, God. Would it never end? All the secrets. The hiding.

"Your mother asked me not to do anything."

"If it wasn't for you pushing your weight around, everything would have been fine. But you pushed him over the edge, and then where were you?" Bonney asked, seemingly completely unaware that anyone else but he and John Lindsay were around.

"Did you know he was hanging around the lake harassing me? No! Did you ever even look him up to make certain he hadn't come back?"

"No." John Lindsay's voice was even, if heavy. Sara, who felt as if she didn't know her father anymore, knew that he was regretting that lapse. That he'd beat himself up over it for the rest of his days.

"He told me about him and my mother. Told me everything. I'm his kid, he says. Sara's his kid, too. And that's why you ran him out of town."

Nausea swept through her. Sara reached for the glass of water she'd been handed when she sat down. Needing it, but afraid to drink.

"I didn't believe him, at first. Thought he was a rambling crazy man. I took pity on him. Brought him blankets to ward off the cold. Gave him money. Food."

She couldn't see her father's face. And she was glad. This had to be hurting him. Badly.

As they'd all been hurt.

She didn't want any more pain. For any of them. Why couldn't it all just be done? Gone?

"But he just kept on saying the same stupid things. I finally told my mother about him one night when my dad was out of town on business. And guess what? The crazy dude had been telling the truth. That fruitcake was my father! Once he knew I believed him, he started blackmailing me. If I didn't do this or bring that, he was going to tell everyone about me. And my mom. Can you just imagine what that would have done to my father?"

The man sounded like a boy going through puberty at this point, and still he pushed the words out with such force that his veins were sticking out all over his face and neck.

The detectives around her were bowing their heads, as if embarrassed for a man who was too far gone to even be aware of himself.

"Bonney always had trouble with self-confidence," Mark said softly.

Like a bystander to a train wreck, she wanted to

leave before the horror was fully known. Yet when she tried, she couldn't move. She was on the train.

"I was out at the lake the day before the party, dropping off the beer tubs. He shows up, just like that, and tells me if I don't get him a girl that night, he's going to tell everyone the truth. I hit him with one of the tubs. I couldn't help it! I had to shut him up. He fell and I just kept hitting him."

Ralph stopped suddenly, as if out of air. He was panting. Staring at the table. "Before I knew it, he was dead."

"What happened next?" Sergeant Miller asked, his voice subdued, and Bonney stared at him. His gaze was wide, innocent.

"I'm a good swimmer," Ralph said. "I swam with him across the lake, and buried him. It wasn't like anyone was gonna miss him. But then I got scared, you know?" The sergeant nodded. "Everyone knew Sheriff Lindsay didn't miss anything. Maybe he'd notice the fresh earth or something."

Trying hard not to throw up, Sara grasped her seat with both hands. And felt Mark's palm slide over one of them.

"But as soon as I saw the sheriff's daughter, *Danielson*'s daughter, show up, it all came to me," Bonney said, smiling now, still a youngster, only now one who'd brought home a perfect report card. "She should pay, too. I wasn't the only bastard kid. And so should Mister High and Mighty, who'd thought he was so special he could just take the law into his own hands." Bonney was gearing up again. "I had these pills. Got 'em from a guy I knew whose dad was a doctor. He'd warned me not to mix them with alcohol. Told me they could make me sexually…irresponsible… and also that I could black out. After that, it was easy. I wait until the guys start hitting on her. I spike their drinks, giving them a double dose just to be safe, and wait for nature to take its course. Sheriff Lindsay's attention was completely absorbed after that."

And the rest was history.

HAVING TAKEN ALL she could, Sara stood, left the viewing room with a quick excuse-me, walked down the hall to the elevator, rode it downstairs, got in a cab and went home. She didn't answer her phone, for once in her life, or acknowledge the knocks on her door.

Eventually, there was silence.

She spent the rest of that night in the only place she could stand to be. Alone with herself.

By morning, Sara was fairly certain she had a

plan for her life. She'd go to work. She'd help people. And eventually, she'd start to smile again.

Where her father fit into the picture, she had no idea. Time would have to sort out that one.

And Mark? He was wrapped up in her best and absolutely worst memories. He'd been drugged. He might not have been found guilty of rape. Maybe had his entire life ruined because of her and her family.

And then again, based on the facts, the drugs might not have made enough difference to free him.

She got up to go to work—or rather, she went in to shower to get ready for work. She'd never actually gone to bed, though she'd dozed on the couch off and on.

But when it actually came time to leave, she called in, canceling her morning appointments. Donna, helpful and concerned, said her father had been by. Several times the day before and again that morning.

She told her assistant that she didn't want to see him right now.

And five minutes later there was a knock on her front door. Fine. She'd take care of this herself.

"What?" she said, pulling open the door with more force than necessary, to stare into the biggest, brownest, most soulful eyes she'd ever seen, attached to a heart-stopping ball of fluff suspended in midair. Or almost.

There was an arm attached. And a note.

Sara grabbed the note.

You need me. And I need you. I potty wherever and whenever I need to, but I can learn better manners. I don't have a name yet. My parents abandoned me. I come with no strings attached. Can I stay?

One look back at those eyes, and Sara smiled, started to cry and reached out her arms.

Apparently waiting until he was sure she'd fallen in love and wasn't going to refuse his gift or otherwise be mad at him, Ryan showed his face.

"I have puppy food and instructions and toys and a kennel in my vehicle," he said.

Sara, completely consumed with the tiny reddish animal wagging its tail and licking her face as if she were its beloved, left the door wide and went inside.

A smart woman knew when she was beat.

"BONNEY'S NOT ONLY FACING charges for murder, but for the rape, as well," Ryan told her as he set up the kennel in her kitchen, showing her how to secure the puppy pads so that her new little friend wouldn't chew them up.

She didn't want to think about Ralph Bonney. Or any other part of her life.

"How big is she going to get?"

"Only five pounds or so." Her son was on his hands and knees, arranging water and food bowls, toys and chew sticks strategically in the little home he'd just assembled.

"Not much protection, then," she said, remembering when she'd first met him, and he'd preached to her about dogs and alarm systems. Seemed like a lifetime ago.

"She'll bark. That's enough."

Brandi was also going to sleep in the bed with her, Sara decided. No one should spend their nights trapped behind bars all alone.

"Mark and I went this morning for the paternity test." Ryan dropped the news casually, as he surveyed his handiwork.

She didn't want to care.

Mark had a life he wasn't going to share with her.

She wanted children. And safety. Dignity and class were what she did best.

"How soon will you know?"

"Should be next week sometime."

She'd think about it then. Maybe. If she couldn't help herself.

"Mom said she called you." He was on his

way out the door now, off to bed before he had to go to work.

"Yeah, there was a message from her."

"She wants you to come to dinner on Sunday."

Sara didn't want to want to go. "That's kind of her."

"She means it."

"Tell her thank you." Sara was about to decline the invitation until two things happened. She met her son's eyes. And Brandi licked her nose.

The heart she'd locked away apparently hadn't been as weak—or as willing—as she'd feared. It opened back up again, right then and there, edges raw and bleeding.

"I'll be there."

AN HOUR LATER, dressed in jeans and a T-shirt, Sara pulled her Lexus into the parking lot of High Import Mechanics. A young man greeted her at the door, asking if she had an appointment.

"No," she told him. "I'd like to see Mark Dalton."

"He's out back, but…" When the twenty-some-thing, greasy-fingered kid looked behind him to an open door leading into a garage, Sara followed his gaze, catching sight of a pair of feet sticking out from beneath a car old enough to have a rumble seat. The feet were about the right size.

Before she could be told she wasn't allowed, Sara hurried through the door.

"Mark?"

He bumped his head. Swore. And wheeled himself out into the open, a supine man, lying on a small piece of board at her feet.

"I just felt it fair to warn you," she started, with no idea what she was going to say next, but trusting herself to get it right, anyway. "I'm not going away. I don't care where we live, or who knows about our past. I don't think I give a damn what anyone thinks, because no one's what they seem, anyway, really, are they?"

And as she spoke, she realized something. Once you've discovered something, you can't go back and pretend you don't know. You could try, but truth was stronger than any opponent and would win in the end.

Even if it took twenty-plus years, as it had with Ralph. And her father.

His head raised at an uncomfortable-looking angle, Mark stared at her. The young man was probably behind her, as well.

"That's all," she said. "Except…I love you. So, there you have it. I'm going home now."

Turning, she brushed past the openmouthed youth, and fled.

TWENTY MINUTES AFTER returning home, Sara answered the knock at her door, trembling, feeling a smile emerging from somewhere deep inside. It hadn't taken him long to clean up.

But it wasn't Mark.

"Daddy," she said, her smile fading.

"I didn't give thirty-seven years of my life to loving you, watching out for you, protecting you, to just walk away. You don't have the right to tell me I can't love you. Or to insist that I can't worry about you. I can. And I do. So…"

With tears in her eyes, Sara leaned forward, wrapped her arms around the perfect sheriff who'd fallen from his pedestal and become a man who she apparently took after more than a little bit. A man who was so much a part of her she'd just that morning handled her own potential rejection just the way he was doing.

"I love you, too, Daddy," she told him, knowing it was going to take her awhile to work through everything in her mind, to square away the betrayal and pain and remember the things that really mattered. Knowing, too, that he'd give her that time, and be waiting at the other end.

While she was still in her father's arms, she heard a car pull up in front of her house. And froze.

Mark was there. If he saw her father, he'd drive

way. Pulling back, she started to run down to the yard, only to stop midstep. Dressed in slacks and button-down shirt, with fancy shoes and tie loose at his neck, Mark wasn't going anywhere but toward her father.

"It's just as well you're here, sir," he addressed the older man. "Saves me a trip from coming to find you."

Worried, biting her lip, Sara noticed her father's inability to look at the man she loved.

"Your daughter's courage is a testament to you, sir. And a lesson to me. Life isn't easy for many people. Probably isn't meant to be. I've wasted enough of mine afraid to face what is. I don't have the best of circumstances to offer her. To the contrary, I can promise there will be hard challenges ahead, but she's done me the honor of giving me her love and I'm going to ask her to marry me."

With tears blurring her vision again, Sara held her breath. How could so much sorrow and so much happiness be rolled into one moment?

"When?" John Lindsay's question was gruff, directed somewhere over Mark's left shoulder.

"As soon as I've let you know."

"You did that."

That's it? Sara glanced from one man to the

other, incredulous. Her father was going to let it go at that?

Mark turned on his heel, facing her. And then he kneeled, right there on her front lawn in his dress slacks.

"Sara Lindsay Calhoun, will you do me the honor of becoming my wife?"

"Yes!" She called the answer out to the entire neighborhood, yanking on his arm until he was standing and she could throw her arms around him. "Oh, yes, Mark. Forever and ever, yes."

ONE WEEK LATER, in a courtroom in Columbus, Ohio, a judge signed the petition offered by the county attorney's office, prompted by the arresting officer of twenty-two years ago, which reclassified the felony on Mark Dalton's record to nonpredator status. He no longer had to register as a sex offender.

And before he'd been a free man for five minutes, the same judge, in front of John Lindsay, Ryan, Glen and Harriet Mercedes, Dana and Jordon Lewis, and Hazel Dalton, took away that freedom as he bound him, for life and all eternity, to Sara Lindsay Dalton.

"You may kiss the bride," his booming voice pronounced, and that's when Mark knew he' inally come home. To a place that would always ecognize him, always welcome him. Always love im.

He pressed his lips to his wife's, uncaring that er father was looking on, closed his eyes and eveled in the first of a lifetime of perfect moments.

He'd traveled a long, hard road to get here. But he steps along the way had made the arrival weeter. He would never be a man to take what e had for granted, but rather, he'd live every day f his life grateful for what he had. Because he new what it was like to have not.

"Uh, excuse us."

Ryan's voice penetrated the fog he'd happily ave sunk beneath forever. Sara pulled back from im, grinning from ear to ear, as she held on. As hough proudly staking her claim.

"This seems like a good moment to tell you omething, now that you guys are legal and all."

"What's that?" Mark couldn't help the jovial esponse, he was just feeling too good to be his sual reticent self. And then he knew.

"Just wanted you to know that…let's see, what as it, almost twenty-two years ago now? You reated a baby."

"Mark's your father?" Sara's shriek resounded

around the gathering in the court room. Judge Keller was still there. And smiling.

"Biologically," Ryan said, drawing Glen and Harriet forward with an arm around each of them. Mark intercepted a long look between Sara and her father right then, too. Biology was important, but living every day was what mattered most.

"I don't know," Ryan continued, cocky as only a young man could get away with being. "I might be out of line, but I'd like to suggest that the two of you get busy and get me a biological sibling on the way. And in the meantime," he held out his hand to Jordon, "welcome to the family, dude."

* * * * *

Every Life Has More
Than One Chapter

Award-winning author Stevi Mittman delivers
another hysterical mystery, featuring Teddi
Bayer, an irrepressible heroine, and her to-
die-for hero, Detective Drew Scoones. After
all, life on Long Island can be murder!

*Turn the page for a sneak peek at the warm
and funny fourth book,
WHOSE NUMBER IS UP, ANYWAY?,
in the Teddi Bayer series,
by STEVI MITTMAN.
On sale August 7*

CHAPTER 1

"Before redecorating a room, I always advise
my clients to empty it of everything but one
chair. Then I suggest they move that chair
from place to place, sitting in it, until the
placement feels right. Trust your instincts
when deciding on furniture placement. Your
room should 'feel right.'"

—TipsFromTeddi.com

Gut feelings. You know, that gnawing in the pit
of your stomach that warns you that you are about
to do the absolute stupidest thing you could do?
Something that will ruin life as you know it?

I've got one now, standing at the butcher
counter in King Kullen, the grocery store in the
same strip mall as L.I. Lanes, the bowling alley-

cum-billiard parlor I'm in the process of redecorating for its "Grand Opening."

I realize being in the wrong supermarket probably doesn't sound exactly dire to you, but you aren't the one buying your father a brisket at a store your mother will somehow know isn't Waldbaum's.

And then, June Bayer isn't your mother.

The woman behind the counter has agreed to go into the freezer to find a brisket for me, since there aren't any in the case. There are packages of pork tenderloin, piles of spare ribs and rolls of sausage, but no briskets.

Warning Number Two, right? I should be so out of here.

But no, I'm still in the same spot when she comes back out, brisketless, her face ashen. She opens her mouth as if she is going to scream, but only a gurgle comes out.

And then she pinballs out from behind the counter, knocking bottles of Peter Luger Steak Sauce to the floor on her way, now hitting the tower of cans at the end of the prepared foods aisle and sending them sprawling, now making her way down the aisle, careening from side to side as she goes.

Finally, from a distance, I hear her shout, "He's deeeeeeaaaad! Joey's deeeeeeaaaad."

My first thought is *You should always trust your gut*.

My second thought is that now, somehow, my mother will know I was in King Kullen. For weeks I will have to hear "What did you expect?" as though whenever you go to King Kullen someone turns up dead. And if the detective investigating the case turns out to be Detective Drew Scoones…well, I'll never hear the end of that from her, either.

She still suspects I murdered the guy who was found dead on my doorstep last Halloween just to get Drew back into my life.

Several people head for the butcher's freezer and I position myself to block them. If there's one thing I've learned from finding people dead—and the guy on my doorstep wasn't the first one—it's that the police get very testy when you mess with their murder scenes.

"You can't go in there until the police get here," I say, stationing myself at the end of the butcher's counter and in front of the Employees Only door, acting as if I'm some sort of authority. "You'll contaminate the evidence if it turns out to be murder."

Shouts and chaos. You'd think I'd know better than to throw the word *murder* around. Cell phones are flipping open and tongues are wagging.

I amend my statement quickly. "Which, of course, it probably isn't. Murder, I mean. People die all the time, and it's not always in hospitals, or their own beds, or…" I babble when I'm nervous, and the idea of someone dead on the other side of the freezer door makes me very nervous.

So does the idea of seeing Drew Scoones again. Drew and I have this on-again, off-again sort of thing…that I kind of turned off.

Who knew he'd take it so personally when he tried to get serious and I responded by saying we could talk about *us* tomorrow—and then caught a plane to my parents' condo in Boca the next day? In July. In the middle of a job.

For some crazy reason, he took that to mean that I was avoiding him and the subject of *us*.

That was three months ago. I haven't seen him since.

The manager, who identifies himself and points to his nameplate in case I don't believe him, says he has to go into *his cooler*. "Maybe Joey's not dead," he says. "Maybe he can be saved, and you're letting him die in there. Did you ever think of that?"

In fact, I hadn't. But I had thought that the murderer might try to go back in to make sure his tracks were covered, so I say that I will go in and check.

Which means that the manager and I couple up and go in together while everyone pushes against the doorway to peer in, erasing any chance of finding clean prints on that Employees Only door.

I expect to find carcasses of dead animals hanging from hooks, and maybe Joey hanging from one, too. I think it's going to be very creepy and I steel myself, only to find a rather benign series of shelves with large slabs of meat laid out carefully on them, along with boxes and boxes marked simply Chicken.

Nothing scary here, unless you count the body of a middle-aged man with graying hair sprawled faceup on the floor. His eyes are wide open and unblinking. His shirt is stiff. His pants are stiff. His body is stiff. And his expression, you should forgive the pun—is frozen. Bill-the-manager crosses himself and stands mute while I pronounce the guy dead in a sort of *happy now?* tone.

"We should not be in here," I say, and he nods his head emphatically and helps me push people out of the doorway just in time to hear the police sirens and see the cop cars pull up outside the big store windows.

Bobbie Lyons, my partner in Teddi Bayer Interior Designs (and also my neighbor, my best friend and my private fashion police), and Mark, our carpenter (and my dogsitter, confidant and ego booster), rush in from next door. They beat the cops by a half step and shout out my name. People point in my direction.

After all the publicity that followed the unfortunate incident during which I shot my ex-husband, Rio Gallo, and then the subsequent murder of my first client—which I solved, I might add—it seems like the whole world, or at least all of Long Island, knows who I am.

Mark asks if I'm all right. (Did I remember to mention that the man is drop-dead-gorgeous-but-a-decade-too-young-for-me-yet-too-old-for-my-daughter-thank-god?) I don't get a chance to answer him because the police are quickly closing in on the store manager and me.

"The woman—" I begin telling the police. Then I have to pause for the manager to fill in her name, which he does: *Fran.*

I continue. "Right. Fran. Fran went into the freezer to get a brisket. A moment later she came out and screamed that Joey was dead. So I'd say she was the one who discovered the body."

"And you are...?" the cop asks me. It comes

out a bit like who do I *think* I am, rather than who am I really?

"An innocent bystander," Bobbie, hair perfect, makeup just right, says, carefully placing her body between the cop and me.

"And she was just leaving," Mark adds. They each take one of my arms.

Fran comes into the inner circle surrounding the cops. In case it isn't obvious from the hairnet and bloodstained white apron with Fran embroidered on it, I explain that she was the butcher who was going for the brisket. Mark and Bobbie take that as a signal that I've done my job and they can now get me out of there. They twist around, with me in the middle, as if we're a Rockettes line, until we are facing away from the butcher counter. They've managed to propel me a few steps toward the exit when disaster—in the form of a Mazda RX7 pulling up at the loading curb—strikes.

Mark's grip on my arm tightens like a vise. "Too late," he says.

Bobbie's expletive is unprintable. "Maybe there's a back door," she suggests, but Mark is right. It's too late.

I've laid my eyes on Detective Scoones. And while my gut is trying to warn me that my heart shouldn't go there, regions farther south are melting at just the sight of him.

"Walk," Bobbie orders me.

And I try to. Really.

Walk, I tell my feet. *Just put one foot in front of the other.*

I can do this because I know, in my heart of hearts, that if Drew Scoones was still interested in me, he'd have gotten in touch with me after I returned from Boca. And he didn't.

Since he's a detective, Drew doesn't have to wear one of those dark blue Nassau County Police uniforms. Instead, he's got on jeans, a tight-fitting T-shirt and a tweedy sports jacket. If you think that sounds good, you should see him. Chiseled features, cleft chin, brown hair that's naturally a little sandy in the front, a smile that…well, that doesn't matter. He isn't smiling now.

He walks up to me, tucks his sunglasses into his breast pocket and looks me over from head to toe.

"Well, if it isn't Miss Cut and Run," he says. "Aren't you supposed to be somewhere in Florida or something?" He looks at Mark accusingly, as if he was covering for me when he told Drew I was gone.

"Detective Scoones?" one of the uniforms says. "The stiff's in the cooler and the woman who found him is over there." He jerks his head in Fran's direction.

Drew continues to stare at me.

You know how when you were young, your mother always told you to wear clean underwear in case you were in an accident? And how, a little farther on, she told you not to go out in hair rollers because you never knew who you might see—or who might see you? And how now your best friend says she wouldn't be caught dead without makeup and suggests you shouldn't, either?

Okay, today, *finally*, in my overalls and Converse sneakers, I get it.

I brush my hair out of my eyes. "Well, I'm back," I say. As if he hasn't known my exact whereabouts. The man is a detective, for heaven's sake. "Been back awhile."

Bobbie has watched the exchange and apparently decided she's given Drew all the time he deserves. "And we've got work to do, so…" she says, grabbing my arm and giving Drew a little two-fingered wave goodbye.

As I back up a foot or two, the store manager sees his chance and places himself in front of Drew, trying to get his attention. Maybe what makes Drew such a good detective is his ability to focus.

Only what he's focusing on is me.

"Phone broken? Carrier pigeon died?" he asks me, taking in Fran, the manager, the meat counter and that Employees Only door, all without taking his eyes off me.

Mark tries to break the spell. "We've got work to do there, you've got work to do here, Scoones," Mark says to him, gesturing toward next door. "So it's back to the alley for us."

Drew's lip twitches. "You working the alley now?" he says.

"If you'd like to follow me," Bill-the-manager, clearly exasperated, says to Drew—who doesn't respond. It's as if waiting for my answer is all he has to do.

So, fine. "You knew I was back," I say.

The man has known my whereabouts every hour of the day for as long as I've known him. And my mother's not the only one who won't buy that he "just happened" to answer this particular call. In fact, I'm willing to bet my children's lunch money that he's taken every call within ten miles of my home since the day I got back.

And now he's gotten lucky.

"*You* could have called *me*," I say.

"You're the one who said *tomorrow* for our talk

and then flew the coop, chickie," he says. "I figured the ball was in your court."

"Detective?" the uniform says. "There's something you ought to see in here."

Drew gives me a look that amounts to *in or out?*

He could be talking about the investigation, or about our relationship.

Bobbie tries to steer me away. Mark's fists are balled. Drew waits me out, knowing I won't be able to resist what might be a murder investigation.

Finally, he turns and heads for the cooler.

And, like a puppy dog, I follow.

Bobbie grabs the back of my shirt and pulls me to a halt.

"I'm just going to show him something," I say, yanking away.

"Yeah," Bobbie says, pointedly looking at the buttons on my blouse. The two at breast level have popped. "That's what I'm afraid of."

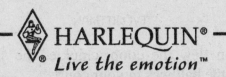

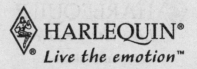

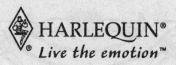

Harlequin® Historical
Historical Romantic Adventure!

*Imagine a time of chivalrous
knights and unconventional ladies,
roguish rakes and impetuous
heiresses, rugged cowboys
and spirited frontierswomen——
these rich and vivid tales will
capture your imagination!*

*Harlequin Historical . . .
they're too good to miss!*

SPECIAL EDITION™

Emotional, compelling stories that capture the intensity of living, loving and creating a family in today's world.

Modern, passionate reads that are powerful and provocative.

n o c t u r n e

Dramatic and sensual tales of paranormal romance.

Romances that are sparked by danger and fueled by passion.

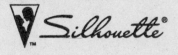